PRAISE FOR

Arsenic and Adobo

"I love to read a well-written and quirky cozy mystery. Manansala has created just that with her debut novel, a tale full of eccentric characters, humorous situations, and an oh-so-tricky mystery. Check this one out for the poetic prose and the mouthwatering recipes that are integral to the plot."

—*The Washington Post*

"This book hits the exact right spot. . . . Mia P. Manansala manages to create a murder mystery where nothing is too horrifying and you know everything will be okay in the end. . . . I've heard it described as a 'cozy mystery,' and that's exactly what it is, a perfectly cozy puzzle to solve."

—Taylor Jenkins Reid, *New York Times* bestselling author of *Malibu Rising*

"This breeze-right-through-it mystery follows baker Lila Macapagal as she investigates the murder of her ex-boyfriend, the town's too-mean food critic, after he dies over a meal in her aunt's flailing Filipino restaurant. Finding out whether or not Lila can solve the crime and save the restaurant is as satisfying as it is climactic, with just the right amount of drama."

—*Bon Appétit*

"[An] enjoyable and endearing debut cozy. . . . Manansala peppers the narrative with enough red herrings to keep readers from guessing the killer, but the strength of the novel is how family, food, and love intertwine in meaningful and complex ways."

—*The New York Times Book Review*

"This debut introduces readers to Filipino-American food and culture, with its emphasis on family. There are cozy tropes (the close-knit community, the food business), but the emphasis on the Tagalog language, the culture, and drug dealing in a small town adds gravity and individuality to this outstanding series kickoff."

—*Library Journal* (starred review)

"A super-fun read that's perfect for the beach, your couch, or any Sunday afternoon."

—theSkimm

"This debut mystery has a snap and sparkle that breathes a bit of new life into the cozy genre. . . . I wholeheartedly hope this is a kickoff to a long-lived series."

—*Mystery Scene*

"Manansala, a Chicago Filipina, has reinvigorated tired tropes to create a multicultural, queer-friendly culinary mystery, making *Arsenic and Adobo* an envelope-pushing, world-expanding debut that goes down easy."

—*Los Angeles Times*

"A delightfully decadent whodunit."

—*Woman's World*

"Mia P. Manansala has crafted a delicious mystery full of wit and wile that kept me laughing and guessing as I devoured every page. . . . I can't wait to read more in this fabulous new series!"

—Jenn McKinlay, *New York Times* bestselling author of *One for the Books*

"Chock-full of food lore, this delicious mystery will leave readers hungry for more of the adventures of Lila, her friends and relatives, and her chunky dachshund (who is named after a kind of short, fat sausage). Cozy fans are in for a treat."

—*Publishers Weekly* (starred review)

"Manansala's fun, fresh voice spins an enchanting fusion of Filipino-American food and culture, artfully and seamlessly woven into a smart, satisfying mystery that made me laugh out loud."

—Olivia Blacke, author of *Killer Content*

"Mia Manansala's debut, *Arsenic and Adobo,* serves up a cozy plate of ube crinkles with a side of murder. Readers are sure to salivate over this Filipino-American mystery as Lila smokes out the food critic's killer." —Roselle Lim, author of *Vanessa Yu's Magical Paris Tea Shop*

"A standout cozy mystery full of heart, the importance of home, and tons of good food. . . . Lila Macapagal is fun, fierce, and all about family."

—Gigi Pandian, Agatha Award–winning author of *The Glass Thief*

"A much-welcome entry into the culinary cozy genre, packed full of mouthwatering food and jaw-dropping reveals. . . . It's guaranteed to be your next favorite cozy series. Just don't read it on an empty stomach!"

—Kellye Garrett, Agatha Award–winning author of *Hollywood Ending*

"Mouthwatering dishes and a funny, smart amateur sleuth make *Arsenic and Adobo* by Mia P. Manansala my favorite new culinary cozy mystery series."

—Lynn Cahoon, *New York Times* bestselling author of the Kitchen Witch Mysteries

"You will be rooting for Lila Macapagal to save the family restaurant and keep herself out of jail while interacting with her interfering yet well-meaning relatives. The first in a lip-smacking series!"

—Naomi Hirahara, Edgar® Award–winning author of *Iced in Paradise*

"*Arsenic and Adobo* is pure murder-mystery fun with a hefty dose of humor and heart. . . . It's an utter delight from the first sentence to the very last page." —Sarah Echavarre Smith, author of *On Location*

"Cozy fans are gonna love this series! Filled with Filipino food; a bevy of meddling relatives; and a plucky, unflappable but admittedly flawed amateur sleuth, Lila Macapagal . . . *Arsenic and Adobo* shines."

—Abby Collette, author of *A Game of Cones*

"Manansala's writing is so approachable that you'll want to be Lila's friend and beg her to feed you. If you love cozy mysteries with a strong dash of large-family dynamics and [a] self-journey all set in the world of delicious food, then this is for you." —BuzzFeed

"Along with Lila's funny and feisty voice, there is a lot to love here: complex clues, mouthwatering food descriptions, and a diverse cast of characters. Fans of Vivien Chien will devour this one and look forward to more." —*Booklist* (starred review)

"A hilarious and delicious mystery that is bound to leave you laughing and wanting more." —Medium

TITLES BY MIA P. MANANSALA

Arsenic and Adobo

Homicide and Halo-Halo

Homicide *and* Halo-Halo

Mia P. Manansala

BERKLEY PRIME CRIME
NEW YORK

BERKLEY PRIME CRIME
Published by Berkley
An imprint of Penguin Random House LLC
penguinrandomhouse.com

Library of Congress Cataloging-in-Publication Data

Names: Manansala, Mia P., author.
Title: Homicide and halo-halo / Mia P. Manansala.
Description: First Edition. | New York : Berkley Prime Crime, 2022. |
Series: Tita Rosie's Kitchen mysteries
Identifiers: LCCN 2021038454 (print) | LCCN 2021038455 (ebook) |
ISBN 9780593201695 (trade paperback) | ISBN 9780593201701 (ebook)
Subjects: GSAFD: Mystery fiction.
Classification: LCC PS3613.A5268 H66 2022 (print) |
LCC PS3613.A5268 (ebook) | DDC 813/.6—dc23
LC record available at https://lccn.loc.gov/2021038454
LC ebook record available at https://lccn.loc.gov/2021038455

First Edition: February 2022

Printed in the United States of America
1st Printing

Book design by Kristin del Rosario

To Mommy,

Thanks so much for your endless support and for introducing me to the wonderful world of cozy mysteries. This series was always meant for you. Love you!

Author's Note

I wrote *Homicide and Halo-Halo* while both me and my protagonist, Lila, were in rather dark places in our lives. I was working through the mental health issues that a worldwide pandemic brought about, as well as the ripple effects from it, such as unemployment, bereavement, added pressure to succeed as an author, etc. Lila is still working through the repercussions from the events of *Arsenic and Adobo,* since they happened only a few months before this book opens. Because of that, this book is slightly heavier in tone than the first.

It is still a cozy mystery, with humor and food and love and a happy ending, but I wanted to prepare you, my dear readers, in case you're not in the right headspace for this book. If you'd like to avoid potential spoilers, stop reading here. Otherwise, I'd like to provide content warnings for PTSD, fatphobia, fertility/pregnancy issues, predatory behavior, unresolved grief, parental death (occurred in childhood), and dismissive attitudes toward mental health.

Author's Note

[illegible]

Glossary and Pronunciation Guide

HONORIFICS/FAMILY (THE "O" USUALLY HAS A SHORT, SOFT SOUND)

Anak (ah-nahk)—Offspring/son/daughter

Ate (ah-teh)—Older sister/female cousin/girl of the same generation as you

Kuya (koo-yah)—Older brother/male cousin/boy of the same generation as you

Lola (loh-lah)/Lolo (loh-loh)—Grandmother/Grandfather

Ninang (nee-nahng)/Ninong (nee-nohng)—Godmother/Godfather

Tita (tee-tah)/Tito (tee-toh)—Aunt/Uncle

FOOD

Adobo (uh-doh-boh)—Considered the Philippines's national dish, it's any food cooked with soy sauce, vinegar, garlic, and black peppercorns (though there are many regional and personal variations)

Arroz caldo (ah-rohs cahl-doh)—A soothing rice porridge containing chicken, ginger, and green onions

Halo-halo (hah-loh hah-loh)—Probably the Philippines's national dessert, this dish consists of shaved ice layered with sweet beans and preserved fruits, topped with evaporated milk and often a slice of leche flan (crème caramel) and ube halaya or ube ice cream. The name means "mix-mix" because it's a mix of many different things and you usually mix it all together to eat it.

Lumpia (loom-pyah)—Filipino spring rolls (many variations)

Matamis na bao (mah-tah-mees nah bah-oh)—Coconut jam (also known as "minatamis na bao")

Pandesal (pahn deh sahl)—Lightly sweetened Filipino rolls topped with breadcrumbs (also written as "pan de sal")

Patis (pah-tees)—Fish sauce

Salabat (sah-lah-baht)—Filipino ginger tea

Sinigang (sih-ni-gahng)—A light, tangy soup filled with vegetables such as long beans, tomatoes, onions, leafy greens, and taro, plus a protein such as pork or seafood

Turon (tuh-rohn)—Sweet banana and jackfruit spring rolls, fried and rolled in caramelized sugar

Ube (oo-beh)—Purple yam

OTHER

Balikbayan box (bah-lik-by-yahn)—Boxes sent by overseas Filipino workers and diaspora Filipinos to their families back in the Philippines. These boxes are filled with gifts such as nonperishable food items, household items, toys, clothes, appliances, etc. that are expensive or difficult to find in the Philippines. "Balikbayan" literally means "returning to the country."

Bruha (broo-ha)—Witch (from the Spanish "bruja")

Diba (dih-bah)—Isn't it?; Right?; short for "hindi ba" (also written as "di ba")

Kain tayo (kah-in tah-yo)—Let's eat

Maarte (mah-art-teh)—Used to mean "artsy" or "creative" but now is used to describe someone who's overdramatic, extra, nitpicky, and/or difficult to please

Macapagal (Mah-cah-pah-gahl)—A Filipino surname

Oh my gulay—This is Taglish (Tagalog-English) slang, used when people don't want to say the "God" part of OMG. "Gulay" (goo-lie) literally means "vegetable," so this phrase shouldn't be translated.

Papansin (pah-pahn-sin)—Attention seeker; self-centered

Tama na (tah-mah nah)—That's enough; Stop; Right/Correct (depends on context)

Tsismis (chees-mees)—Gossip

Homicide and Halo-Halo

Chapter One

Curls of smoke drifted around the Brew-ha Cafe, a pleasant floral aroma filling the space while hints of an unknown herb tickled my nose, making me sneeze.

"Salud," said Elena Torres, the pierced-and-tattooed woman holding the smoldering bouquet, as she wafted a bit more smoke toward me. Adeena Awan, Elena's girlfriend and my best friend, stood next to her, breathing the mixture in, bathing in the smoke.

I held back a cough. "Didn't we already cleanse the place?"

Elena nodded, circling me with the smoke cleansing stick in her hand. "Yes, but I did some research and saw that guava leaves were used in ancient Filipino practices the same way the indigenous people here use sage. Thought it would bring some good energy into the shop and be something nice for your ancestors, without us having to appropriate white sage. This is a special blend of guava leaves, rosemary, and lavender my mom and I grew in our greenhouse."

Ah, so that explained the floral scent my trusty nose detected. I wasn't as into the woo-woo stuff as Adeena and Elena, but I appreciated how thoughtful Elena was being. Besides, the place could use a good cleanse after what happened here back in March.

She continued, "I'm really liking the vibes this blend is bringing. I'll need to make more for the altar."

We all glanced toward the employees-only corner of the shop. It used to be the back room of the cafe, but after the events that happened a few months ago, neither Adeena nor I could stand to look at it, so we had the walls knocked down and converted it to a semiprivate alcove. Elena wanted to use the space to set up an altar, to both pay homage to those who came before us and to have them bless our business venture. She'd been bugging me to give her something to add to it, but I kept putting it off. I knew what she really wanted were photos of my dead parents, but I refused to put them on display, even if the only other people who'd see them were Adeena and Elena. They weren't for public consumption, even in a way that was meant to honor them. Besides, I wouldn't even look at the photos of them inside my own home—what made her think I'd be comfortable seeing them in my place of business?

"It's getting way too hot in here. I'm gonna close the door now. Can you turn on the AC and make sure it's not acting wonky anymore?"

Adeena had propped open the door earlier to "let out the negative energy" and the sweltering summer heat rolled in, the temperature having already reached a stifling eighty-six degrees at seven in the morning. Any of the bad juju Elena had managed to cleanse would be replaced with my dark mood if it got any hotter.

The air conditioning kicked in, and I breathed a sigh of relief as the cool air washed over me. Summer had just started and the cafe had been closed since the . . . unpleasantness, but we were finally ready for our soft opening in a few days.

I looked around the room, once a monochrome minimalist space, now full of color and life. We'd outfitted the area with Adeena's artwork, Elena's plants, and my . . . well, OK, so I hadn't added any personal touches to the cafe yet, but I was more of a back-of-the-house person. I handled anything involving organizational skills, such as ordering, sourcing suppliers, bookkeeping, etc. I was also the baker, so my contribution would be more evident once we opened.

If we opened.

I couldn't shake the feeling that we were missing something, that we were rushing into opening too soon. This was my dream, after all. It needed to be perfect. It needed to be a success. It needed to be *right*.

Before I could voice these doubts, Adeena said, "Stop it. We're not pushing back the opening."

I struggled to keep my facial expression neutral. Had I been thinking out loud or had Adeena finally progressed to full-on mind reader? "What are you talking about? I didn't even say anything."

She studied my face. "You didn't have to. I know you and I know the way you think. Plus, you had that look on your face."

I crossed my arms. "What look?"

"The one where you don't know whether to run away or puke. You really need to start dealing with your anxiety and stop sticking your head in the sand over every little thing."

"What Adeena is trying to say," Elena cut in, giving her girlfriend a warning look, "is that we're worried about you. You've seemed really stressed out and—"

"Of course I'm stressed out! We're opening on Monday and we're so not ready. We haven't even—"

"Haven't what? We've done everything possible." Adeena ticked off the list on her fingers. "We've replaced all the furniture because neither of us could stand to look at it anymore. We hired industrial cleaners to go over the entire place," here her eyes flicked over to a particular spot near the door, "and the space is sparkling. It's even cleaner than your family's restaurant, which is really saying something. We've registered the business with Illinois, had my brother draw up all the legal papers, gotten every freakin' license possible. We could've opened even sooner if it hadn't taken the county so long to replace Mr. Nelson."

Mr. Nelson was the previous health inspector, currently in jail after I'd exposed his shady dealings with the help of Adeena, Elena, and some of the other Shady Palms restaurant owners.

She continued, "And it's not even our official opening on Monday, just the soft opening. Which you conveniently won't be present for since you decided to take that judging position without consulting us." She put her hands on her hips. "You know. Us? Your business partners? Who have just as much riding on this as you do?"

I sighed and toyed with my necklace, already tired of the conversation. I'd agreed to judge the Miss Teen Shady Palms Pageant yesterday, after one of the judges had to drop out at the last minute. The pageant committee had wanted me, a former winner, to be part of the original lineup, but I'd turned them down. I'd already had my hands full preparing for the cafe opening and didn't need to be reminded of my pageant past, especially with Elena harping on about remembering those we'd lost.

However, with the pageant down a judge and the first event happening later tonight, the committee had decided to play dirty. They not only offered the Brew-ha Cafe the catering contract for all the pageant events plus a free booth and advertising at the Founder's Day Festival, our town's biggest celebration, but they also brought in the big guns: the Calendar Crew, aka my godmothers—Ninang April, Ninang Mae, and Ninang June.

Nobody, but nobody, wielded guilt and tsismis the way these three women did. Once those aunties got involved, it was all over.

How could I have possibly said no when Ninang June, my mother's best friend, said things like "Ay, Lila, it would mean so much to Cecilia, God rest her soul. You know how much she loved the pageant and believed in helping the community. Paying it forward, diba?"

Nothing like conjuring up the name of my dead beauty queen mother to convince me to do something that I absolutely did *not* want to do.

Which was what made Adeena's comment so unfair. If anyone knew my complicated feelings about the pageant and my mom, it would be her.

"You act as if me taking on the position is a huge inconvenience for you. May I remind you that I'm the one stuck dealing with this for the next three weeks? And that my sacrifice ensures a strong opening since we'd never have been able to afford a booth or the kind of advertising that they're providing? Not to mention the catering contract, and that I was able to convince them to hire Terrence to design everything!"

Terrence Howell was one of our closest friends, and a freelance graphic designer. He'd finally quit his construction job to do his design work full-time and I wanted to support him as much as possible. He'd already designed the Brew-ha Cafe logo, website, and social media banners, and did the same for my aunt's restaurant, but it wasn't enough. I knew he was hurting, both emotionally and financially, after the mess his fiancée, Janet, got him into a few months ago.

Elena, ever the peacemaker, stepped in. "She's right, Adeena. Besides, it was my idea to do the soft open, remember? We agreed it was the best way to work out the kinks in the system before officially opening since we could test what our customers are drawn to. Plus, I'm still trying to figure out the shop's energy. Without it, I won't know what other plants to bring in."

The three of us brought very different skills to the table. Adeena was our potion brewer/barista and had come up with an impressive menu that offered the usual cafe staples as well as more creative drinks, drawing from our collective Pakistani, Filipino, and Mexican backgrounds. Elena was our green witch, providing not just the decor, but also ingredients from her family's greenhouse and garden. The herbal remedies, teas, and natural bath and beauty products that she and her mom made lined the shelves, scenting Elena's corner of the shop with a lovely, subtle aroma. And I crafted the baked goods, putting a Filipino spin on coffee shop classics.

Or at least, that was what I was supposed to do. One of the biggest reasons I was hesitant to open was something I could never admit to Adeena, something that pained me to even think about. Something that proved the timing wasn't right. Because *I* wasn't right.

And as if on cue, Adeena asked about it. "OK, fine, I'm sorry. I do appreciate all the publicity you're drumming up for us. But we still haven't seen your part of the menu. When do you plan on getting it to us?"

The tinkling of the door chimes interrupted us, announcing the arrival of an unexpected savior, my not-related-by-blood cousin, Bernadette. The sight of her got my adrenaline going, as if my body were gearing up for a fight, but I tamped it down. A year older than me, we'd been rivals almost our entire lives, but had formed a truce a few months ago back when things were bad and I needed her help.

"Hey, Ate Bernie. What's up? Do you need me to let you into the restaurant?"

My family's restaurant, Tita Rosie's Kitchen, was conveniently located next door to the cafe. I technically still worked there since the cafe hadn't opened yet, but my aunt and grandmother only called me in on the weekends and the occasional lunchtime rush. They'd even hired a new server, which was the first time a non-Macapagal worked at the restaurant. She was the sister of one of Bernadette's old college friends and also Filipino, which in the eyes of my aunt made her family, so it was close enough.

Bernadette shook her head. "This isn't a social visit. You're needed next door."

I'd barely succeeded in calming myself down and those words got my blood pumping again. "What happened? Are Tita Rosie and Lola Flor OK?"

A look I couldn't read crossed her face. "Detective Park is there and he wants to speak to you. He needs your help on a case."

Chapter Two

Tita Rosie's Kitchen was most famous for our breakfast platters and Sunday lunch specials, and usually at this time of day, Tita Rosie and Lola Flor would be busy preparing for the Saturday-morning breakfast rush.

Instead, they were setting platters of garlic fried rice, sunny-side up eggs, and Filipino breakfast meats on the large table where Detective Park and the Calendar Crew sat waiting for me and Bernadette.

"Took you long enough." Ninang April looked me up and down, then gestured toward her eyes. "You look tired. Staying up late is bad for your skin, diba? And you're getting too much sun."

I sighed. "Good morning, everyone."

Tita Rosie waved me over to the seat between her and Detective Park, who'd quickly become part of the family. Shocking, considering a few months ago he got me locked up for murder and tried to convince everyone I was a small-town drug queenpin (it's a long story). Anyway, I caught the real killer—at no small risk to my own life, I might add—and as if to make up for his mistake (and possibly to get back into my aunt's good graces), the detective had been nothing but kind and solicitous ever since, which I appreciated. He also insisted on referring me to a therapist and talking about feelings, which was not appreciated.

My aunt shoved a piece of pandesal that she'd thickly coated with my grandmother's special coconut jam, minatamis na bao, into my hands. "You look hungry, anak. Kain tayo!"

She gestured to the plates on the table, urging everyone to help themselves to the do-it-yourself silog platters. I dished up a big plate of longsilog—longganisa (the delicious sausages I loved so much I'd named my adorable dachshund after them), sinangag (garlic fried rice), and itlog (fried egg). Traditional Filipino breakfasts typically included sinangag and itlog, as well as some form of protein, and the name of the dish changed depending on which protein you chose—tocilog, tapsilog, spamsilog, bangsilog, etc. It sounded intense, but this hearty meal was the only real way to start the day. No bowls of cereal or skipping meals in the Macapagal household. We worked long, hard hours and needed the delicious fuel to get us through the day.

Once plates were full, everyone except for Detective Park crossed themselves, which I copied belatedly, before tucking into the food. Joy Munroe, the teenager my family hired to help out at the restaurant since I was busy with the cafe, came out with a tray of drinks, her willowy arms straining as she tried to place the carafes of coffee and tsokolate on the table without spilling anything.

I offered to help her, but she demurred politely. "Thanks, Ate Lila, but I've got it. This is good training for me."

Bernadette smiled at her as she accepted a mug of tsokolate, our version of hot chocolate. "Love your positive thinking, Joy. Remind me to work more strength training into your routine in addition to your lessons on grace."

Joy beamed at her. "Great idea, Ate Bernie. Does anyone need anything else?" We all shook our heads at her. "Then, Tita Rosie, I'm going to do my homework in your office. I ate before coming here and want to make sure my work's done before the first pageant meeting tonight."

After she left, Detective Park said, "Diligent girl. But shouldn't she be on summer break?"

"She's going to summer school to make room for more AP classes when school starts. She's hoping to get an early acceptance into one of Chicago's top schools for civil engineering," Bernadette said, her chest puffing up as if she were bragging about her own daughter. "I'm coaching her for the pageant. She could really use the scholarship that comes with the crown. Lord knows, her parents are no help."

Joy was the younger sister of Bernadette's best friend, Pinky, a fellow Filipino nurse at the Shady Palms Hospital. I didn't know much about Pinky, other than she worked hellish hours to provide for her family, so it was nice that Bernadette had taken Joy under her wing.

Detective Park cleared his throat. "Now that we have privacy, we should probably get to business. What we talk about here doesn't leave this table. Am I clear?" He leveled a look at my gossipy godmothers, who had the nerve to look affronted.

"Detective, shame on you. We would never share classified information," Ninang Mae said, lying with the face of a saint.

"You better not, because if there's a leak, I know exactly who to blame. I called you here since you're all either good sources of information," he nodded at the aunties, which seemed to mollify them, "or directly involved with the pageant."

This he directed at me and Bernadette. He continued, "Ordinarily, I wouldn't get civilians involved, but according to the chief there isn't even a case. I wanted to get your take on the problem."

He pulled a sheet of paper out of his pocket and put it on the table between us. At his nod, I picked it up. It took me a minute to decipher the cursive script before reading aloud,

Cancel the pageant if you know what's good for you

I looked up at him. "That's it? Ominous, but not particularly threatening. Is the SPPD taking this seriously?"

Detective Park made a noise of frustration. "I tried, but the chief is blowing it off as a prank. Won't even add extra guards until the final event because it'd be 'bad optics' and 'there's no room in the budget.'" Even without the gesture, I could hear the air quotes in the detective's voice. He continued. "Rob Thompson invested fifty thousand dollars and has devoted hundreds of hours on the planning committee to make sure it's a success. Plus, the mayor has been making a big to-do about it for months. Thinks it's the perfect opportunity to sweep away the last bits of bad press from, well, you know." He paused, softening his tone. "How are you doing, by the way? Did you ever get in touch with Dr. Kang? She can do a quick virtual session with you, see if she's a good fit for—"

I was spared from answering when Lola Flor cut in. "She's fine. She doesn't need to talk to a doctor. Now what exactly do you want us to do about this?" she asked, pointing to the note with her lips.

"I was hoping you could tell me all you know about this pageant and the people involved. Has there ever been a problem before? The department may think it's a hoax, but I'll be damned if I let any of the kids get hurt."

Tita Rosie frowned at his use of a swear word, but said, "I'm glad you're taking this seriously, Jonathan. Miss Teen Shady Palms is very important to our town."

That was an understatement. Shady Palms lived for this pageant. So many girls tried out for it—or were forced into it—that it had weekly elimination rounds so there'd be a manageable number of contestants for the final event that took place at the Founder's Day Festival. Momtestants attempting to bribe the judges and getting into fistfights over the evening dress selection at the nearby mall were not unheard of. But actual threats against the pageant itself? Never. As much as I hated the concept of beauty pageants, I knew Miss Teen Shady Palms was a necessary evil. It promised a generous college scholarship, which had allowed quite a few ambitious women, like me, to make it out of this tiny town situated a few hours outside of Chicago and see what the world had to offer.

Something I'd felt extremely guilty about since I officially quit school at the end of last year just a few credits short of receiving a degree. I had already taken a leave of absence to help my ex-fiancé set up his new restaurant, but had planned on going back once we were more settled. After catching him cheating on me, though, I'd high-tailed it back to Shady Palms to lick my wounds in peace, leaving my entire Chicago existence, and responsibilities, behind me. Not that that'd been going so well.

Tita Rosie continued, "Other than that, I'm afraid there's not much I can help you with. I don't really follow the contest the way everyone else does."

Not sure if it was Lola Flor's influence, but Tita Rosie had never been big on the pageant scene. From what I remember, it was my mom who had given her the idea to have special viewing parties for the Big Four (Miss Universe, Miss World, Miss International, and Miss Earth, obviously) to drum up business for the restaurant. If you wanted to draw a large Filipino crowd, the surest way to do so—outside of karaoke, of course—was to have a viewing party for a beauty pageant, a basketball game, or a boxing match.

"Don't worry, we've got it covered. How much time do you have, Detective? We can give you a rundown on all the past winners and judges, plus the rivalries and scandals. We could write a book about the Thompson family alone," Ninang Mae said.

The Thompson family was one of the oldest and most prestigious families in Shady Palms and had funded the pageant since its inception. They owned several businesses and dabbled in construction, but the most lucrative was their sporting goods store that had adopted the athleisure trend early on. The current head of the family, Rob Thompson, had been the subject of several scandals in his youth, many involving the pageant his family ran. Now in his early fifties, he seemed to have calmed down and reveled in the role of pillar of the community—his generous donations and fundraising attempts had increased tourism, brought sports and the arts back into our local schools, and his grants for local farmers and gardeners had enabled Elena and her mom to build the greenhouse that housed their various edible plants and herbs.

At the mention of the Thompsons, Detective Park gave a smile that looked suspiciously like a grimace. "I'm afraid I don't have time for all that right now, but let's make an appointment to go over your information in depth. Before I go, Lila," he turned to me, his gaze so direct and intense, I flinched instinctively, "keep your eyes open when you're around these pageant people. Let me know if you hear anything suspicious. Even if it doesn't seem like a threat, I want to know about anyone who may have a beef with either the pageant or the people involved."

"Ooh, you want me to go undercover?" I gave him a mock salute. "Miss Congeniality, reporting for duty."

Bernadette snorted. "Miss Congeniality, yeah right."

Detective Park held up his hands, signaling it wasn't the time for a fight. "You're not going undercover. I just want you to be vigilant. I'm hoping it all comes to nothing and we have a great Founder's Day Festival. But you're a smart girl. Observant. We'll have increased security on the day of, but I'm hoping to nip this thing in the bud before then. You are not to take action in any way, just report to me if you see or hear anything suspicious. Are we clear?"

I nodded. "Crystal. The first meeting is in a couple of hours, so I'll let you know if I learn anything."

"Good." Detective Park drained his mug and wiped the crumbs from his face. "Thanks for breakfast, Rosie. I'll stop by again soon, OK? Maybe we can grab dinner sometime."

My aunt smiled at him and said that would be great. She stood to let him out, but he paused at the door.

"I shouldn't have to say this, but watch yourself, Lila. We don't want a repeat of last time."

And then he was gone.

Chapter Three

After Detective Park left, the breakfast party broke up. Bernadette needed to get to the hospital, and the restaurant would be opening soon. I spent the next few hours going over my aunt's books, getting so into my task that I lost track of time. I had planned on baking something for the first pageant committee meeting, but it was too late now. I grabbed a tray of my grandmother's freshly fried turon to bring with me and hurried out to my ancient SUV.

As I drove, I helped myself to the sweet banana spring rolls, the crisp wrapper crackling in my mouth, little shards of caramel littering my dress and clinging to my freshly painted lips. I probably should've waited to eat, but I needed to fortify myself. This snack was meant for the pageant committee, but the thought of reentering that world left me scrambling for comfort food.

A world I hadn't been a part of since my mother died. One where beauty was the only commodity a girl had, where a single slipup—in heels, in hitting the wrong note during your talent portion, with a boy—could somehow be enough to derail all the hopes and dreams your mother had heaped onto your shoulders. My mom had pushed me into one contest after another when I was a kid, determined that I would pick up where she had left off. Her winning her Philippine province's big beauty pageant had gotten her to the U.S. and no further. Her dreams for herself had ended once she reached the safety and security of a life with my father in quiet, safe Shady Palms.

"But you, Lila," she'd say to me at night, as she tucked me in after making me recite my prayers, "are American. There's no limit to what you can accomplish here. You can be so much more. And I know how to get you there." These memories of my mother always stirred up something uncomfortable in me, both tender and resentful.

She'd been gone so long that I sometimes forgot what she looked like. The sound of her voice. The feel of her hand stroking my hair. The warmth of her smile when I won another competition. Yet all the memories I didn't want to keep stayed, jagged pieces lodged into my brain and heart. The rivalry she constantly stoked between me and Bernadette. Her blind faith in the lie that was the American Dream. The narrow way she defined beauty, and her belief in its power. Her desire to mold me into whoever she thought she should've been—and my yearning yet constant failure to be the girl she wanted me to be.

I shook my head. It didn't have to be that way. I wasn't a kid anymore, my mom was gone, and Bernadette and I were friends. Joining—and winning—the pageant as a teen had been more about using the scholarship to get out of Shady Palms than anything to do with my mom. Just like back then, I needed to stay focused on my goals and away from the drama of that world. This pageant had no power over me. I repeated that last statement over and over to myself like a mantra as I drove to the community center, but it took two more turon before I started to believe it.

• • •

The Shady Palms Community Center was newly renovated, one of the pet projects of the illustrious Thompson family, and housed a swimming pool, basketball court, gym, craft room, meeting rooms, a party room, and an auditorium. This last room was where the pageant committee was meeting. It was also where we'd hold the majority of the contest, with the big final event taking place at the town square's Main Stage on Founder's Day.

I arrived right on time, a first for me, but everyone else had already assembled. William Acevedo, the head of the chamber of commerce, was in conversation with a tall White woman, who was dressed like she was about to go hiking and looked to be in her mid- to late fifties. She looked vaguely familiar, but I couldn't quite place her. A few paces away from them were Rob Thompson and Mayor Gunderson, both of them laughing it up like two good ol' boys, dressed in matching outfits of crisp, tucked-in white button-down shirts, slacks, and navy blazers. A gorgeous Black woman I'd never seen before kept an eye on the proceedings from a distance. She was also turned out in business casual attire, but her blazer was a shade of coral I'd never wear (dark color palettes were more my thing) that glowed against her lovely dark skin. She'd paired it with form-fitting capris, and her matching suede open-toed booties completed the look.

Mr. Acevedo noticed me coming down the aisle and waved me over. "Lila! So glad you could make it!"

The mayor flashed his campaign smile and made his way forward with his hand out as if for a handshake. He must've realized that was impossible since my hands were full, and smoothly changed his gesture to seem like he was helping me with the tray.

"How lovely! Did you bring us a treat from your restaurant? It'll be nice to have something decent to eat during these meetings. For once," he added under his breath. A small table near the stage held a couple of carafes as well as a fruit salad and a box of donuts.

"Oh? It looks like there's plenty of food for a group this small," I said, as he set down the tray and pulled back the foil. "My grandmother's special turon, fried shortly before I got here. The spring rolls are stuffed with saba banana and a strip of jackfruit."

I waited until everyone had helped themselves, then grabbed a paper plate and piled a bit of fruit salad on it, as well as a chocolate cake donut and another piece of turon. I'd had more than my share already, but I couldn't help myself—the crisp, sweet coating and firm-yet-creamy inside were wonderful. The donut, in contrast, was not quite so wonderful. Dry, with an odd, crumbly texture and not a bit of chew. I tried to set it aside discreetly, but the mayor noticed and laughed. "See what I mean? Valerie brings those things to every meeting and she's the only one who'll eat them."

Valerie, the woman who'd been talking to the head of the chamber of commerce, lifted her chin. "Well, I'm sorry that my gluten ataxia is so trying for you, Mayor Gunderson." It was then that I noticed the mobility device propped up against the stage next to her. She turned her gaze to me. "I'm Valerie Thompson. Lovely to meet you, Lila."

We shook hands, and as I studied her closely, it was easy to see the resemblance between her and Rob, particularly regarding the famous Thompson nose. I always forgot Rob had an older sister, since she didn't work at the Thompson Family Company and never appeared in any of their press releases.

"Sana is kind enough to bring fruit to every meeting, but since the men seem to think it's beneath them to provide food for us, I don't see where they get off complaining." Valerie stared longingly at the turon. "I'm guessing those aren't gluten-free?"

I shook my head. "I'm sorry. I didn't realize anyone here would have dietary restrictions. I'll make a note of it for next time."

She lifted an eyebrow. "You know that's not necessary. I'm capable of providing my own snacks."

I shrugged. "I want everyone to enjoy my food. Dietary restrictions aren't a burden. Plus it lets me be creative. It'll be fun."

The other woman came over to us and held out her hand. "I'm Sana Williams, one of the judges for the pageant. I like your attitude. Love your lipstick as well," she added with a wink.

Her silky soft skin encased my hand in an iron grip—this woman was strong. And possessed great style as well as an excellent skincare routine. Clearly this was someone who understood the importance of exfoliation. "Nice to meet you, Sana. I'm Lila Macapagal. My family runs Tita Rosie's Kitchen, and I'm the owner of the Brew-ha Cafe, opening soon."

She smiled even wider. "Oh, you're friends with Adeena and Elena! I've been wanting to meet you." At my confused look, she explained, "Elena is a regular at my fitness studio. She started bringing Adeena around recently and they talk about you often."

"Only good things, I hope," I said, in a clichéd attempt at a joke. Knowing how Adeena had been feeling about me lately, I doubted everything she'd said had been complimentary. She wasn't the type to hide her feelings or mince words.

Sana made a noncommittal noise and gestured to Valerie. "Valerie's part of the pageant committee and her brother, Rob, is our fellow judge."

Rob had been chatting with the mayor and chamber head, but made his way over to us after hearing his name. "So, this is our lovely third judge, eh? Pleasure to meet you, Lila."

He winked at me, an appreciative gaze sweeping over my body. I wore my favorite summer outfit, a simple fit-and-flare dress in a deep shade of maroon, the closest to a summer shade I owned in my decidedly winter-toned wardrobe. The only good things about summer were these dresses and that it was finally sandal weather. I had paired the dress with intricately laced black leather sandals, whose stacked heels added another three inches to my five-foot-three-inch frame. Those additional inches, along with the dress's very forgiving fit, made me look nice and voluptuous. I tried hard to embrace my curves and dressed in a way that showed them off, though it was still difficult to shut out my grandmother's judgmental voice and the cruel taunts from other girls that had been on the pageant circuit. Another reason I wasn't eager to reenter the pageant world.

"Anyway," Rob said, breaking into my train of thought, "now that we're all here, we can get started. I'm eager to begin."

Mr. Acevedo handed Rob a sheaf of papers. "Here are all the contestants. Your first job is to screen the ones who haven't supplied a satisfactory volunteer position so you can talk to them tonight. Remind them they have until the end of next week or they're out of the competition."

"Sorry, before we begin, what are the rules? And the schedule?" I asked. "Have they changed in the past seven or eight years? I know the pageant was on hiatus for a while."

The Miss Teen Shady Palms Pageant had been relatively unchanged since its inception in the late 70s, but after Rob and Valerie's parents passed away in a plane crash a few years ago, it had been put on hold to give the Thompson family time to mourn as well as get back on its feet, business-wise.

The mayor and chamber head frowned at my question, but Valerie lit up. "You bet they have! Those rules were so antiquated. I told the mayor that the only way the Thompson family would restart the pageant again is if we changed the rules."

She threw a look at the mayor, who was grumbling under his

breath. "The rules are rather simple this year. Contestants have to be self-identified young women between the ages of thirteen and eighteen. Currently enrolled in school, with plans on continuing their education after high school. They must volunteer a minimum of ten hours a week throughout the course of the pageant and provide signed proof they've completed their hours. Finally, they must read through and sign the Code of Conduct, stating the behavior we expect from our scholarship contestants."

She reached into her oversize leather satchel and handed binders to me, Rob, and Sana. "These are your expected duties over the next three weeks, as well as the rubrics you'll be using to judge each category."

We looked over our sheets. My pageant days involved the typical Q&A, talent show, and evening gown contest, which even back then I thought was weird. What high schooler needed an elegant evening gown outside of the prom? There had also been a sportswear modeling portion, where we had to parade up and down the runway wearing the latest Thompson Family designs, a blatant bit of self-promotion from the pageant organizers.

Valerie had kept the Q&A and added essay and speech contests, plus a display of what the contestants had learned during their time volunteering. The sportswear modeling had morphed into a "Design Your Own Athleisure Outfit" segment—still self-serving, but at least it was creative. I liked it. I liked it a lot. It still wasn't perfect, but at least now this was a competition I could be proud of.

I smiled. "These changes are amazing! I wish it had been like this when I was competing. I especially like that you got rid of the rule saying that a girl couldn't compete if she had a boyfriend or had ever been pregnant or whatever."

Valerie pursed her lips. "What good would that do? Punishing girls for things that men are rarely held accountable for? Take away the only chance many of them have to improve their lives and get an education? Who does that help?"

Mayor Gunderson said, "I don't like it. We had those rules for a reason. It seems like you're telling these girls it's OK to make bad decisions. There need to be consequences."

I raised an eyebrow. "And that involves denying them a chance at a good education?"

The mayor spluttered and looked as if he were preparing a rebuttal, but Mr. Acevedo stepped in. "We've got a lot to do if we want to start the kickoff event on time. Maybe we should start preparing the room?"

Valerie looked at her watch and clapped her hands. "He's right. OK, everyone, let's get to work!"

A few hours later, after the room looked like every streamer in Knotting Hill, our local craft store, had given its life to make the party room look festive, Rob stood up and stretched. "I don't know about you ladies, but I'm famished. I had to skip lunch to make it here on time. Would either of you care to join me?"

He looked between me and Sana, clearly not including his sister in the invitation. Valerie rolled her eyes, probably used to her younger brother leaving her out when other women were around.

"Why don't we all grab lunch at my aunt's restaurant?" I suggested. "I convinced my aunt to get gluten-free soy sauce a while ago, and I can warn you away from any recipes that might contain gluten. We have a very rice-based cuisine, so it'll be easy."

Valerie smiled at me. "That would be lovely. I've never had Filipino food before, but I've heard good things about your restaurant."

Rob looked a little put out at having his sister tag along but tried to make the most out of the situation and rope in Sana as well. The look he gave her was just as appraising as the one he'd given me earlier, and she shuddered a bit as she stepped closer to me. "I have to teach a yoga class later, so I probably shouldn't eat anything."

"You don't have to eat, then. Just come keep us company. I'd love to get to know my fellow judges better, especially when they're as lovely as the two of you," Rob said, putting an arm around me.

Sana and I exchanged a look, me begging her with my eyes to join us. She sighed. "Sure, why not? I'd like to chat more with Lila anyway. I'm always interested in meeting more women of color entrepreneurs."

"Great! Full disclosure though, one of the contestants is a server at my family's restaurant. That's not going to be a problem, is it?" I bit my lip, worried I might be messing up Joy's chances by telling them this.

Valerie waved my concern away. "Everybody in this town is connected to everybody else through blood, marriage, or business. We'd have to disqualify everyone whose family has been here for more than a year."

"I guess that's one of the good things about having me as a judge, right? I've only been here a few years, so you don't have to worry about me being biased," Sana said.

Valerie nodded. "That's part of it, I won't lie. But I also wanted you on the team because you're a young female entrepreneur running successful businesses that focus on wellness. You're a great role model for the girls who enter the pageant."

Sana blushed and waved away the compliment. "Let's head out, shall we? I'm starting to feel a bit peckish and could use a nibble before my class."

We each took our separate cars to Tita Rosie's Kitchen and joined the busy lunchtime rush. It was after two, but most of the tables were still full. I managed to snag a booth for four near the kitchen and excused myself to greet my aunt and grandmother.

They were hard at work, churning out lunch platters and smaller plates for meryenda, or snack time.

"Oh, anak, are you done with your pageant duties?" Tita Rosie brushed her old-fashioned bangs out of the way to look at me.

"Sort of. I brought some of the pageant people over for lunch. Thought it'd be good to get to know them and see if I can get any information for Detective Park."

She smiled. "Good idea. Are they ready to order yet? Any special requests?"

"One of the members can't eat gluten, so make sure to use the gluten-free soy sauce and keep all wheat products away when you prepare her food."

I said this to Tita Rosie, but it was really directed at Lola Flor, who was in charge of the baking and sweets, and not so careful when it came to people's dietary restrictions. She ignored me, but my aunt gave me a knowing smile.

"I'll handle it. Now go back to your guests. Joy's probably waiting to take your order."

She was right. Joy was giving the pageant table recommendations on what to order and guiding Valerie to safe menu options when I joined them.

"As long as you order a dish that says it's served with rice or rice noodles, you should be fine. And the majority of our desserts are made with glutinous rice and rice flour, so it shouldn't be a problem."

"Great job, Joy," I said, taking my seat next to Sana. "I'd planned on being their guide but needed to talk to Tita Rosie really quick."

She smiled, her dimples making her look extra sweet. "No problem, Ate. Are you all ready to order?"

Rob ordered my aunt's signature mixed adobo lunch platter, while Sana echoed my order for shrimp sinigang, a delicious, tangy soup that managed to be both comforting and refreshing. Valerie went with one of our breakfast platters, available all day due to their popularity. She couldn't decide which meat to choose—I kept pushing her toward longganisa, the most delicious sausage ever—so Joy told her she could get a sampler platter with small portions of the sweet, garlicky longganisa, sweet, cured tocino, and salty, lightly dried tapa.

Joy left to give our orders to the kitchen, and Rob's eyes followed her every step. Valerie dug her elbow into his side and he turned his attention back to us, wincing slightly.

"She's the pageant contestant I mentioned earlier. Practically a member of the family. I will, of course, be completely objective when it comes to judging, but I'm glad that I took this position. I remember from my own pageant days that older creeps loved hanging around the girls," I said, looking him in the eye to make sure he got my meaning. His scowl told me that he did.

Satisfied, I turned toward Valerie. "I've been meaning to ask. You said it didn't matter that I have a personal connection to one of the contestants. So then why was Bernadette rejected?"

"Bernadette?" she repeated, brow creased.

"Bernadette Arroyo. She's my cousin and the runner-up from my year. She said she couldn't be the judge because she was coaching Joy."

When the Calendar Crew put the pressure on me to accept the position, I tried to redirect them and have Bernadette take on the responsibility. She cared about the pageant way more than I did and should've won the year we competed together. She wasn't happy about having to admit that she'd already volunteered, and they'd turned her down.

"Oh. Well, coaching involves training a specific candidate to win, so that's more of a conflict of interest than your family employing a contestant. Though I don't remember talking to a Bernadette about being a judge. We were pretty adamant it be you."

Ouch, no wonder Bernadette's pride was hurt. This woman

must've dismissed her with barely a glance, considering how she couldn't even remember her. "Why? I mean, I get that she didn't win, but she would've taken my place if I hadn't been able to fulfill my duties. Plus she's a nurse. She'd be a great role model for these girls."

Valerie shrugged. "That was probably the mayor's call. I introduced quite a few changes to the rules and events and vetoed the judge who was chosen after you first turned us down. I insisted the last position be filled by a female professional, and the mayor said it had to be a former winner since that was tradition. You're the only one still in Shady Palms who fits both criteria, so we were at a bit of a stalemate. It was either you or no one."

I wasn't quite sure how to take that. "I thought the previous judge dropped out. Why did you replace them?"

Rob, Sana, and Valerie all seemed to have a sudden need to drink from their previously untouched water glasses instead of answering my question. Interesting. Before I could push further, Joy arrived with our meal.

After serving us and checking if we needed anything else, she left to go wait on some new customers and we dug into our food. The weak air conditioning in the restaurant was no match for the ninety-degree heat outside, and combined with the big bowl of steaming sinigang that Sana and I were consuming, I was soon dripping with sweat.

"This tastes so familiar!" Sana said. "That sourness . . . is it from tamarind?" When I nodded, she grinned, the dazzling smile lighting up her whole face. "I knew it. My family's originally from Trinidad, and we use it in a bunch of dishes. This soup is new to me, but somehow it tastes like home, you know?"

She attacked the soup and rice with new vigor, and so did I, both of us patting sweat away with the paper napkins on the table.

Rob noticed this and frowned. "I don't understand how you two can eat soup on such a hot day."

I snorted. "What, do you think people in hot climates never eat soup?"

Sana added, "Why do you think so many tropical countries eat spicy food? Sweating is healthy and helps us cool off. Removes toxins from the body, too. Though it does do a number to my hair," she said, dabbing at her edges.

"I'll stick with ice cream to cool off, thanks. Or an ice-cold beer. Speaking of which, with the way I drink, no amount of sweating will detox me." He chuckled at his little "joke."

Joy came by to refill our water glasses. "If you want something cold, you should order Lola Flor's special halo-halo for dessert. It's so good!"

At the pageant group's confused looks, I said, "Halo-halo literally means 'mix-mix.' Think of it as a combination of shaved ice and an ice cream sundae. It's one of my favorite desserts and my grandmother makes almost every component of the dish herself instead of relying on jarred or canned ingredients."

Everyone agreed that sounded wonderful and ordered the dessert, including Sana, who said, "I'll probably regret it come yoga time, but it sounds too good to pass up."

Large fountain glasses arrived at our table, layered with sweet beans, caramelized saba bananas, jackfruit, palm fruit, nata de coco, and strips of macapuno topped with shaved ice, evaporated milk, a slice of leche flan, a healthy scoop of ube halaya, and a scattering of pinipig, the toasted glutinous rice adding a nice bit of crunch. This frosty rainbow confection raised my spirits every time I saw it, and both Sana and I pulled out our phones to take pictures of the dish.

She laughed. "This is almost too pretty to eat, so I wanted to document its loveliness before digging in."

"This is for the restaurant's social media pages. My grandmother only prepares this dish in the summer, so I need to remind our customers to come while it lasts."

"How do we go about this?" Rob asked, looking at his rapidly melting treat in trepidation.

"Up to you. You can mix everything together like the name says so that you get a bit of everything in each bite. Or you can tackle it layer by layer. I'm a mixing girl, but you better figure it out fast or you're going to be eating dessert soup."

We all dug in, each snowy bite punishing my teeth and making me shiver in delight. I loved the interplay of textures—the firmness of the beans versus the softness of the banana and jackfruit mingling with the chewiness of the palm fruit, nata de coco, and macapuno. The fluffy texture of the shaved ice soaked through with evaporated milk, with the silky smoothness of the leche flan matched against the creaminess of the ube halaya and crispiness of the pinipig. A texture eater's (and sweet tooth's) paradise.

"This is so strange," Valerie said. "I never would've thought of putting all these things together, especially not in a dessert. But it works. I mean, I don't love the beans, but they're certainly interesting. And what are these yellow strips?"

"Jackfruit. When ripe, they're yellow and very sweet and fragrant, so they make a nice addition to lots of Filipino desserts. They were also in the turon I brought to the meeting earlier. Unripe jackfruit is green and used in vegetarian recipes, usually."

The rest of the meal passed in inane chitchat—anytime I tried to get Valerie or Rob to talk about themselves, the conversation devolved into a bragfest with the siblings trying to outdo each other with their various academic (on Valerie's part) and business (on Rob's part) achievements. Sana seemed used to this and spent the rest of the time alternating her attention between her dessert and her watch, probably wondering when she could finally escape. Rob graciously paid the bill at the end, and neither Sana nor I bothered fighting him for it. Considering how much the Thompson family was worth, he could afford it.

When Joy came to clear the table, he grinned and slipped her a thick, folded set of bills. "Great job, sweetheart. Your recommendations were top-notch."

Joy gave him a tight smile and slid the tip into her apron pocket. "Thank you, sir. See you later tonight for the kickoff event. I hope you all have a great day."

Sana glared at Rob, then turned toward me. "It was great meeting you, Lila. Why don't you stop by my yoga class later? The first week is free and I think it'd be good for you."

Before I could reply, Joy said, "Are there student discounts? My friend Katie loves your classes and I've been thinking about joining. Just thinking about all the exams I have to take this year stresses me out, but I want to deal with it in a natural way."

"My six o'clock class is open to all ages and levels, and I accept payments on a sliding scale, so we can talk about that." Sana paused, choosing her next words carefully. "Yoga, and exercise in general, is wonderful for both physical and mental health, but I hope you know it's not a cure-all. It's just a way to help deal with the symptoms. If you—"

"Your class ends way before the potluck tonight, right? I don't want one of our own judges showing up late to the event," Valerie interrupted.

"I'm surprised you're holding the event so soon. You only notified the contestants a few days ago," I said. I was hoping for a bit of downtime today, but they were really throwing me into the deep end with this position. When I was a contestant, there were a few weeks between the announcement of who made it in and the kickoff event. I also remembered the pageant being a whole month long. Seemed like they were running behind on planning this year and trying to make up for it by packing everything into a shorter time frame.

"Everyone knows the pageant potluck is how we kick things off, so they should've planned for it if they were serious about competing. We start at seven p.m. sharp and I expect you to be there, Lila. As the newest judge and a former winner, I'm sure the girls are dying to meet you." Valerie grinned, tenting her fingers. "I bet the moms are, too."

A flashback to what my mother and Ninang June were like during my and Bernadette's pageant days had me crossing myself and offering up a prayer: Heaven save me from Shady Palms's scheming stage moms.

Chapter Four

Before I knew it, seven o'clock had rolled around and it was time for the annual "Getting to Know You" potluck for the contestants and their parents. Just like all those years ago, I entered the community center with huge trays of lumpiang shanghai and pancit—meat-filled fried spring rolls and stir-fried noodles—courtesy of Tita Rosie, and a small tray of Lola Flor's cassava bibingka, a treat I'd carefully marked "gluten-free" for Valerie.

I dropped off the trays and went around the room greeting everyone I knew, then stopped short when I came across a group I'd been avoiding for months: the PTA Squad. Led by Mary Ann Randall, and the main reason I'd been avoiding church lately. They'd long been in competition with my family—or I should say, they saw my family as competition since we usually didn't bother with them—for the good graces of Father Santiago. He was everyone's priest, but he was also our family friend, and the PTA Squad hated that we had this personal link to him when they should've been the favored bunch. They had been only too happy to spread rumors about me when I got in trouble earlier in the year, and even though I had proven my innocence (which the aunties had rubbed in their faces), I was in no mood to deal with their snide remarks. I'd planned on moving on after acknowledging their presence with a nod, but they moved as a pack, trapping me inside a circle of athleisure-clad moms.

"Lila!" Mary Ann squealed, the pleasure (and pitch) in her voice stunning me in place. "We haven't seen you in so long. How have you been?" Without waiting for me to answer, she said, "How exciting that you're going to judge this year's Miss Teen Shady Palms Pageant!"

She lowered her voice as she said the name of the pageant, the title uttered with the reverence of a prayer. So there it was, the real reason she was so happy to see me, and with so little subtlety, too. Then again, with Mary Ann, there was rarely any subtext, just text. To be honest, that was something I appreciated about her. I liked knowing where I stood with people, and she'd always been very clear about that.

"What did you bring? It smells absolutely divine." She made a big show of sniffing the air and clutching her hands to her chest in ecstasy.

"Hello, Mary Ann, and . . ." I trailed off, realizing I didn't know the names of anyone else in the PTA Squad.

Mary Ann gestured to a pretty blonde girl standing behind a table full of casseroles. "Oh, this is my daughter, Sharon. My little girl's going to be Miss Teen Shady Palms, just like her mom!"

Ah, so that explained why Mary Ann behaved the way she did. One of the reasons I hated the pageant was because the winners who stayed in Shady Palms acted like they deserved special treatment, as if they were above everyone else. Though according to Bernadette, I'd acted that way even before winning the crown. I wished she were here with me now. She was way better at putting people in their place than I was, and I had little interest in playing nice with any of these women.

Sharon had a pained smile on her face, but came around the table to shake my hand politely. She then grabbed her friend's hand and pulled her forward. "And this is my best friend, Leslie. We both want to win, but if we don't, we know it's not the end of the world."

She stressed those last few words very carefully, directing them toward her mom without losing her smile or breaking eye contact with me. Hmm, maybe there was more to Sharon Randall than I'd first thought. I was going to write her off as just another blonde-haired, blue-eyed beauty queen, but if she wasn't just a clone of her mother, maybe she warranted a closer look.

Leslie, however, seemed to be made of the same stuff as her nameless mother, shrinking behind Sharon and offering a limp handshake. At first, I thought her hiding behind Sharon mirrored her mother's deference to Mary Ann as the head of the PTA Squad, but then I noticed the way Leslie looked at her friend. Oh. I see. I made a mental note to get to know this pair better, but before we could continue the conversation, the whine of a microphone cut through the room, making everyone wince.

"Sorry about that! And welcome, everyone, welcome to the beginning of the fiftieth Miss Teen Shady Palms Pageant!" The mayor was up onstage, addressing the crowd. "Before we all fall upon our delicious repast, I'd like to introduce the people who are making this possible. Could the judges and pageant committee please come up here?"

Ugh, I hoped he wasn't going to make us give speeches. The mayor was notoriously long-winded and loved to make everything a big to-do, probably to make himself (and Shady Palms) seem more important than they were. Rob and Valerie were already standing behind the mayor, so Sana and I went to join them.

"I'm sure you all know William Acevedo, the head of our chamber of commerce, who has been wonderful about finding sponsors for our program. Let's hear a round of applause for his efforts." The mayor paused as the crowd cheered for Mr. Acevedo. "I'd also like to introduce Valerie Thompson, a powerful force on the committee. I—"

Valerie stepped forward and took the mic from the mayor mid-speech. "Thank you, Mayor Gunderson, for your kind introduction. And yes, I'd like to think of myself as a powerful force of change, not just for this pageant, but for the futures of all the young women in Shady Palms. Before we introduce our illustrious judges, I'd like to point out the changes we've made to this year's program and let you know our expectations regarding the behavior and performance of these young women."

She then went on to delineate, step by step, what the girls had to do, droning on and on despite all this information being covered in the hefty information packets the contestants had received after being accepted. Then again, after seeing how many people couldn't follow basic instructions on the application, maybe Valerie knew how few of them would take the time to read over the documents she had so carefully put together.

Based on the number of gasps and murmurs that accompanied some of Valerie's announcements, most of the crowd hadn't even bothered to crack open the envelope. Removing the modeling and evening gown sections seemed to be a popular move, but when she mentioned the thirty-hour volunteering portion of the program, which counted for 40 percent of the total score and also required an essay of reflection, there was almost a mutiny.

"What does that have to do with Miss Teen Shady Palms? This is a beauty pageant!" Mary Ann Randall said, clutching her actual pearls in rage.

Valerie looked at her coldly. "And we want to make sure our winner is beautiful inside and out. Brains, ambition, and spirit are what will win this contest. Miss Teen Shady Palms is more than just a pretty smile."

Mary Ann reared back as if she'd been hit. Her friend stepped up beside her. "But that's unfair! How are the girls supposed to get thirty hours of volunteer work done in such a short time? They're just kids!"

Valerie pinched the bridge of her nose. "The requirements were clearly listed on the application form. If you didn't bother reading it before filling it out and checking the box, you have no one to blame but yourself."

I looked around to see how everyone was taking that statement, and as my eyes swept the crowd, I finally found Joy, who was standing next to Bernadette. Joy and I made eye contact and she smiled brightly at me, nodding her head to let me know she already knew about the requirement. Of course she did. When she'd applied to work at Tita Rosie's Kitchen, her resume said she'd been volunteering at the local animal shelter since freshman year of high school, so this was nothing to her. Good girl. I wondered why she was with Ate Bernie instead of her parents—I would've liked to meet them.

"And now I'd like to introduce our judges," Valerie continued. The mayor stood behind her, arms crossed and expression stormy. I got the feeling that he'd planned on being the emcee that night and Valerie had stolen his thunder.

"I'm sure you all know my brother, Rob Thompson, the benefactor of this pageant." Rob moved forward to say something, but Valerie steamrolled on. "And while his generosity is wonderful, I'd like to focus on these two very inspiring young women: Sana Williams and Lila Macapagal!"

The room broke out in applause, while Sana and I awkwardly smiled and waved at the crowd. I guess this was why Valerie had asked how to pronounce my last name earlier that day, a gesture I definitely appreciated.

"Sana and Lila are both women of color and they've gone on to do great things. That's why I was so eager to get them on the judges' panel," Valerie said, beaming at the crowd.

Sana and I exchanged glances at Valerie's well-intentioned yet unflattering surprise at our success as "women of color," glances that spoke of the frustration we felt at moments like this. Moments that happened far too often.

Valerie continued, oblivious to her obliviousness, "Miss Teen Shady Palms contestants, this is the perfect opportunity to take advantage of these women's expertise. Ask questions. Be curious. Be ambitious. And good luck!"

After another round of applause, Sana, Rob, and I left the stage together. As I waited for my turn to descend the narrow stairs off to the side, I heard the mayor say, "Interesting speech. But I am to be the emcee at all the major events from now on. You may be a Thompson, but you don't run this town."

I strained to hear Valerie's response, but it was impossible without making my eavesdropping obvious.

I followed Sana and Rob to a table where George and Nettie Bishop were laying out tray after tray of their amazing Southern-style comfort food. They both paused what they were doing to wrap me up in a big Bishop hug. Big Bishop's BBQ was a Shady Palms institution and one of the first Black-owned businesses in town. If Valerie wanted to acknowledge women of color who had made it in Shady Palms,

Nettie Bishop was the OG. Her husband, George, may have been the one who manned the grill, but everyone knew it was Nettie who reigned over the restaurant.

"Miss Nettie! Big George! I didn't expect to see you here," I said, accepting the heaping plate Big George pushed on me.

"Mr. Thompson hired us to cater his portion of the potluck," Miss Nettie said, winking at Rob.

Rob shrugged. "There's no way anyone would want to eat something I made, and the Bishops make the finest food in town. Oh, uh, present company excluded, of course."

I smiled at him. "Considering how much time I spent at Big Bishop's BBQ in high school, I'm happy to share that honor."

Sana said, "Well, this is my first time trying your food and it's amazing! I don't normally indulge like this, but this mac and cheese is so worth it."

Big George grinned at her. "Why, thank you, miss. You should stop by the restaurant sometime. A pretty lady like you is sure to drum up business."

Miss Nettie swatted his arm. He winced, and added, "You too, Lila. We miss having you around."

He gave me a sad smile, likely asking for forgiveness. We'd had a bit of a falling-out due to my ex-boyfriend. Or more like, Big George hadn't wanted to see me since I reminded him of my ex's betrayal. So I'd been avoiding his restaurant the last few months. Guess this was his way of welcoming me back.

"Thanks, Big George. I'll stop by later this week with Terrence. We need to talk about the flyers I want him to design for the new cafe anyway."

"And what about your business partners? Will Adeena and her lovely lady friend be there as well?" Miss Nettie gave me a knowing look. Somehow, she always knew when Adeena and I were on the outs.

I shrugged. "I'll ask, but she and Elena might have their hands full with the cafe's soft opening, plus preparing the catering for all the pageant events." Before they could ask more questions about Adeena or the cafe, I said, "Excuse me, I see my friend Yuki and her daughter. I should go say hi."

I hurried over to Yuki Sato, who was arranging a tray of vegetable tempura on the table. Her daughter was pouring iced green tea into individual cups, but stopped when she saw me approaching, sloshing tea all over the table.

"Oh no! I'm so sorry, Ms. Macapagal!" She grabbed a bunch of paper towels and mopped up the mess, her eyes begging her mother to take over.

Yuki sighed but obliged. "Lila, this is my daughter, Naoko. The pageant has been all she's talked about for the past month, so please watch over her."

"Nice to properly meet you, Naoko," I said. We'd met before, since I was a regular at Sushi-ya, the restaurant Yuki and her husband ran, but had never really talked. She was usually too busy helping her parents and I was too busy stuffing my face to make polite conversation. "I didn't realize you were old enough to be in the pageant."

Naoko's eyes shone behind her giant red plastic-framed glasses. "I turned thirteen last month! Mommy thinks I'm too young, but Dad said it's never too early to start saving for my future." She ducked her head, her high, off-center ponytail (wait, were scrunchies back in fashion?) swinging in front of her face. "I don't think I'll win, but it's good practice for next year. And the year after that. And the year after—"

"As you can see, Lila, my daughter is both diligent and practical." Yuki's tone was teasing, but she couldn't hide the pride shining in her eyes. My heart twinged at that open affection. My mother had only looked at me like that if I won something so she could brag about me to Ninang June and her friends. "And considering she wants to go to art school, I'm happy to let her try for the scholarship, as long as she doesn't let it interfere with other, more traditional scholarship opportunities. Like getting good grades," she said pointedly.

Looking at Naoko, I wasn't surprised that she was an artist. Her round, oversize glasses, which might look frumpy or geeky on someone with less style, framed her intense eyes. And unlike yours truly, she didn't seem to shun bright colors. In fact, her clothes were a cacophony of colors: yellow overall dress on top of a red short-sleeved shirt, blue belt bag covered with pins slung across her chest, and glittery, rainbow-sequined sneakers that looked like she'd bedazzled them herself. An armful of beaded bracelets and beaded, fringe-like earrings topped off the ensemble.

"You have a very distinct sense of style, Naoko. I'm getting Claudia Kishi vibes. Did you make that jewelry yourself?"

"I did! I'm saving up to get a 3D printer so I can start designing more pieces and sell them on Etsy." She lit up, pleased that I'd noticed. "You have a nice style, too. Just . . . dark. Jewel tones would go well with your tan skin too, but I don't know if that's you."

I smiled at her. Finally, someone who understood. "I prefer playing with pattern and texture than color," I said, gesturing to the starry knit black shawl I'd thrown on over my shimmery black wrap dress and peep-toe booties with star cutouts. I'd painted my nails a glittery black color to match. The only pops of color on me were my gold and jade necklace, plus my signature burgundy lip shade.

She nodded sagely. "Monochrome doesn't have to be boring. Good for you."

Fighting off laughter, Yuki said, "Sorry to interrupt fashion talk, but there are quite a few people waiting to chat with Lila." She gestured toward Joy and Bernadette, who were standing with a pretty East Asian woman in her early thirties and her teenage daughter. As I walked over to join them, I heard Naoko ask her mom who Claudia Kishi was.

I laughed to myself as I greeted this new group. "Hey, everyone! Having a good time?"

"Hi, Ate Lila! This is my friend Katie Pang, and her mother, Winnie," Joy said. "Katie's the one who convinced me I should apply to the pageant. Well, her and Ate Bernie, of course."

"It's so nice to meet you, Ms. Macapagal! Joy talks about your family all the time, saying how kind your aunt is and how good the food is. I keep trying to get Mom to take me there, but she's busy, I guess." Katie grinned at me, her open smile, light brown hair with blunt-cut bangs, and smattering of freckles across her prominent nose and round cheeks lending her a very cute girl-next-door vibe. Judging by her features, she was also mixed Asian, just like Joy, and the two made an adorable duo.

"We don't eat out much. I work long hours at the salon and prefer to save money where I can. Restaurants are more of a special-occasion thing in our family. Plus, I'm a pretty good cook, if I do say so myself." Winnie smiled, gesturing to the platter of jiaozi she'd brought. Her black hair and dark brown eyes contrasted with her daughter's much lighter coloring, but they had the same sweet smile.

"What salon do you work at? I've been meaning to do something with my hair." I loved my shiny black hair and had always worn it long and straightened, but months of neglect left me with split ends and a sense of blah that was new to me. Maybe it was time for a change. Or at least a trim. No need for anything drastic.

"I'm the owner and main stylist at the Honeybee Salon, but I also do lashes and makeup." Winnie circled me, eyeing my hair. "Your hair is gorgeous but could use a little . . . refreshing. I'd love to get my hands on it."

"Good luck with that. Lila's kept her hair exactly the same since she was five. Tita Cecilia insisted on the two of them getting matching haircuts every year." Bernadette's smirk was replaced by a look of horror when she realized why I hadn't changed my hairstyle in over twenty years. "Oh, sh—sorry."

Katie, completely oblivious to what was going on, asked, "Who's Tita Cecilia?" stumbling slightly over the pronunciation of "Tita."

"'Tita' means 'aunt' in our language," I explained. "She's referring to my mom. She passed away when I was eight."

Katie's eyes widened. "Oh. I'm so sorry."

"I'm sorry too, Ate." Joy put her hand on my arm, the concern in her eyes sweet but discomfiting.

I forced a smile. "It was a long time ago. Don't worry about it."

Bernadette said, "Tita Cecilia loved beauty pageants. I'm sure she's so proud that Lila won and is a judge now. She always said the point of being a beauty queen is giving back to the community."

My mom had grown up in Tondo, one of the poorest areas of Manila. Her neighbors had all chipped in to pay the fees and other expenses it took to enter a pageant because they knew she had what it took to obtain the crown. After she won and moved to the U.S., she sent money and balikbayan boxes home every year until she died. Tita Rosie still sent a yearly balikbayan box, even though we had our own money problems and they weren't her blood relations. I hadn't thought about that side of the family in a long time.

As annoyed as I was that Bernadette was still talking about my mom and making me think about things I'd left in the past, the fact that she was, dare I say, *comforting* me was new and a little bewildering. We'd spent most of our lives looking for ways to compete and weak points to exploit. Maybe we really were becoming friends.

Then again, she knew how I felt about my mother and the way she'd phrased what she said could be a jab at me, trying to hint that even though I'd won the crown, I'd never given back to the community. Just because she felt guilty about my mom didn't mean she wasn't still pissed about me beating her.

"Thanks, Ate Bernie. I appreciate it." I even added a little smile to show her no hard feelings, and that I totally wasn't wondering if she was plotting against me.

"So your mom was a beauty queen, too?" Katie asked.

Maybe I shouldn't have said I was OK with it. Katie seemed to think that gave her carte blanche to ask all kinds of questions, and talking about my parents was something I did not do. Which Bernadette knew. I shot her a dirty look but she just shrugged.

I sighed. "Yeah, she won a local pageant and had a shot at the Miss Philippines title. She didn't win, but she did well enough to save money for her move to the U.S."

"So then she met your dad here, right? Because beauty queens can't be married when they're competing?"

"Those rules depend on the competition, actually. She and my dad had been a thing back in the Philippines, but they broke up when he moved to Shady Palms with my grandparents. After she moved here, they were able to reconnect and got married a few months later."

Against the wishes of my grandmother, I didn't add. Lola Flor had held her only son in high regard and thought he could do much better than a small-time beauty queen. I could tell by the sighs both Joy and Katie were letting out that they found the story romantic.

"A second chance at love! Those are my favorite kind of stories,"

Katie said. "I used to dream that my dad would come back to Shady Palms to win back my mom."

"And I told you that I didn't come to this country for a man. You should never rely on one for anything. You're young and pretty—use those assets to make your own way." Winnie sighed. "Besides, you never even met your father and it's probably better that way. Romance is for books. In the real world, it's about your brains and your looks. So use them."

Katie hung on to her mother's words, eyes widening in what she probably thought was the wisdom in them. I'd gotten a similar speech when I was a kid. "Yes, ma'am. Don't you worry, I'm going to win this thing, go to college, and become a high-powered businesswoman to manage a chain of our salons. Just like we always talked about."

"That's my girl." Winnie threw her arm around her daughter's shoulders and kissed her head. "Now go practice your networking skills."

As Joy and Katie wandered off to talk to the other contestants, Winnie motioned toward the other moms. "Need to check out the competition," she said with a wink.

"That woman is something," Yuki said. She'd wandered over to join our group and held out a piece of sweet potato tempura, which I gladly accepted.

"She reminded me of Tita Cecilia," Bernadette said.

I shot her a look. She'd brought up my mom one time too many. "Why are you here anyway? Where are Joy's parents?"

Bernadette pursed her lips. "They're not particularly involved in their children's lives. To put it mildly. Pinky's usually the one who attends the kids' functions, but she had a late shift at the hospital today and asked me to come."

"That was nice of you," I admitted.

She shrugged. "I wish Pinky could've gotten some time off, but she's the moneymaker in her family. And their parents only care about themselves. Joy's a good kid. She deserves to have someone who cares about her here with her."

We both turned to watch Joy laughing across the room with her friends, and my heart went out to her. I wondered what was worse: to grow up without your parents or to have parents who didn't give you the time of day? Or to be like Katie and not even know who one of your parents was?

I took a deep breath. No need to go down that path, especially now. "I should probably get to know the other contestants as well. See you two later."

I made my way over to Sana, who was chatting with Winnie Pang, Mary Ann Randall, and a few other women I didn't know.

"Hey, Lila, come meet some of the women in my yoga class. Maybe they can convince you to join us," Sana said.

"Sana's classes are the best. I don't know what we'd do without you," one of the women said, almost purring as she stared lovingly at Sana.

"They leave you so relaxed, even though your body knows you just had an intense workout," Winnie said. "Katie and I are both in her class. A little mother-daughter bonding, plus it doesn't hurt to stay fit, especially at my age."

The other moms in the group, clearly older than Winnie, stiffened at that comment. Sana rushed in to smooth over the situation. "That's the beauty of yoga, it's for all ages and levels! Great for the body and mind. You really must stop by sometime, Lila."

"Oh yes, please! We'd love to get to know you better," the moms begged.

I groaned inwardly. Though if I took better care of my health, maybe Detective Park would get off my back about that therapist. After all, Sana said it was good for the body *and* mind. "You know what? That sounds great. I'll talk to Adeena and Elena and try to join them for a class."

"Yoga class, huh? Maybe I should check it out, too," Rob said, strolling over to our group. "Lord knows it's taking more and more to get this old thing working properly." He gestured toward his body, which, at fifty-plus years of age, was still trim and fit and he knew it. I swear on everything, the group of momtestants squealed like a bunch of young girls at a K-pop concert.

Sana rolled her eyes and walked over to the refreshments table, and to my surprise Winnie joined her. She'd seemed the ambitious sort, so I figured she'd use any opportunity to get in good with the head judge. Though maybe she was playing it smart by trying to appeal to me and Sana. The others were too busy foaming at the mouth over Rob to notice. I tried to engage them in conversation, but it was clear they only had eyes for him.

I wandered around the room, wondering who to talk to next (or if enough time had passed to politely leave) when a commotion at the door drew my attention. Valerie and the mayor, speaking in low, hurried voices, were blocking someone from entering.

"Oh come now, Oskar. Don't make a scene!" the mayor said. "I understand why you're upset, but you're being a bad sport about this."

"The deli in my grocery store has helped cater the Miss Teen Shady Palms potluck for years! You gonna stop an old man from trying to deliver sandwiches?" The owner of the One Stop Shop, Shady Palms's combination grocery store/deli/convenience store, stood at the doorway, a full tray in his hands.

Valerie sighed. "Why are you even here, Mr. Weinman? You are no longer part of the pageant, and as far as I know, you have no relation to any of the young women participating. I'm going to have to ask you to leave."

Mr. Weinman lowered his voice. "Look, I just want to donate some sandwiches and hand out some coupons, OK? Business has been slow and I could use the opportunity to remind everyone I make the best damn sandwiches in Shady Palms."

He raised his voice for the last part of the sentence, drawing the attention of most of the people in the room.

The mayor grunted in frustration. "Fine, Oskar. Thank you for your donation, but this is the last time, OK?"

Valerie said, "But, Mayor—"

The mayor cut her off. "I'm serious, Oskar. After this, you pay to advertise or sponsor the pageant, just like everyone else. You hear me?"

Oskar glared at Valerie, as if this were her fault, but said, "Yeah, yeah. Whatever you say, Mr. Mayor," and went to go set up his sandwiches.

"I'm not sure that was a good idea, Bill," Valerie said. She crossed her arms, her eyes following Mr. Weinman's path through the room, watching him interrupt conversations to hand out coupons.

"And I'd like to remind you that this wouldn't even be an issue if you hadn't stuck your big Thompson nose in pageant business that had nothing to do with you. Your ridiculous crusade is ruining an honored Shady Palms tradition, and we don't need any bad press right now. Just play nice for once, will you?" And with that last condescending remark, Mayor Gunderson went to go grab a sandwich.

Valerie, as if in reaction to the mayor's insult, pinched the bridge of the offending feature while watching the two men, her eyes narrowed. She must've felt my gaze on her because she dropped her hand and turned to me.

"I'm not offended by what he said about my appearance, just so you know," she said, reading my mind. "It's always been a family joke, us sticking our large noses into everyone's business, always wanting to be part of everything going on in Shady Palms. It's his dismissive attitude I don't care for."

We both watched as Rob approached Mr. Weinman and slapped him on the back in greeting. In response, Mr. Weinman threw off his arm and shoved him. Valerie made a move toward them, but before she got more than a few steps away, Rob had his hands up in surrender and Oskar was leaving, bumping into both me and Valerie in his haste toward the door.

"Rude," I muttered.

"You're not wrong, but there's some history there," Valerie said. "My brother may have slept with Oskar's wife and caused their divorce. Well, honestly, it had been coming for ages, but Rob was probably the last straw. I just wanted to make sure they didn't cause a scene."

I gaped at her, but she just shrugged. "Just about everybody knows, so it's not like I'm revealing sensitive information. Surprised you hadn't heard about it yet. Anyway, whatever happened is between them, but this is an official pageant event. I don't need any liability issues because my brother doesn't have a loyal bone in his body."

"I heard that, Big Sister," Rob said. He looked utterly unfazed by what had just occurred.

Valerie snorted. "And was I wrong?"

He grinned at us. "We just have different ideas of loyalty and commitment, that's all. Beth understands."

"Beth likes being a Thompson enough to forgive your failings. Not exactly the same."

"Who's Beth?" I asked.

"My wife," Rob said, his eyes already wandering, looking for his next target.

"Your wife?!" I couldn't keep the judgment off my face or out of my voice.

He shrugged. "She knew who I was when she married me. It's not like any of this is news to her. We have an understanding." He paused, looking away to watch the crowd around Sana. "She's the only one who really gets me."

Valerie shook her head. "I'm so glad I have no romantic urges. The Thompsons have always been terrible at love."

Rob looked back at us and grinned, tapping his nose. "What can I say? Thompson family genes. Always sticking our noses in places they don't belong."

I watched him walk over to a group that included Joy. "What the heck did he mean by that?"

"No clue, but knowing him, I'd suggest not trying to figure it out." She glanced at her watch. "Excellent, the potluck is past its official ending time, which means we had a successful event and I can take the last of your grandmother's dessert home to enjoy in peace. See you tomorrow, Lila."

She paused, watching Rob stand next to Joy. He didn't do anything, didn't even seem to be talking to her, but she still said, "You might want to have a word with her. Just in case."

As she said that, Bernadette materialized between Joy and Rob, creating space between the two. I couldn't hear what she said from where I stood, but Rob's response obviously didn't jell with her because she started taking her earrings off. Joy pulled Bernadette away before she could start swinging on Rob, saving me the trouble. I had no idea what just happened, but our family didn't need an assault charge, especially against one of the Thompsons. Our lawyer was good, but no one was *that* good.

"You need to get your brother under control," I said to Valerie.

"You think I haven't tried? I just hope he doesn't do anything to ruin the pageant," she said, watching her brother grimly. As he slid his arm around one of the moms, she added, "But ruining things is what he does best."

Chapter Five

I woke up the next morning in a funk, one that persisted through my solitary breakfast, since my aunt and grandmother were at church. Well, not completely solitary since my dachshund, Longganisa, was with me. She'd eaten her diet kibble at lightning speed and was now curled up at my feet, waiting to pounce on the inevitable dropped bits of food. I'd just broken the yolk on my perfect sunny-side up egg when I got a text from Adeena, reminding me to stop by the cafe later to finish setting up the altar space Elena had planned, and oh, where was my part of the menu?

Well, there went my appetite. I pushed my barely touched plate away, knowing it was time to face the truth. I'd been avoiding this for months, hoping it'd all work itself out in the end (my usual way of handling things) but there it was: I'd lost my baking mojo.

I couldn't explain it. Normally, I brimmed with baking ideas and my aunt couldn't keep our kitchen stocked with enough eggs, butter, flour, and sugar since I ran through them so quickly. But for the last few months, I'd felt blocked while the ingredients piled up in the fridge.

I flipped through the beautiful leather-bound bullet journal I used to jot down my recipes, hoping something would catch my eye. I needed something spectacular for my part of the menu, something that would bring people to the cafe in droves. Something that would put us on the map. This was my dream and it needed to be perfect. But as I scoured the book, trying to find something worthy of the Brew-ha Cafe, I grew more and more dissatisfied with the simple recipes I'd compiled. But Adeena and Elena were counting on me. I had to figure this out.

I slammed the book shut and racked my brain to remember the last time I was wowed by a pastry. Images of a gorgeous croquembouche, a cake composed of filled cream puffs stacked with caramel and spun sugar, filled my head. If I filled them with ube, coconut, and pandan pastry creams, it'd be a wonderful Filipino-French fusion dessert that was sure to stop people in their tracks. Picturing it as the centerpiece of our stall for Founder's Day, I hurried off to research the various components and create my own award-winning recipe.

Five hours, an ungodly amount of eggs and sugar, plus several caramel burns later, I had a hideous stack of soggy pastry balls in front of me. It was not elegant. It was not beautiful. It wasn't even tasty. What it was, as I stared in anger at the mess I'd made, was a colossal waste of time and good ingredients. The counter, stove, table, and I were covered in flour and caramel drips. The sink was piled with dirty dishes. And as I stood there, trembling with the urge to smash some plates, who should walk in but Tita Rosie and Lola Flor.

"Ay nako! Anak, what happened? Are you OK? Did you burn yourself?" Tita Rosie rushed over and examined me for injuries. She pulled out a handkerchief and dabbed at my face, which was when I realized I was crying.

I sniffed and wiped at my face, smearing even more mess across it. "I'm OK, Tita. Just frustrated is all. I was trying to figure out a new recipe for the cafe and ended up with a big failure. I'm sorry, I'll clean it up soon."

"Don't worry about that right now." My aunt hesitated. "We missed you at church. Father Santiago was asking about you. He said that—"

My ringing phone cut her off. I glanced down and was surprised to see Sana's name flashing across the screen. Normally I would've ignored it since Tita Rosie was still talking, but I didn't want to hear about how I was disappointing Father Santiago, our priest and my former running buddy. "Oh sorry, Tita! This might be pageant business; can you give me a minute?"

She nodded and moved to clean up my mess, my grumbling grandmother joining her while I stepped into the living room to answer the phone. "Hey Sana, what's up?"

"I'm about to go for a run down the Riverwalk. I remember you mentioning it was your favorite spot. Would you like to join me? I'm in the mood for some company."

I wasn't the most athletic person around, but I enjoyed a good run. Something about the simple, rhythmic motion helped clear my mind—I hadn't gone on a run since the summer heat started, but maybe this was what I needed to get over my baking funk. Nisa and I could use the exercise, too. People said that dogs tended to resemble their owners, and considering that my little wiener dog was a super cute brown girl with stubby legs, great fashion sense, and a tendency toward plumpness, I had to agree.

"Sure! Give me a few minutes to change and get my dog ready and we'll meet you at the entrance to the Riverwalk." She agreed and we both hung up.

I went upstairs to clean myself up and change into workout clothes, then got Nisa into her matching gear. I was at the front door putting on my shoes when Tita Rosie came out of the kitchen.

"Oh hey, Tita. I'm going to meet Sana for a run. Is it OK if I clean up the kitchen after?"

"Don't worry, anak. Just go have fun with your friend. I think it'd be good for you. Invite her back for dinner, too. I'd like to get to know her."

I told her I'd ask, and Tita Rosie waved me and Nisa off as we jogged over to the Riverwalk. Sana was standing at the entrance in a yoga tree pose, smiling brightly as Nisa and I hurried over to her.

Wow, I was out of shape. I bent over, hands on my knees as I took in deep breaths and tried to greet her. "Sorry, just let me catch my breath. Maybe I really should check out your classes if that short sprint has me this winded."

She smiled and bent over to pet Nisa. "Well, hello there, cutie. What's your name?" She glanced at Nisa's nametag. "Longganisa? Nice to meet you, Longganisa."

Nisa flopped on her back and enjoyed belly rubs from Sana while I worked to regulate my breathing.

"You should put your hands on your head and stretch a little. It'll improve your breathing," Sana advised.

Once I was a little more comfortable, I gestured for Nisa to get up and follow me along the Riverwalk. Sana and I sauntered along the path, dodging the occasional cyclist, jogger, and stroller-power-walking mom. After a few minutes of walking in a comfortable silence, Sana subtly picked up the pace until we were both jogging along the path, Nisa keeping up at a light trot alongside us.

"How've you been? Adeena said your cafe is open now, so you must be really busy these days."

I faltered at the question, stumbling over a nonexistent crack in the sidewalk. "Oh, um, it's just the soft opening. I mean, we're not officially open yet, so not all that busy."

"I'll stop in sometime this week. Adeena and Elena have been talking about it so much lately, and I can't wait to check out the space. What's it called again?"

"The Brew-ha Cafe." I spelled it out for her. "It's a play on words. In Tagalog and Spanish, 'bruha/bruja' means 'witch.'"

She laughed. "So that's why Adeena insisted that you all made magic in that shop."

Except the magic was gone now. At least mine was.

Picking up on my mood change, she asked, "Something wrong?"

Should I tell her? Just spill my guts to this woman who was still kind of a stranger about how I was failing my friends and my family and my dreams all because I sucked at baking now?

Her voice casual and friendly, Sana said, "If it's about the cafe, you can talk to me without worrying about me saying anything to your partners. I'm a life coach for female entrepreneurs, so I'd like to help if I could."

With the caramel burns still fresh on my hands and my earlier failure still fresh on my mind, I figured I had nothing to lose. "I need to come up with my side of the menu for the cafe and I want it to be spectacular. Something that'll bring people in from all over, not just Shady Palms. But everything I've made lately has been terrible."

"Are you sure you're not being too hard on yourself?"

"You wouldn't be saying that if you saw the monstrosity I made earlier." I described the failed cream puff cake and the mess I'd made, ending with, "My regular recipes are too boring, but anytime I try something fancy, it's terrible."

"Are you sure fancy is what you should be trying for? You're not a trained pâtissier, are you?"

"Well, no. My restaurant training was on the business management side. Baking was more of a hobby," I admitted.

"I understand wanting to make an impact with your menu, but there's more than one way to do that. You don't have to go the fancy route if that's not your brand. In fact, it can actually hurt your business if your vision and brand aren't aligned. So take a minute to think about who you are as a baker and business owner."

We jogged in silence for a few minutes, Nisa's tiny legs working hard to keep up with us, as I turned that question over in my mind. Who was I as a baker and business owner? I'd thought the fusion croquembouche was me: creative and sophisticated yet fun. Bernadette would accuse me of being too bougie with that bake, but what did she know? Though if I really thought about it, Sana was right to bring up my lack of technical training. Since I didn't have the education or equipment, I usually nailed down basic recipes and put a Filipino spin on them. As much as I admired fancier pastries, my style of only-kinda-sorta measuring and never using a scale was probably not going to work. Maybe if I worked on my decorating skills, it would be OK to stick to the simple cookies, brownies, cakes, and scones that made up a typical coffee shop menu. That way they'd be tasty as well as pretty.

I must've been silent for too long since Sana changed the subject by saying, "So how do you feel about being part of the pageant committee? I know you won years ago, but I'm sensing a lack of enthusiasm from you about judging."

There was way too much history to get into there, so I asked her a question instead. "How about you? How did you get roped into judging?"

"Well, like Valerie said, I'm a 'woman of color and business owner,' so she asked me to judge months ago."

I laughed at her impression. "Oh, so you already knew Valerie before this?"

"I do some coaching work for the Thompson Family Company."

"I thought she didn't work there?" Rob was the head of the company, despite being the younger sibling. Valerie worked at the Shelbyville Community College, if I remembered correctly.

"She doesn't, but she attends the sessions anyway. Rob was the one who hired me."

Her voice had gone flat as she said her client's name, making me think I could confide in her.

"Rob Thompson, huh? There've been rumors going around about him for years, but you know him better than I do. Do you think . . . do we have to worry about him being around the girls?"

Sana stopped so suddenly that a biker had to swerve around her to avoid a collision. After calling out an apology, she said, "Why? Have you seen something? If so, we need to report it immediately."

"No, nothing like that. He hasn't done or even said anything all that blatant. The most he's done is look at Joy, but I . . . something about him makes me uncomfortable. I just can't shake the feeling that he's bad news."

Nisa started whimpering and pulling on her leash, so Sana and I resumed our jog.

She was quiet for a moment before admitting, "I don't trust him, either. I think we should keep an eye on him and make sure he's never alone with the girls for any of the events. And the minute we see something shady, we report him to the committee. He may be her brother, but Valerie would back us up."

I nodded, and a steely resolve came over me. I wasn't alone in this—together, Sana and I (with Valerie's support) would keep the girls safe. "I'm so happy I said something to you. This has been bugging me since yesterday and I—what's that?"

We'd just circled the bend and were getting close to the little footbridge that would lead us across the river. Nisa started barking and pulling on her leash, leading me toward something wrapped around the pillar at the foot of the bridge. I sped up to get a closer look, but was forced back by the arm Sana suddenly threw out.

"Stay back, Lila! And call 911." Sana jogged toward the river and carefully leaned over the footbridge to get a closer look at what was in the water.

I didn't have to ask her why. There in the water, bobbing against the bridge with the current, was Rob Thompson.

Guess we wouldn't have to keep an eye on him after all.

Chapter Six

"I'm sorry you had to go through this again, Lila. This isn't what I had in mind when I asked you to keep an eye on the pageant."

Detective Park had arrived minutes after the ambulance. After issuing orders, he took me aside while another officer questioned Sana. "Lila, are you OK?"

I'd been shaking my head back and forth for the last few minutes. Again. I couldn't believe I'd found a dead body again. "What happened to him? Was it an accident? Or was he . . . ?"

Murdered? No, that wasn't possible. He'd probably slipped and fell, hit his head or something. There were no guardrails on that bridge, so it wouldn't be the first time. The Shady Palms Lounge was just on the other side of that bridge, and many a drunk had stumbled and ended up in the river.

None had ever died though.

Detective Park echoed my thoughts. "It's hard to say without an autopsy, but he had a head injury. Likely he fell, hit his head, and got knocked out. Drowned when he couldn't get back up."

"So this is just a tragic accident? It doesn't have anything to do with the pageant or those threatening letters?" The desperation in my voice was obvious even to me. I picked up Nisa and clutched her to my chest. She struggled (she hated being picked up), but I needed her near me.

Detective Park let out a breath. "I sure hope so. The sheriff's going to have a fit if there's another murder in this town, not to mention the mayor and his precious pageant. Still, I'm uncomfortable with you being involved with these people. Is it too late to drop out?"

I frowned. "Way too late. Besides, I can't abandon those girls. You've met Joy. You know how badly she needs this. And I promised Yuki I'd watch over her daughter. They've got so much riding on this. If someone is targeting the pageant, who's going to watch out for them?"

"The Shady Palms Police Department, Lila."

I shifted Nisa to my other arm. I didn't understand how such a tiny dog could have the density of a dying sun. "Do you really believe that? I know you care, but the rest of the department has proven as inept as usual."

He didn't answer for a moment. "Officer Clarkson has a daughter in the pageant. There's no way he'd let anything happen to her."

"His daughter's name is Abigail, right? Yeah, no, she tried to use the fact that her dad's a cop to 'convince' me and Sana to vote for her. Valerie kicked her out of the pageant after we reported her." That was a particularly fun part of the evening, happening shortly after Rob's scene with sandwich guy.

Detective Park cursed, then collected himself. "Sorry about that. But don't worry, I'll handle it. Now tell me everything you saw, starting from the beginning of your run until I arrived."

After the police had taken down our statements, Detective Park dropped Sana off at her studio and took me and Nisa home. He came inside with me and pulled Tita Rosie aside while I headed straight to the kitchen. All evidence of this morning's failure was gone, and the kitchen was its usual sparkly, inviting self.

I sank down into a seat and laid my head down on my arms on the table. How could this have happened? I had just seen Rob the other night and he had been so . . . full of smarmy charm and himself, yes, but also full of life. So confident. So sure of his place, not just in this town, but the world. Yet all it took was one drunken mistake and he was gone? Just like that? If accidents like this could end the lives of people as rich and important as the Thompsons, and as good and simple as my parents, then—

I shook my head. No need to go down that road. I needed to focus on some sort of mindless activity—dwelling too much on Rob Thompson's death could lead to a panic attack. I'd had more than I cared to count in the last few months. No, I just needed to deal with my pain the Macapagal way—work through it.

My thoughts suddenly turned to Valerie. She'd just lost the last member of her family. She didn't seem particularly close to Rob, but that didn't mean she wouldn't be devastated. I understood how complicated love and family could be. I couldn't do much to ease her grief, but I wanted to whip up something delicious, something that would bring a little sweetness during a bitter time.

As I racked my brain for a suitable gluten-free treat, I remembered Sana's advice. I could easily bring her some kakanin, the various Filipino rice cakes that my grandmother was known for, but then that'd be a gift from her. Besides, she'd likely be seeking the comfort of something familiar. And what was more comforting than warm chocolate chip cookies? But I couldn't resist mixing it up, just a little.

My style was hybrid Filipino-American desserts, giving a Filipino spin to what we think of as American and vice versa. It wasn't about being fancy or technique-driven—it was about creating something delicious that made people happy. Period. I already knew that ube worked well in cookies, thanks to the ube crinkles I'd created earlier in the year. But would the subtle earthy sweetness of the purple yam pair well with chocolate? Guess there was only one way to find out. I grabbed my keys, hoping Mr. Weinman carried gluten-free flour at the One Stop Shop.

A couple of hours later, the cookies had cooled enough to pack in plastic containers: one for the regular ube chocolate chip cookies and one for the ube white chocolate chip. I wanted to see if the lighter, sweeter flavor of white chocolate worked better than the semisweet. Also, I was stalling. There was no way to avoid how awkward and tense this visit would be.

I located Valerie's number on the Contacts form in the pageant info packet and called to see if she was up for some company. If not, I'd just drop the food off at her place. When she answered, she informed me she was at Sana's apartment above her studio.

"I came here after I heard the news. I wanted to talk to you anyway, so thanks for saving me the trouble of looking up your number. Can you come over?"

This was even better than I'd hoped. I hadn't been looking forward to being alone with her since I didn't know her like that, but Sana did. Sana would be the perfect buffer for the sad, uncomfortable conversation that was sure to happen.

"Heading over now, and I've got some snacks."

"Better make it quick. Sana's whipping up her famous sangria slushies and I can't promise there will be any left by the time you get here."

Sana's sangria slushies were exactly what I needed. Both to help me unwind and also remove any last bits of awkwardness among the three of us. Before leaving, Tita Rosie had given me a huge tray of chicken adobo and rice, which was delicious but did nothing to combat the effects of our drinks. We were already on the second pitcher and showed no signs of stopping.

The ube chocolate chip cookies I'd prepared were a hit, though I wasn't sure if it was because Valerie truly loved them or if the wine had made her maudlin.

"These are so delicious! They remind me of this dessert I tried in Hawaii. Such a pretty purple color." Valerie made a noise of appreciation as she picked up another cookie.

Sana took one as well. "When were you in Hawaii?"

Valerie tilted her head. "Maybe five or six years ago? It was right before Mom and Dad died. Family trip to attend a wedding. We all had such a lovely time." Her expression changed. "Rob was there, too. Probably the only time the whole family was together and we didn't fight."

I put my hand on her arm. "I'm so sorry about Rob."

She turned to me, eyes bleary, and a wave of alcohol fumes rolled off her, overwhelming my sensitive sense of smell. I tried not to gag as I braced myself for the question I knew was coming. The first pitcher had passed in small talk, and I guessed Valerie was relying on liquid courage to get her through this.

"What happened? What did you see? I know you both were there. The officers told me you were the ones who found the body."

Nothing but professionalism from Shady Palms's finest.

Sana and I exchanged looks, but she then busied herself with filling Valerie's glass. Guess she was leaving this to me. "There's not much I can tell you. Sana and I were jogging along the river and my dog started barking and pulling me toward the bridge. That's how we found the . . . found Rob. Once we realized what we were looking at, I called 911. That's pretty much it."

"Sana, you saw the body, too? What were you doing while Lila was on the phone?" Valerie leaned forward, as if what she said next could be crucial.

"I leaned over to see if he could be saved, but it was pretty obvious it was too late. I didn't want to move him in case the cops needed to preserve the scene, so I just sat on the bridge by him until the ambulance came."

"Obvious how?" Valerie asked.

Sana bit her lip. "You don't want to know. I wish I didn't know. I can't get it out of my head . . ."

Her voice had gone all far away and hollow-sounding, so Valerie dropped the subject. She held out her glass to Sana, who silently refilled it, emptying the pitcher. Sana left for a few minutes, leaving Valerie and me to sip our drinks in silence. Wow, were they delicious. And potent. I made a note to ask Sana for the recipe.

Sana returned with cups and another pitcher, this one full of ice water. "Time to hydrate."

We grumbled but complied since we needed to sober up before going home. Valerie ran a finger around the frosty rim of her glass. "Sana, you said you didn't want to disrupt the scene. Do the police think Rob was murdered?"

Sana, who'd been pouring herself a drink, sloshed the water all over herself. Valerie apologized, handing Sana a clean handkerchief from her bag to dry herself off.

I scooched a little closer to Valerie. "You probably know more than we do. Since you're family and all. What did the police tell you?"

"Just that he was found dead by the river. No cause of death or anything like that. I wonder if Beth knows more."

I couldn't place the name at first, but then I remembered Rob was married. "Oh sugar, his wife. Does she like sweets? Have any dietary restrictions? I should probably pay my condolences to her, too."

Valerie gulped down her glass of water and poured another. "What for? You didn't even know her."

There was a sulkiness to her voice that spoke volumes about Valerie Thompson and her relationship with her brother's wife—a childishness and pettiness that I recognized. She did have a point, though. It wasn't my place to investigate, and after the last time, I couldn't say I was all that eager to jump back in. But I had to admit to a morbid curiosity. And I couldn't shake the feeling that I was already involved somehow. It wasn't just finding his body—Detective Park showed me letters threatening the pageant and then a day or two later, one of the judges was dead. Could these things possibly be linked? Maybe it was a coincidence, but I couldn't ignore the timing. Did this mean the rest of us involved were in danger?

Even if there was no nefarious plot surrounding the pageant, this was Shady Palms. Not sending a condolence casserole during times of distress was our version of a slap in the face. Whether or not you knew the person, etiquette dictated that a grieving person should not be expected to prepare their own meals and it was up to the community to provide.

I ran my finger down the condensation on the glass, trying to look nonchalant. "She just lost her husband. A little bit of kindness wouldn't hurt, right?"

Valerie snorted again. "Kindness won't get you far with Beth. But good luck. Let me know if she tells you anything interesting." She put down her glass and sighed. "I bet she gets everything. All these years and I still have no say in what happens with my family's legacy."

I nudged the cookies closer to her. She'd had way more to drink than me and could use something in her stomach.

"You're older than Rob, right? How come he became the head of the company after your parents passed instead of you? You seem much more responsible than Rob. No offense to your brother," I added.

A sad, bitter smile tilted Valerie's lips as she reached for another ube cookie. "You're right about that. I'd be damn good at running the company. But my parents didn't think I was a good fit. I didn't study business, after all. Plus my 'radical politics' might upset our investors."

She paused to take a large bite of her treat, and I did the same, savoring the light sweetness and crisp yet chewy texture that I loved.

Sana also helped herself to a cookie but broke it in half before indulging. "Forgive me for asking, but what exactly did your parents consider 'radical politics'?"

Valerie rolled her eyes. "You know, wild things like decent pay and benefits. They also hated that I got a master's in women's studies and wanted to teach at a community college before taking over the company. A waste of time and money, according to them. Still, they might've gotten over it if . . ."

"If what?" I prodded.

Valerie straightened up, looking at me and Sana carefully. "If I hadn't told them I had no interest in marrying to strengthen our business and political connections, or in producing an heir. My parents stressed that we were the Thompson *Family* Company. If I didn't have a family, who would it go to? They couldn't risk our legacy being passed down to an outsider. My brother may not have had a head for business, but he could produce an heir. Or at least, that's what we thought." Valerie shook her head, letting out a bitter laugh. "And here he is, dying without any kids. Typical Rob."

Sana shook her glass, watching the ice cubes clink against each other. "I can understand that. You said you have no interest in marrying for connections, but what about love?"

Valerie poured herself more water, keeping her eyes on her glass. "I don't have any interest in those kinds of relationships. I'm not of that particular persuasion, I guess you could say."

I didn't know how to respond to that kind of revelation, one that couldn't have come easily and showed a level of vulnerability I wasn't prepared for. But Sana did.

She placed her hand on Valerie's and said, "Thank you for sharing that with us. I appreciate that you trust us enough to share that side of you."

I echoed Sana's sentiments.

"Thank you. Not many people know. Most don't understand. My parents always assumed I'd grow out of it, and they'd welcome me back when I did. Rob had his faults and I hated so much about him. But he was always accepting of who I was. And he took care of me. So I guess I loved him, too."

There was so much more I wanted to ask. So much more I needed to know about Rob and what could've led to his death. But this wasn't the time. So Sana and I just held Valerie's hands and let her cry.

• • •

After Valerie broke down, Sana kept the sangria slushies flowing. "After all that, I think we need a full-on girls' night. You can either sleep over or call a ride, but nobody's driving home. Now drink up."

I sipped at my glass, noting the mixed berries, citrus, and heady red wine she'd used for the drinks. Tons of antioxidants and vitamin C. Practically a health tonic.

The thought made me smile. "You'll have to give me your recipe, Sana. Adeena and Elena would love this."

"I'll have you all over soon. I would've invited them, but this wasn't the right time." She nodded her head toward Valerie, who had fallen asleep on Sana's couch.

"I'm glad she had someone to talk to. I can't imagine the shock the news must've given her. Didn't realize you two were such good friends though." I took another drink, a shiver from the icy beverage running up my spine, followed by a warmth from the alcohol radiating out from my stomach.

Sana, who was still sitting cross-legged on the floor with me, leaned her back against the couch, careful not to wake up Valerie. "I don't know that I'd say we're 'good' friends. We admire each other, run in some of the same circles. We have a professional relationship. That makes things difficult."

At my questioning look, she explained, "She's one of my coaching clients, remember? Due to the nature of the coach-client relationship, I try to keep a professional distance because the lines can get blurred very easily. But in a town this small, it's hard to avoid."

"Oh right, you said you were a life coach earlier." I wrinkled my nose and spoke before I thought to watch my tone.

Sana laughed. "I know what you're thinking. I hate the name, too.

Really what I do is provide guidance to female entrepreneurs and business leaders, particularly women of color. I coach them through negotiations, and how to both understand and ask for their true worth. I help them learn how to lead without feeling like an impostor, build up their confidence and intuition, things like that."

"Oh wow, that actually sounds really cool. No wonder Valerie wanted you to be a judge." Though why would Valerie need Sana's services? "Valerie isn't involved with the Thompson Family Company though. What were you coaching her on?"

"Sorry, that's client-coach confidentiality. Can't talk about that."

"Oh, of course. Sorry, I should've known." I studied her, curious to learn more about her. "What made you decide to be a coach?"

Sana leaned her head back, eyes on the elegant wood-and-bronze ceiling fan that turned lazily above us. The sun was setting outside and golden light filtered through the large windows, casting a warm glow around her. She was quiet for so long, I thought she wasn't going to answer me, so I also leaned back against the couch and closed my eyes to enjoy this peaceful moment. The light breeze conjured by the fans and the hazy feeling from the strong drinks left me feeling relaxed in a way that I hadn't in a long time.

"I wanted to help people." Sana's voice, barely above a murmur, floated toward me. I kept my eyes closed but nodded to show I was listening. "I thought I could do that with my original career, but it didn't work out. So I did some volunteer nonprofit work for a while and realized how many young women of color struggled with running their own businesses. I started unofficially coaching this Black-owned beauty business, though I didn't know that's what I was doing at the time. The owner couldn't afford to pay me, but referred me to some friends who could, so I thought I'd do some research and see if I could turn it into a career." I opened my eyes to take another drink and Sana turned to me and smiled, holding up her wineglass in a salute. "Turns out I could."

I clinked my glass against hers. "It's great that you found your niche. I thought I did too, but now I'm not sure."

"With the Brew-ha Cafe? You mentioned earlier that you were having trouble with your recipes, but you seemed to figure that out. Is there something else bothering you about this business venture?"

I'd already spilled way more than I was comfortable with during our run earlier—after all, my problems were my own. But enough of my feelings must've leaked through into my expression because Sana set her glass down and leaned toward me. "You're more than your work, Lila. More than whatever contributions you think you're supposed to be making." She paused. "More than whoever people think you're supposed to be."

She was getting dangerously close to things I never talked about, so I faked a yawn. "Thanks, Sana. I appreciate it. I'm getting tired though, so I think I'm just going to wash my face and go to sleep if that's OK with you."

Sana sighed but didn't push me. "Of course. You can borrow anything of mine that you need. Spare toothbrushes are under the sink. But think about what I said, OK? Good night."

I agreed and went about my usual nighttime routine. But after she headed to her room, I downed the rest of the sangria pitcher and waited for red wine–fueled oblivion to take me.

Thinking was the last thing I wanted to do.

I woke up the next morning with the rug imprint creasing my cheek, a dry mouth, and an aching head, made worse by the relentless ringing of my cell phone, which was . . . somewhere in the room. Inching my sore body off the floor, I spotted my purse next to the couch and crawled over to it. I somehow managed to dig out my phone and answer it before it went to voicemail.

"Hello?"

Tita Rosie's panicked voice shook off the lethargy that had settled into my bones. "Anak, you need to come over to the restaurant right now! They just arrested Bernadette for Rob Thompson's murder!"

Chapter Seven

I wasn't arrested, Tita. They just took me in for questioning."

Bernadette sat at the table sipping coffee and munching on pandesal with my aunt, grandmother, and godmothers, everyone looking mighty calm after nearly giving me a heart attack with that phone call.

Adeena's older brother, Amir, was there too, and he greeted me with a warm smile. He was a lawyer and had saved our family countless times in the past. Guess it was Bernadette's time up at bat.

I waved at him and slid into the seat next to him, ignoring the fuzzy feeling in my stomach that smile gave me. Adeena had finally given us her blessing, but after years of crushing on him, I suddenly wasn't ready to make it a reality. Feelings were complicated, and I'd had my fair share of complications lately. Right now, what I needed was his friendship.

Tita Rosie placed a bowl of arroz caldo, a soothing, chicken-and-ginger-laced rice porridge, in front of me and I smiled at her. My stomach wasn't up for a heavy silog breakfast, but it needed more than the light bread rolls and coffee the others were consuming. Without my saying a word, my aunt knew exactly what I needed.

"Thanks, Tita Rosie. I have to say, you gave me quite a scare with that phone call." I nodded at Bernadette. "Glad you're OK, though. I wouldn't want a repeat of last time."

Amir's smile faltered a little at my lack of attention, and he picked up another pandesal to dip in his coffee. "She's not out of the woods yet. They didn't have enough to hold her on, but they made no secret of the fact they consider her a suspect."

My godmothers, who had been suspiciously quiet this whole time, erupted at his words.

"They've always been incompetent, but to think my Bernie had anything to do with this!"

"Everyone knows it was the wife, why are they even wasting time on this?"

"Hoy, Rosie! What's your detective going to do about this?"

This last question, phrased so indelicately, came from Ninang April. Of course. Tita Rosie turned bright red, though whether from embarrassment or frustration, I wasn't sure.

"He's not my anything. I haven't had a chance to talk to him yet, but you can be sure he's going to hear from me." Tita Rosie cleaned her glasses, not looking at us. "I'm sure this is all a misunderstanding. Like Bernie said, they just took her in for questioning. They're probably going to do that for everyone involved with the pageant."

At that, Ninang June turned to me. "Have they questioned you yet?"

I shook my head, regretting the action when the dull ache in my head became sharper from the sudden movement. "Only when we first found the body. There hasn't been any follow-up. So it's official then? Rob was murdered?"

Amir nodded grimly. "They haven't released the details yet, but the police department says it's definitely murder. Considering Rob Thompson was an important Shady Palms citizen, and his connection to the town's beloved pageant, the mayor is putting the screws to the department to solve this as quickly and discreetly as possible."

Ninang June's nostrils flared. "Which means they're going to do anything to pin this on my Bernie rather than Rob's high-class wife. Don't want the Thompson name being dragged through the mud."

I squeezed some calamansi over my bowl of arroz caldo. "Beth Thompson? Why are you so sure it's her?"

Ninang June sniffed. "Because it's always the spouse. Especially when the victim is a no-good cheating as—"

"June!" my aunt interjected. "No speaking ill of the dead. It's not seemly."

Ninang June rolled her eyes and shoved an extra-large piece of pandesal in her mouth to keep herself quiet, but there was no stopping Ninang April.

"He's already dead, Rosie. There's nothing we can say that'll hurt him more, especially when it's the truth. Besides, if it wasn't his wife, it was probably the husband of one of the women he was having an affair with. I heard one of the original pageant judges was forced to leave after he confronted Rob about the affair."

Thinking back to the pageant potluck, I said, "Whoa, was Mr. Weinman the original judge? Nobody would tell me anything when I asked, but he crashed the event the other night. Valerie told me Rob slept with his wife, so she and the mayor were worried about him making a scene. He mostly just wanted to promote his store though."

Lola Flor made a dismissive noise. "I always knew that pageant was no good. Adulterers. Murderers. Shameless women. At least now you can quit judging. Bernadette, tell Joy she should quit, too."

Bernadette and I reacted at the same time. "What? No! She needs this!"

"Lola, I made a commitment. I can't back out now, it would reflect poorly on the cafe and Adeena would kill me."

"You want to die for real? A man is dead. I've told you and your mother time and again that those pageants are a waste of time and full of bad people. I don't want you involved." Lola Flor picked up her dishes and walked back to the kitchen, ending the conversation. She expected me to just fall in line, no arguments, no listening to my side.

Tita Rosie cleared her throat. "May I ask . . . if it was indeed a murder, why aren't they shutting down the pageant? Or at least postponing it? It seems so unfeeling for them to keep pushing forward with the contest."

Amir sighed. "The mayor as well as the board of directors at the Thompson Family Company think it'd be bad PR to focus on Rob's 'untimely death.' That's a direct statement from the company, by the way."

He cleared his plate and stood. "Thanks for breakfast, Auntie. I'll be in touch again soon. Don't hesitate to contact me if anything comes up."

Bernadette also stood up. "I need to get ready for work, so I'll head out with you. Lila, you got a second? I have that book about medicinal plants that Elena wanted to borrow. You mind dropping it off for me?"

"Sure. Today's the soft opening, so I should head over to help out anyway." I thought I'd want to head home and nap, but the arroz caldo did its job, soothing my throat and tummy, and caffeine would dull the ache in my pounding head. I checked my purse to see if I still had the baggie of ube chocolate chip cookies I'd set aside for menu sampling. Hopefully they were enough to get Adeena off my back. "Let me know if you need anything later, Tita."

We waved goodbye to everyone and walked out to Bernadette's car, Amir following us over. I sensed this was more than needing my help with an errand. "What's going on, you two?"

Bernadette sighed. "I didn't want to freak everyone out, but it's more serious than we made it seem. My mom was right when she said I was the main suspect."

I stared at her, waiting for her to go on.

"Joy told me that Rob had hit on her and Katie at the potluck. She says he was pretty subtle about it, but it made her really uncomfortable." Bernadette's fists balled up. "She'd waited to tell me till after the potluck was done because she didn't want to cause a fuss, but I tracked him down at the Shady Palms Lounge later that night. Seems an entire bar full of witnesses told the cops I'd threatened Rob shortly before he died."

"And did you?" I asked, knowing what her answer would be. Bernadette in a mood was not to be trifled with.

"Yes, but you know I'd never actually kill anybody! But my shift supervisor called me earlier, saying not to come in. That the *Shady Palms News* staff was already sniffing around the hospital trying to get the dirt on me. They're going to paint me to be the villain, just like—"

"Just like they did to me," I said, suddenly exhausted again.

She grimaced. "Look, I didn't want it to be like this, but I helped you out last time. Now I need you to help me. Please."

I hated to admit it, but she was right. She'd risked her job standing by me last time, and if nothing else, I prided myself on paying my debts. I usually avoided conflict, but there was something about my family that fired me up every time. Though if I was back in the sleuthing game, I knew I couldn't do it alone.

Guess it was time to go next door and beg forgiveness so we could get the gang back together.

Chapter Eight

"I come bearing a peace offering," I declared, holding up the cookie bag as I stepped into the Brew-ha Cafe.

"Ooh, what did you bring us?" Elena abandoned the framed photo she'd been hanging above what seemed to be . . . an altar. I knew she said she was putting one up, but I didn't realize she meant a full-blown altar, with cloth, candles, flowers, framed photos, the works.

I stared at her work. "Wow. That's . . . a lot. I guess it fits our brand, at least."

Elena reared back like I'd slapped her. "I didn't do this for a brand! This is to give thanks and remember those who came before us. The customers aren't allowed back here, so don't even think about putting this on social media."

Adeena jumped in before it could go any further. "So you're finally ready to share your side of the menu?"

I handed over the cookies and fiddled with the clasp on my purse so I wouldn't start wringing my hands. Sana and Valerie had loved them, but were they good enough for the Brew-ha Cafe? "I thought I'd start with the classics and then expand from there. I present to you ube chocolate chip cookies two ways: one with semisweet chips and the other with white chocolate chips. Tell me which you prefer. I'm honestly a little torn."

They took turns sampling my offering, giving each cookie their undivided attention. Elena said, "If you're going to serve the cookies as is, I'd say the semisweet gets my vote. It plays well with the earthiness of the ube, but is still a chocolate chip cookie. The white chocolate is a bit too sweet for me."

Adeena, whose capacity for sugar was probably some kind of Guinness World Record, said, "I disagree about the white chocolate being too sweet. It's so good! But it lacks oomph, you know? If you're playing with the classics, why not add macadamia nuts? Then it could be your take on white chocolate macadamia cookies. Which are my favorite cookies, FYI," she said to Elena.

Now this I missed. The creativity, the collaboration, the sheer inspiration I got from working with people who knew me well. "Love that idea! Thanks, Adeena. We've got our beginner cookies down, so I'll make a large batch for today. Any idea what I should tackle next?"

I put it out there in the spirit of collaboration, not because I was completely idealess and needed their help or anything.

Elena raised her hand. "Well, one of my favorite treats are those lemon poppyseed muffins every coffeeshop has, but they're a little too sweet and too big for me. They should taste like breakfast, not dessert."

I jotted this down in the Notes app on my phone. "I love those muffins! And while a healthy version makes me sad, I'm sure other people would appreciate the option. I could replace the lemon with calamansi for extra kick, maybe have a glaze or curd on the side for those who want something sweeter. Anything else?"

"Since it's summer, Adeena and I thought we should offer a frozen treat. We don't have an ice cream maker, but paletas are super easy. We just need ice pop molds."

Adeena nodded. "We figured we should start small. One flavor each to represent us. I already told her I want a kulfi-inspired ice pop."

"Mine's going to be arroz con leche since it's my favorite dessert. You need to think about what your signature paleta flavor will be."

My mouth watered as I remembered the Mexican ice cream carts that were everywhere in Chicago, the tinkling bells announcing the arrival of the paletero with ice pops in all sorts of delicious flavors, such as the rice pudding Elena was so fond of. A paleta that would represent me, huh? That would require some serious thought. Though one thing occurred to me.

"Paletas sound great, but a bit time-consuming since we'll need to get the molds, freeze the mixture, unmold the paletas, and then wrap them up to sell. Why don't we sell ice candy instead?" I explained that ice candies were basically ice pops with the mixtures poured into a slim plastic bag then frozen and sold as is. "I saw a Filipino food blogger on Instagram post about these new heavy-duty plastic zip bags that would be perfect for our shop."

I found the post on my phone and showed it to Adeena and Elena. Adeena nodded. "I like it. And because they're smaller and faster than paletas, we can play around with more flavors."

"I still need to think about my ice candy flavor, but I can get started on the cookies now." I paused, remembering why I had originally come over and the huge favor I needed to ask them. "Also, we need to talk. When do we open?" We still hadn't agreed on an opening time last time we met, so I left the decision up to them since they were the ones running the shop this week.

Adeena glanced at the clock. Nine a.m. "Now, actually. Elena and I decided that we'll start earlier once we have our official opening, but wanted to stick to a simple nine to five this week."

As she said that, a tall figure knocked on the glass and waved at us. She hurried to let him in. "Jae! How are you?"

Dr. Jae Park owned the dental clinic a few doors down and had become a good friend after I'd moved back to Shady Palms. I could tell that he hoped for something more than friendship, but at this point in time, it was all I was able to give. Though sometimes I wished I could. Like when he stood in front of me, glistening from the heat, filling out his scrubs in a way that made those shapeless bits of cloth Bernadette was always complaining about look downright sexy. Though with Adeena standing there watching us, I couldn't help but think of Amir and his suit-and-tie perfection waiting for me to make a decision. Guilt pooled in my stomach, effectively stopping my ogling—I turned my mind to more pressing matters.

Jae stepped into the shop, briefly turning his face toward the air conditioner on the wall before smiling at us. "Why, hello, my witchy women. Do I get the honor of being your first customer?"

He'd taken to calling me a witchy woman after he'd heard me singing the Eagles song at karaoke one day. He said it suited me, so I'd laughed and told him about the meaning of our cafe name, which cemented the nickname. It was cheesy, but I didn't mind. His cheesiness was part of what made him so sweet.

"You do! And for that distinction, you can have the rest of these cookies that I'd prepared as a sample. I was about to go in the back to make a fresh batch for the cafe." I handed over the bag. "Tell me what you think so I can make any tweaks before getting started. I already know I'm adding macadamia nuts to the white chocolate version."

He took his taste-testing job seriously, scrunching up his face in concentration as he tried each cookie. "Man, these are good. I think the macadamia nuts are a good call for the white chocolate chip. Coconut might also be nice, either in addition to the nuts or as a replacement for those with nut allergies. The regular chocolate chip cookies are fine."

There was something about the way he said it that prompted me to ask, "Just fine?"

He shrugged. "I mean, they're delicious. But something seems like it's missing. I don't know, maybe I'm just comparing them too much to my idea of what a chocolate chip cookie should taste like."

"Hmm." I made a noncommittal noise as I tried to decipher what was missing from my recipe. Just when I thought I had finally nailed the baking thing. At least I had a jumping-off point. Perfecting those cookies was what I needed to get out of my funk and they were going to be glorious, so help me . . .

"By the way, are you OK? I heard about Rob Thompson." Jae, probably noticing the troubled look on my face, changed the subject.

I groaned. "How much did you hear?"

"That you stumbled across another dead body."

"What?!" Adeena rounded on me. "How could you not tell me?"

"I was going to tell you the whole story while I prepped the cookies, but then, you know." I gestured toward Jae.

He smiled gently. "It's OK. My brother told me everything."

"Really? I didn't think Detective Park would talk about a case with family."

"He usually wouldn't, but he knows we're friends. He wanted me to check up on you. Make sure you were doing OK, 'processing things well,' was the way he put it."

I crossed my arms and huffed. "So you're my keeper now?"

He put his hand on my arm. "Don't be like that. He was worried about you. *I'm* worried about you. It must've been an awful shock."

I put my hand on his and squeezed lightly before stepping back. "Thanks, Jae. And you're right. I don't know what I would've done if I hadn't had Sana with me. And Longganisa."

Though if Nisa hadn't been with me, maybe I wouldn't have found the body in the first place. No, I couldn't blame my poor puppy for this. She was just doing her job, using her sniffer to find potential threats and keep us safe.

"The cookies can wait," Adeena said. "You need to tell us what happened before anyone else shows up."

"Whip me up an iced coconut milk latte and you're on."

Adeena winked. "I'll do you one better. I created a new spin on my cold brew just for you. I want to see if you can figure it out."

"Can I get one, too? It's so hot outside and I need to open the clinic soon. I could use the caffeine boost."

"Two Lila Specials, coming right up!"

While Adeena worked, Elena turned her charms on Jae. "Now, Jae, don't you think the clinic could use a bit of redecorating? I've got the perfect plant over here that would really brighten up the reception area. And that herbal tea your mom loves."

I hopped on a seat by the counter as those two debated between a tall, palm tree–looking thing (what? Plants were Elena's thing, not mine) or several hanging pots with dangling vines. "So what's this special drink that bears my name?"

"You tell me." Adeena placed two frosty drinks in front of me. "There're two versions, sweetened and unsweetened. The sweetened one is for Jae, but I poured you a sample so you can try both."

I sipped at my drink first so I could fully experience the beverage without the sugar dulling my palate. Adeena's bold, rich cold brew flooded my tongue, tempered by the creamy sweetness of my beloved coconut milk. There was something else lingering in the background, but I couldn't quite place it until I took a deep breath and the herbal flavor mingling with the coconut became familiar.

"Pandan! You used fresh pandan leaves for my drink. And coconut water instead of plain filtered water?"

Adeena grinned. "I also added a tiny bit of homemade pandan extract since the flavor isn't as strong without the syrup. I got the idea after trying the coconut and pandan jellies in Grandma Flor's halo-halo."

She sighed. "I could really go for some right now, actually. Think you could grab us a couple to-go cups once your cookies are in the oven?"

"The dough needs to chill for at least half an hour, so I'll get it then. I love that the jellies were an inspiration—we can make our own as an add-in for the drinks, like they do at boba tea shops. Tapioca pearls, jellies, and other fun stuff." I picked up the small sample cup. "Now for the sweetened version." I sipped at the creamy, sweet liquid, rolling it over my tongue to get the full flavor of the drink. The light, floral sweetness of the pandan simple syrup played surprisingly well with the coffee, considering what a delicate flavor pandan had. It'd be a winner even without the coconut milk, but that extra touch brought a sense of decadence without heaviness. And just like the last drink, there was a hint of something familiar . . .

I raised an eyebrow. "You added vanilla to the pandan syrup?"

Adeena clapped her hands. "You got it all! Yeah, for the sweet version, I wanted to stick with water to not muddle the flavors too much, but I remembered what you said about pandan being the vanilla of Southeast Asia. I figured the two would work well together."

"Well, they're both excellent. Definitely worthy of being named after me."

Jae ambled over, hands full of herbal teas, a potted plant, and various bath products. "As your number one customer, I think it's only right I have a drink named after me, too." He heaped the products on the counter near the register. "Especially since Elena is taking me to the cleaners right now. Oh, can you add both our drinks to my tab?"

He grabbed his drink and leaned against the counter, taking a long, slow sip. His full lips pulled into a satisfied smile as he took in all the flavors Adeena had pulled together. "I call dibs on this one! It's so good."

"I figured my two lactose-intolerant buddies would love it." Adeena winked. "It's settled. The Brew-ha #1 and the Dr. Jae."

She wrote the names and descriptions out on the Specials chalkboard, adding little flourishes around the names, then pointed at me with the chalk. "OK, I've entertained you long enough. Now spill. What's this about a dead body?"

So I laid out the whole sordid tale, adding that Bernadette was now their prime suspect and Amir was once again our family's counsel.

By the time I was finished, Jae's eyes were wide and he'd crushed the sample cup I'd left on the counter in his hand. "Hyung didn't tell me all that. I didn't even know Rob was murdered, just that he was dead and you found the body. Poor Beth. Hope she's holding up."

"At least your brother told you something. I can't believe Amir didn't say anything! Or at least stop by to wish us luck. He was right next door." Adeena scowled and I could tell Amir was in trouble. The Awan siblings loved each other fiercely and bickered just as fiercely. This fight was going to be a doozy.

"How do you know Beth?" I asked Jae, trying to divert Adeena's attention for Amir's sake.

"She's one of my patients. Rob's wife," he added, for Adeena's and Elena's benefit. "One of my very first patients, in fact, and a diligent one."

He paused, blushing slightly, and warning bells started ringing in my head. "What do you mean by diligent? Like, you see her a lot?"

"Fairly regularly. Can't say much more than that. Patient confidentiality and all that." He adjusted his glasses, avoiding my gaze by reading the instructions on the tin of lavender bath salts he was buying.

"Seems like she's more than a patient," I said, looking away and sipping at my coffee.

"We're friends," was all he offered as explanation.

"Do you think you could set up a meeting between me and this *friend*?"

Elena had been arranging photos and a candle on her altar while sipping a glass of iced calamansi-ade, our Filipino spin on lemonade, but she looked up at my request. "Are you investigating again?"

Adeena's eyes lit up at the thought of sleuthing, but the frown on Jae's face told me to tread lightly. "Not exactly. I'm a little worried about Bernadette, but they have no evidence against her. I was with Rob's sister, Valerie, last night and figured it's only right to extend my condolences to his wife, too. After all, Rob was an important part of the pageant."

Jae smiled at me before finishing his drink. "That's sweet of you. I can't promise anything, but I should also offer my condolences. I'll let you know if I can arrange a meeting." To Adeena and Elena he said, "Thanks for the refreshments and the personal shopper experience. I'll stop by for a pick-me-up after lunch. Good luck with your opening!"

The three of us waved him off. Once the bells chimed behind him, Adeena turned to me. "OK, now that he's gone, you're investigating, right?"

I rolled my eyes. "Bruha, please. This is my family on the line. You know we're investigating."

Chapter Nine

"I can't believe we're having a committee meeting so soon after Rob's death."

The mayor studied the selection of sweets I'd laid out on the table before replying to me, as if death were way less important than pastries. It had only been a few days since I found out Rob had been murdered, and now that I no longer had baker's block, I'd channeled my anxiety over the case into my baking. Still had ninety-nine problems, but at least baking wasn't one.

"This pageant meant a lot to Rob and even more to this town. He would want us to forge ahead. Besides, what better way to honor his memory than to dedicate this pageant to him?"

I wasn't sure taking an event meant to uplift young women and dedicating it to a problematic older man was the way to go, but again, his family money was what kept the pageant running.

"I also think it's a bit soon, but dedicating a special scholarship prize to the girl with the best presentation on their volunteer experience is a lovely thing to do. Great idea, Valerie," Sana said as Valerie threw her a grateful smile. Valerie's dark eye bags and shaky hands as she attempted to sip a cup of coffee filled to the brim with cream and sugar told me all I needed to know about how she was doing. But before she could respond, a voice that managed to be equal parts melodic and flinty interrupted.

"Yes, well, *my* Rob was a good man, and Valerie knows how much I love charity. I'd planned on doing something similar in lieu of flowers at his service, but as always, Valerie was quicker." A woman I'd never met before marched up to us, a smile frozen across her perfectly painted mauve lips.

"Beth! So glad you could join us." The mayor went over to give her a hug. The woman moved as if to dodge it, but recovered her poise and gave him a church hug. Plenty of space for the Holy Spirit between the two of them.

Beth Thompson was not what I expected. I'd asked the aunties about her, and they informed me that it was a fairly recent marriage—two years at most—and that Beth was fifteen years younger than her husband. Considering this information, Rob's personality, and his admission that his wife knew and accepted his infidelity, I pictured a shrinking violet. You know, blandly pretty, quiet, happy to accept her husband's disrespect in exchange for being a kept woman. And with Rob gone, I figured his widow would be wallowing in grief. Or at least playing the part. But Beth Thompson was *radiant*.

Close to six feet tall, she moved with the grace of a model. There was nothing overtly sexy about the way she walked or dressed, but the confidence she exuded drew your eye to her. She reminded me of Sana in a way, and not just because they were close in age. There was something magnetic about them, something that seemed to say they'd earned their place in life and were comfortable with who they were. I longed for that air of self-assuredness.

I'd planned to observe from the side, see if I could glean the inner workings of this group and how it all connected to Rob's death, but I felt Beth's pull. Against my better judgment, I walked over to introduce myself. "Beth? I'm Lila Macapagal, owner of the Brew-ha Cafe and one of the pageant judges. It's lovely to meet you, though I wish it were under better circumstances."

"You're a polite one, aren't you?" Beth smirked, looking me over. "So you're the former beauty queen Rob mentioned. Not quite what I was expecting, honey."

The spell she'd cast over me lifted a bit at that remark—I didn't need her reminding me I wasn't beauty queen material. I felt Bernadette's and Adeena's influence stirring in me and returned the smirk. "Same goes for you."

"What, because I'm young and Black?"

"No, because you seem like you have self-respect."

I almost clapped my hands over my mouth like a child. Oh my gulay, Lila, what was wrong with you? This woman just lost her husband, who she might have killed, by the way. Watch your mouth.

I cringed. "Sorry. I'm so sorry. Um, my condolences."

I did an awkward head nod/bow and tried to exit the group, but Beth grabbed my arm. "No, it's fine." She looked me up and down again, reappraising me. "You're feistier than I expected. And you do have some style, at least. Maybe this pageant won't be a waste of my time."

Mr. Acevedo, the chamber head, cleared his throat. "Thank you for agreeing to take over Rob's spot on the judging panel, Mrs. Thompson. Are you sure you're OK with holding the first event tonight? We can postpone it if—"

She waved her hand. "No, we should continue as planned. We can have the news team here and release an official statement, as well as drum up press for the event. We want to nip this in the bud before the *Shady Palms News* spins their own story."

Noting the surprise on my face, Valerie leaned over. "She headed the PR department for the Thompson Family Company before marrying Rob. She understands damage control."

Huh. Guess she really did know what she was getting into. But did that give her more or less of a motive to want Rob dead? Maybe she thought she could change him, or that she wouldn't be hurt by him since she already knew about his behavior. But then the years went by and she finally snapped. If so, what would've been the trigger?

Beth looked at her Cartier watch. "I need to meet with the funeral home to plan Rob's memorial and want to make sure we're all on the same page in case the media has questions for any of us."

Sana raised an eyebrow. "You want us all to spout some predetermined company line? Won't that seem a bit cold?"

"Trust me, when it comes to talking about Rob, it's always best to have a little practice beforehand. I'm not saying to read line by line from a card, but maybe don't rhapsodize on what a saint he was. Anything too effusive will come off fake."

"And to avoid sounding fake, you want us to have a prepared script to use in public?" I lifted an eyebrow.

Beth gave a bitter smile. "The irony, huh?"

"We all have our roles to play, especially in a town like this," Valerie said, a resigned look on her face. "Don't worry, Beth. You won't have to coach me on what to say."

"Yes, I'm sure that's what your 'life coach' is for. You can't seem to make a decision without her anymore." Beth turned to Sana, a condescending smile on her face. "For what she's paying you, you must be very good at what you do."

"I am." No elaboration, no explanation from Sana as she met Beth's look head-on.

Beth tilted her head. "And what exactly is it that you do? Besides take money from weak women with no business sense?"

Before Sana could defend her work, the mayor butted in. "Ladies, can you save this little squabble for another time? We need to finalize our statements and go over the procedure for the Q&A portion of the pageant."

Between Beth and Mayor Gunderson, there was so much condescension in the room, I had no idea how Sana could keep her cool. Maybe I really should check out her yoga class if it meant I could deal with conflict as gracefully as she did. My usual method of avoiding it or running away hadn't been all that effective lately.

"Of course, Mayor. Like Valerie said, we all have our part to play. Just interested in seeing what roles everyone here fits into."

Beth grinned at Sana's response, flashing a perfect set of pearly white veneers. Which should've added to her beauty, but instead came off as intimidating, predatory almost, and left me wondering who Beth really was. It'd be easy to cast her as the downtrodden widow or even the villain. But something told me there was more to her than that, and I needed to break past that perfect facade and soon—before anyone else got cast as the victim.

"Thank you so much for being here today. I'm sure you're all just as shocked and saddened as I am by the loss of Rob Thompson, one of our esteemed judges and a true pillar of our community."

The mayor looked out over the crowd who'd assembled for the opening ceremony of the pageant, pressing his hand against his heart in a show of emotion as he enumerated the many ways Rob helped Shady Palms. "However, I know how much this pageant meant to him, so we will be moving forward as scheduled. Taking his place as judge is his lovely wife, Beth Thompson. Beth, would you mind saying a few words to kick things off?"

He handed the mic to Beth, who flashed a winning smile, with just the right hint of sadness, at the crowd. "Thank you, Mayor Gunderson. And thank you, Shady Palms community, for all the kindness you've shown during this horrible ordeal. The outpouring of support would've meant everything to Rob. We will be holding his memorial on Saturday, where we can all say our final goodbyes."

She paused for a moment and took a deep breath. I tried to figure out if this was an act she was putting on, or if it was all genuine. She looked every inch the grieving widow putting on a brave face—her hair was freshly pressed but understated, her black sheath dress flattering yet modest, her classic black pumps increased her already impressive height and highlighted her legs without making it seem like she was trying to attract attention, and she wore the barest covering of makeup that let a hint of dark under-eye circles come through.

As a cosmetics lover, I could tell Beth was a woman who knew how to wield a makeup brush, so the fact that her dark circles were visible was a calculated move. But was it meant to convey *I know the people in this town will judge me if I look too perfect after my husband's death* or *Look at this poor grieving widow who's been without sleep since losing the love of her life, of course she's not a killer*? I couldn't overlook either option.

While I ruminated on her appearance, Beth continued. "This pageant not only meant a lot to my husband, but it also means a lot to me. Education and opportunity are the most important things we can give to our girls, so as sad as I am about the circumstances, I'm thrilled to be part of such an important event. We'll kick off Miss Teen Shady Palms with a quick photo shoot, and then move directly into the Q&A session, which I'm afraid is a private event. However, you're free to socialize in the common area, where we have refreshments from the soon-to-be-opened Brew-ha Cafe."

After news of Rob's murder got out, some parents pulled their kids from the pageant, so we were down to a little over thirty contestants, but the majority seemed content to let their daughters continue competing. All pageant events were usually open to the public, but the mayor was finally taking some precautions. There were too many contestants to keep an eye on with our limited security, so until the semifinal events, the pageant programming was closed to the public.

The contestants lined up according to the photographer's instructions, grinning and shifting poses every few shots. After about half an hour of that, the photographer waved the judges in, seating me, Sana, and Beth in the middle and having the girls crowd around us.

"Yes! Absolutely gorgeous. Maybe we can do individual profiles on all the judges as well?" the photographer asked.

Beth agreed, but I hesitated, remembering the trash they printed back when my aunt's restaurant was in trouble a few months ago. Sana also looked uncomfortable with the idea of a profile centered around her. The photographer must've sensed this because he added, "You'll see everything beforehand and it'll only go to print if you approve it. We'll even sign something attesting to that if you want proof."

Signed paperwork might not stop them if they found anything too juicy, but it was better than nothing.

"All right, but I also want you to throw in an advertisement for the Brew-ha Cafe." If I had to subject myself to invasive questions on the pageant and myself, I was going to milk this for all it was worth.

"Not a problem. If the rest of the menu is as good as the samples you provided today, the *Shady Palms News* team would be happy to run an endorsement."

With the photos done, everyone had a half-hour break before the individual Q&A sessions started. Sana and I dashed to the Brew-ha

Cafe table, where Elena was handing out my ube chocolate chip cookies, calamansi-chia seed mini muffins, salabat-spiced banana bread, and other goodies, as well as coupons, to the people helping themselves to the cold brew and house blend coffee dispensers.

"Caffeine!" I poured some cold brew into my insulated water bottle and chugged it, then refilled it. "If I'm going to interview three dozen teenage girls on their beauty queen aspirations, I'm going to need to take this entire thing back with me."

Sana laughed. "I'm sure it won't be as terrible as you think. Valerie came up with some pretty insightful questions, so hopefully we'll avoid the usual cookie-cutter replies."

"Where is Valerie?" I asked as Sana poured herself some of the house blend and accepted a muffin from Elena with a smile.

Valerie had been present for the first few group photos, but had slipped away while we were talking to the photographer. She'd been oddly quiet throughout the event, letting the mayor and Beth handle all the talking.

Sana looked around, but nobody was near enough to overhear us. "I think Valerie's upset that Beth has taken over as head Thompson. You saw how she was when she talked about her place in the family business. She probably thought this was her chance to make an impact on the company."

She paused, fiddling with her recycled paper cup. "It hasn't been made public yet, but I think Beth is the new head of the company. I can't even imagine how Valerie feels, considering her relationship with Beth and that she isn't even blood."

"How do you know all this?" Elena had finished handing out samples and wandered over to where we stood.

Sana's smile didn't quite reach her eyes. "I do coaching work for the Thompson Family Company, remember? Not that Beth has ever bothered attending any of the sessions. She's smart enough to not say anything too obvious since there hasn't been a press release yet, but she's not the most subtle person in the world. The life I've had, you really learn to look past the marketing copy to discern the true intent."

It hadn't occurred to me that with Rob gone, there would be a shift in leadership in the Thompson family business. Would Valerie have killed her brother for a shot at taking her rightful place in the family hierarchy? Or had Beth known she'd be the likely successor and wanted to speed up her rise to the top? Since Sana did coaching work for the company, would she have a better insight to the company's power dynamics? Remembering Beth's earlier remarks, the two seemed to have a rather contentious acquaintance, with Beth having little respect for Sana's profession. I wondered what the story was there. Maybe something for the aunties to sniff out? The Calendar Crew must know something about all this.

"Did you make these muffins, Lila?"

Beth slipped into our circle so seamlessly, I let out a yelp, worried she'd overheard our little tsismis session.

"Uh, yeah?" I cleared my throat and attempted to speak with more confidence. "Yes, one of my partners," here I gestured toward Elena, "requested that I make my own version of her favorite muffins. I replaced the usual lemon with calamansi, which is a small citrus fruit native to the Philippines."

OK, so that came out more encyclopedic than confident, but at least it was an improvement from uptalking and that weird noise I'd made. Knowledge was power, right? OK, maybe that didn't fit here, but Beth kept catching me off guard.

She smiled, ignoring my awkwardness. "Whatever it is, it's delicious. Remind me to talk to you about publicity for your little shop. Maybe we can have you cater some of the Thompson business meetings as well. I think you might have something special."

I didn't know whether to bristle at her minimizing comment

about the cafe or be thrilled that a woman with as much power and influence as Beth wanted to help me out, so I just changed the subject. "Is it time to go back yet?"

Beth glanced at her rose gold watch and grimaced. "Indeed it is. All right, ladies, let's go interview the future leaders of Shady Palms."

Chapter Ten

If these girls were the future of Shady Palms, maybe it was a good thing I'd moved back here.

We filed into one of the small classrooms housed in the community center, this one dedicated to arts and crafts, if the various paintings and collages lining the wall were any indication. Most of the surfaces were covered with a dusting of glitter, which would soon be coating us as well. Beth pulled a lint roller out of her purse and went over her outfit to try and remove every little sparkle, but I didn't bother. Fighting glitter was a losing battle.

We took our seats at the long table at the front of the room, in front of which sat five chairs. The first Q&A was done group-interview style, and the contestants were not only being graded on their answers, but their posture, poise, confidence, and ability to lead a conversation as well. Each judge had the same list of twenty-five questions in front of them, and we would each ask a question off that list at random, so that no contestant group received the same three questions.

Beth, as head judge, went first, followed by Sana, then me. By the usual pageant rules, I should've ranked higher than Sana, but because I was technically a replacement judge, I was at the bottom. Not that it mattered, since our scores all carried the same weight, but pageantry sure loved enforcing hierarchy and so did Beth.

"OK, I've marked the questions I'm going to ask each girl, so cross-check your list now so you don't get mixed up. Since this is in groups, it's easy to get confused or off-topic, but we don't have time for that." Beth showed us her questionnaire, her bold handwriting listing a contestant next to each question.

"Wow, you're very organized," was all I could say. I figured I'd just wing it and choose my questions based on the vibe I got from the group.

Beth had a lovely smile, but there was always a touch of disdain in it. "We're interviewing three dozen teenagers over the next couple of hours. The only way I'm not going to run screaming from this room after the millionth inane answer is if I stay organized and keep us on schedule."

She ran her hands lovingly over her champagne-colored planner. "It's no different from a job interview. Study the candidates ahead of time, prepare the questions accordingly, and shunt them out on time so you can move on to the next one."

I nodded as if I understood, when in reality I'd never been on a real job interview, let alone run one. I'd worked at Tita Rosie's Kitchen most of my life, and even the internship and odd restaurant jobs I'd had in college were because of my ex-fiancé, Sam. Over the past few months, I'd had to deal with people (mostly my family) pointing out how spoiled and privileged I was, but it wasn't until that moment that I'd realized that maybe they were right.

This point was driven home when one of the contestants, a lovely Puerto Rican girl named Sara Colon, answered the question, "How do you plan on juggling the responsibilities of the crown with the demands of your current life?"

I thought it was a silly question because how busy could these girls be? At their age, I was pulling straight As, taking exam prep classes, working at Tita Rosie's Kitchen, and still found plenty of time to hang out with Adeena, Terrence, and my then-boyfriend, Derek.

Sara paused for a moment, studying the other girls in her group, before saying, "I have a kid. My daughter will be a year old soon and her father isn't in our lives anymore. I'm lucky enough to have a supportive family who watches her when I'm at school and work. So I know what responsibility is. I juggle school, a part-time job, and parenting, and know that being Miss Teen Shady Palms is more than a title and shiny tiara."

She straightened up, ignoring the whispers of two of the fellow contestants in her group. "But I want to go to college. I want to show my little girl that I have what it takes to be a success, and that being a teen mom doesn't ruin your life. People always say they don't have time, but they just mean they won't make the time. I know how to make time for what's really important. And I know being Miss Teen Shady Palms is an important platform, both for me and my community. I would never waste this chance."

I wanted to stand and applaud, and I could see the warmth and approval radiating off Sana as well. Beth, however, was unmoved until the girl added, "On top of that, I'm super organized. If I could show you my phone, you'd see that my calendar is color-coded and has alarms and notifications and stuff so I don't forget anything."

Beth grinned, this concrete piece of information finally winning her over. "You should also invest in a physical planner. I love my online calendar and scheduling system, but if something went wrong or the Internet was down, then where would I be? Technology is fickle. Always have backup plans. Also," her eyes cut to the two girls who'd been whispering about Sara, "don't waste time worrying about what others think or say about you. You're clearly intelligent and driven. Haters are insignificant and whether you win here or make your own way, your success will show them how little they matter."

Sara's eyes widened before she let out a joyful laugh. "Thank you, Mrs. Thompson. I'll make sure to write that down as my inspirational quote once I get a planner."

When it was time to question the gossipy girls, Beth was ruthless and their answers proved to be as thoughtless as they were. The rest of the interviews ebbed and flowed, some just as fascinating as Sara's, others as inane as Beth said they'd be. I swelled with pride when it was Joy's group's turn and she managed to hold her own against Beth.

Beth lobbed what should've been a softball question to the group—What do you want to study in college and why?—until I realized how many of them just didn't know. They'd obviously prepared for the question, but weren't able to explain why they'd chosen those majors other than "It sounds like fun!" and "I don't know, it makes a lot of money." When Beth pressed them to elaborate, one of them actually burst into tears.

Joy, however, looked as if she'd been waiting her whole life for someone to ask her that. "I want to study civil engineering in Chicago. People don't realize this, but designing and building a city's infrastructure is so important for the safety and quality of life of its citizens. Chicago is an amazing city with some of the best architecture, but there's so much work that needs to be done on a systematic level. Or is it systemic? Anyway. You know what I mean, right?"

That sincerity. That passion. That belief that she could actually make a difference. I'd forgotten how strongly I had felt everything as a teenager, but Joy was bringing it back in full force.

Beth leaned forward. "So you plan on moving to Chicago? Then how would your winning the scholarship benefit the people of Shady Palms?"

Joy started chewing on her lower lip, but a raised eyebrow from Beth made her stop. "Civil engineers go where their work is needed. Chicago is my goal because it's the biggest challenge, and could really use this kind of change. But Shady Palms isn't perfect. I mean, it was here that I noticed which areas get the benefits of the town's services. Working in Chicago is my dream, but Shady Palms is my home. I want to make Shady Palms the safest and most equal place possible."

"By overseeing construction projects?" Beth didn't bother to keep the mocking tone out of her voice, which made the other girls in the group snicker, but it didn't seem to affect Joy.

Her earnestness shone through as she said, "You work for the Thompsons and are a member of their family. You know that construction projects are political—both in who gets them and which areas benefit from them."

Beth reared back, but rather than look offended, her eyes gleamed in satisfaction at Joy's response. Her only comment was, "So you're not as naive as you seem. Sana, time for the next question."

Just over two and a half hours later, the final group was gone and Beth, Sana, and I were *done*.

"Lord, I need a drink," Beth said as she stood and stretched, the perfectly tailored blazer she wore over her dress rising and falling back into place with her movements.

I checked the time on my phone. "Why don't we grab some food at my aunt's restaurant and drinks at the Brew-ha Cafe? It's not on the menu yet, but we do have a liquor license and a limited selection."

"The Brew-ha Cafe? Now, why does that sound familiar?" Beth tapped her chin a few times, apparently forgetting she'd enjoyed our food and drinks so much a few hours ago that she'd offered to help us with marketing. Guess I knew where I stood as a priority. "Oh, it's right by Jae's clinic, isn't it?"

"You know Jae?" When Jae mentioned her earlier, I'd gotten the feeling there was more to their friendship than he was letting on. Her response confirmed my suspicion.

"Oh, I know him *very* well. I have another appointment, so I'll have to take a rain check for drinks at your place, but only if you invite him, too." Beth draped a silk scarf over her hair and wrapped the ends around her neck before picking up her large Birkin bag and heading toward the door.

She paused at the doorway, hand trailing down the wooden trim. "Oh, by the way. Next time you see him, let him know he left his tie at my place."

A tiny smile quirked at the edge of her lips and she walked away, knowing full well the impact of her words on me.

Chapter Eleven

"I have to say, Lila, when you invited me over for dinner, this isn't quite what I had in mind."

Jae stood in the doorway, clutching a bunch of my beloved lilacs as he eyed all the action going on behind me. He'd taken care with his appearance, dressed in a baby blue Henley and fitted shorts, with his medium-length dark brown hair tousled just so to take advantage of the messy texture. The light, clean scent of his aftershave mingled pleasantly with the lilacs as I leaned forward to give him a hug and accept the bouquet.

I glanced over my shoulder at the Calendar Crew peeling and cutting up fruit at the dining room table with Detective Park and Amir while Bernadette and Joy set out the plates and utensils. My aunt and grandmother wandered in and out from the kitchen, laying out dish after dish as if they were feeding a crowd of thirty instead of ten.

"I'm sorry, I didn't think it'd be a big deal. We were already having everyone over and I thought you'd enjoy the company," I said as I led him to the table before going to get a vase for the flowers.

Of course I knew that he was going to misconstrue my dinner invitation, but I didn't care. He could have his close friend Beth Thompson console him if he didn't like it. I had a murder to solve.

After checking to make sure Longganisa was comfortable in my room (poor Amir was allergic), I emerged from the kitchen with the vase to see the Calendar Crew had already surrounded Jae and were grilling him about Beth Thompson.

"What do you know about her?"

"Do you think she killed her husband?"

"When did you two start your affair?"

This last question from Ninang April had Jae choking and spilling water all over himself. Most of the time, my godmothers' nosy bluntness was a huge pain, but I appreciated it at times like this. The Calendar Crew absolutely did not care what you thought about them, and they would stop at nothing to get to the bottom of the latest bit of tsismis.

Watching this six-foot-tall man shrinking into his chair and clutching his empty water glass for protection against my aunties shouldn't have been so satisfying, but I'd been in a mood since leaving the pageant event and this was definitely helping.

Jae turned panicked eyes toward me, seeking assistance, but I busied myself with arranging the flowers on a nearby shelf. Detective Park cleared his throat and Jae turned toward him, likely thinking his big brother was going to save him.

"I didn't realize you were involved with Beth Thompson, Jae. Care to explain the nature of your relationship?" Detective Park folded his hands on top of the table, gazing at his little brother with that penetrating stare of his.

Jae looked at everyone else in the room. Joy was at least pretending to be busy, straightening the forks and spoons next to each plate, but everyone else's undivided attention was on him.

He rubbed the back of his neck. "It's not what you think, OK? We've had dinner together a few times, but that's it. Nothing is going on between us."

"Dinner with just the two of you? At which restaurants?" Amir asked, taking the chair next to Jae and leaning close.

"We usually went outside of Shady Palms to hang out. Not that we had anything to hide!" Jae was quick to add, as he leaned away from Amir. "I just wanted to try new places and Beth said she knew some good restaurants in Shelbyville. She introduced me to a great Ethiopian place."

I knew that restaurant. It was a small, intimate, and intensely romantic space. He'd taken me there a few times, and while those were friend hangouts, I guess I considered it one of our places. The fact that he'd gone there with Beth first hurt in a way it shouldn't have.

I crossed my arms. "So she was the one who introduced you to Demera?"

Jae flinched. Amir, noting the involuntary movement, tried to drive the wedge further between me and Jae.

"So you've been sharing this special date spot with two different women? One of whom was married? I thought better of you, Doctor."

"They weren't dates," Jae muttered. "Lila and I are friends, and so are me and Beth. I don't exactly know a ton of people in this town, OK? Besides, I have made it very clear to Beth that I'm not interested in being the other man."

I crossed my arms. "Well, she's single now. Guess you get to be the one to console her."

Jae tilted his head, studying me. "Why are you being like this?"

"Why was your tie at her place?"

The room stilled.

"What?" Jae's eyes widened and his hand went to his chest as if to check for the missing tie.

"After the pageant interviews, Beth told me to remind you that you'd forgotten your tie at her place." I leaned over, putting a hand on the back of Amir's chair to stabilize myself. "Why were you there?"

I was being unfair to him. So, so unfair since Jae was being honest when he said he didn't know many people in Shady Palms. Adeena and I were among his first friends in town, and I knew he still struggled to put himself out there and meet new people. I knew how hard he'd been trying to break out of his shell and make new friends. But I just couldn't get the image of his tie at Beth's place out of my head—maybe I cared more than I let myself believe.

"Why am I under interrogation? Is that why you invited me here? To ambush me?" Jae stood up, his face redder than the time he'd downed a whole bottle of soju at karaoke. He was mad at me. Me, as if I were the one hiding secrets and information about a potential murderer.

"Bro, this isn't an interrogation. We're all here to share information that will hopefully shed light on what happened to Rob Thompson." Detective Park's tone was soothing, meant to assuage his brother into telling us what we wanted. "Out of all of us, you know Beth Thompson the best and she's a person of interest right now. Nobody's accusing you or her of anything. Isn't that right?"

He glared at me and my godmothers and raised his eyebrows at Amir, but we all just shrugged at him.

Jae ran his hand through his hair, somehow making it even messier and sexier than before. "Look, I'm not going to pretend that she's not an attractive woman and that she hasn't made it obvious she's interested in me. But I wasn't going to be a piece in the Thompsons' weird game."

"What do you mean by that?" his brother asked.

"Beth said that I shouldn't let the fact she was married stop me since it was an open secret that they both had relationships on the side. I could respect polyamory, but I know people in polyamorous relationships, and the way she was talking made it seem like this wasn't it. That it was a competition between the two of them and they got off on flaunting their latest conquest." Jae grimaced. "I was flattered, but had no interest in being part of that, especially with a town this small and a couple that powerful. I was looking for a fun hangout, not some weird *Eyes Wide Shut* thing."

"And she was cool with you turning her down?" I asked. Beth Thompson did not seem like the kind of woman who took rejection lightly.

"She said she valued my friendship, so she'd let it go for now."

I didn't miss those last two words. Beth was probably smart enough to know that (1) Jae cherished his friendships and (2) he did not do well if you pushed him too far outside his comfort zone. She was playing the long game with him, I was sure of it.

"So would you say their marriage was contentious? Was she unhappy?" Detective Park pressed.

Jae fiddled with the cutlery next to him. "I mean, that's not really for me to say, is it? They seemed fine. Just . . ."

"Just what?" Detective Park and I asked at the same time.

"Beth is the kind of person who's never truly satisfied. So happy or unhappy, I can't really speak to that. Not sure that even matters to her. But I think she enjoyed competing against her husband. I never once got the feeling she wanted out, if that's what you're asking."

Ninang Mae snorted. "That's just because she signed a prenup. If she left Rob, she wouldn't have seen another dime of his money."

"Probably would've been kicked out of the company as well," Ninang June added.

This was the first time I'd heard of a prenup, though it did make sense. "Wait, if she signed a prenup, does she get Rob's money now that he's gone? Or does it stay within the family?"

Wanting to get out of a prenup was a decent motive for murder, but only if she could expect a payday. Otherwise, she was in far worse shape than before and with a murder charge on top of that. But if the money stayed in the family, would that give Valerie a motive? I asked Amir as much.

He sat up, probably trying to look as lawyerly as possible. "A prenup doesn't mean someone can't inherit. It just means certain property that a person holds doesn't become marital property, which is more about divorce than death. That being said, it all depends on what he put in his will. Just because a prenup doesn't stop her from inheriting doesn't mean Rob provided for her in his will. So prenup or no, unless Rob left a provision about what assets go to Beth after he's gone, she might not get anything. Of course, she could always get a lawyer to contest it, but it'd be tough to get a better lawyer than the ones the Thompson family employ."

I turned to Detective Park. "Has the will been read yet? The contents will probably help with seeing who has a motive."

"Not yet. I already got the OK from Mrs. Thompson to be there for the reading later this week. Valerie Thompson should be there as well."

"Do you think—"

"Hope you're all hungry!" Tita Rosie came out with the last of the dishes and stood behind her chair, forcing everyone to find their seats.

"Oh, thank God," Jae said, sinking back into his chair in relief.

Lola Flor eyed him. "I'm going to assume you're giving thanks to God for this food and not using his name in vain. Am I correct?"

"Of course, Grandma Flor," Jae said, addressing my grandmother the way Amir and Adeena did. "And thanks to you and Auntie Rosie as well."

I eyed the spread, wondering where I should start. Skewers of pork barbecue, the slightest hint of char releasing a delicious, smoky aroma, beckoned me, as did the platter of grilled adobo chicken wings next to it. As I loaded up my plate with meat, my aunt reached over to put a tofu-and-mushroom skewer on my mountain of rice.

"Can you tell me what you think of this, anak? I'm testing the recipes for our Founder's Day booth and this will be our main vegetarian offering. I used a similar marinade as our barbecue, but it's not quite right."

Looking at the array of food on the table, I noticed it was all pica-pica, or finger food. Things that could easily be prepared at the booth and eaten while wandering the festival. The barbecue skewers were obviously the mains, but she also had fish balls (so much better than it sounded) and my favorite, kwek-kwek. The hard-boiled quail eggs were skewered, dipped in a bright orange batter colored with annatto seeds, and deep-fried. So simple and so delicious, especially if you dipped it in my aunt's sweet and spicy vinegar sauces.

"Sure, Tita!"

My aunt was an intuitive cook, and it was rare for her to ask for my help with her food. But once in a while, something stumped her and it was up to my trusty nose and palate to figure out what was missing. I first took a bite of the tofu alone, then the mushroom alone, and finally the two together. It was good, but it wasn't the explosion of flavor or layers of nuance that I associated with my aunt's cooking, even after dipping them in the sauces. The Shady Palms residents would happily chow down on it, at least those who weren't afraid of tofu, but Tita Rosie didn't believe in sending out mediocre food. Mediocre food made the Macapagals sad and cranky.

"The marinade is too sweet for something this delicate. I would make it saltier and add chiles, similar to what you'd use for tokwa't baboy or sisig." I tasted the tofu again, thinking about what would make it pop. "Marinate it for a couple of hours and then brush the reserved marinade on the skewers while grilling them so the sauce will caramelize a bit. With all the sauces you'll have on the side, that should be more than enough to keep our customers happy."

"Wow, you were able to figure it out just like that? You're a real pro," Jae said as he grabbed a tofu-mushroom skewer for himself. I thanked him, but my tone let him know he wasn't off the hook just yet.

"Everything is delicious, Auntie! I can't get enough of this chicken." Amir was attacking the chicken wings with his hands, like he was supposed to, his plate piled high with a little of everything—minus the pork barbecue, of course. "Can't wait to see what Grandma Flor gives us for dessert."

"You'll get nothing unless we get back on topic," Lola Flor said, jabbing an empty skewer in Detective Park's direction. "How did Rob Thompson die, what evidence do you have against Bernie, and who are the other suspects?"

Lola Flor really knew how to kill the vibe in the room. Still, her bluntness got results. I wondered at what age you stopped caring what other people thought about you and just spoke your mind.

Detective Park cleared his throat. "Officially, he drowned. I can't say anything else about an active case, especially when—"

"When the main suspect is here? Even though I know you don't believe that?" Bernadette said. She'd been quiet all night, sticking close to Joy and helping my aunt and grandmother, but I'd be a fool to think any part of the conversation that night had escaped her notice. She had a sharp mind, a wide circle of friends, and a vengeful side—maybe we needed to schedule a hangout day to compare our notes on the case, because I didn't believe for a second she'd left it all up to me.

Detective Park used his fork to remove a piece of barbecue from his skewer, not meeting her eyes. "You of all people know what one can and can't talk about regarding sensitive information."

Ninang June scowled at him. "Then why are you even here?"

Detective Park opened his mouth, but it was Tita Rosie who responded. "Because he's a friend. We all help in different ways, but only if it can be done safely. I don't want anyone getting hurt or losing their jobs, diba? It's bad enough Marcus got fired last time."

Marcus was Ninang Mae's youngest son and a former correctional officer with the Shady Palms Police Department. He was a big help when I was accused of murdering my ex-boyfriend a few months ago.

Detective Park said, "Rosie, he wasn't fired. He quit. It had nothing to do with his involvement with the previous case."

I snorted at that, as I dipped my millionth kwek-kwek skewer in the spicy sawsawan. "I mean, he quit because of how incompetent and low-key corrupt the SPPD is. So it's kind of connected?"

"You're not helping, Lila."

"Neither are you. You know the department is going to rush this. Sheriff Lamb cares more about saving face and impressing the mayor than making a difference. And you're still the only one on the force who has experience investigating murders."

"That's . . ." Detective Park trailed off, then paused to take a sip of water. "Anyway, I'm not one to speak ill of my colleagues."

His words were firm enough, but there was a hesitance to his voice that let me know how he really felt. "And you have full confidence that the SPPD will be objective, methodical, and thorough in its search for Rob's killer?"

Detective Park drew his lips into a thin line. "No comment."

"Fine, we will share information about the people we think are involved and you can tell us if we're hot or cold," Ninang June said.

"That's not—"

"So let's start with Rob's scandals. There was his affair with Oskar Weinman's wife. Last I heard, they're getting divorced. There've been allegations of Rob flirting with the contestants every year, but I don't think it's ever moved past that. Though I do remember hearing about a contestant who had to be pulled one year because she became obsessed with him. Started stalking him, made all kinds of accusations against him."

I nearly choked on a chunk of barbecue. "What? I never heard about that! When was this?"

Ninang June checked her notes. "At least a decade ago. Maybe two."

"Oh." I grabbed another skewer, tamping down my disappointment. "Then it probably has no bearing on this case. Let's focus on recent scandals."

"So there's Oskar Weinman's divorce."

"He beat out William Acevedo for a construction deal."

"I didn't know that," Joy piped up. "I usually follow those things."

"Apparently, Mr. Acevedo wanted to renovate one of the old farms to turn it into a B and B for all the guests who stop by after visiting the state park nearby, but Mr. Thompson scooped him," Detective Park said, looking over the notes the Calendar Crew had given him.

"He's been sniffing around the pageant contestants this year too, so an angry parent might've killed him." Ninang June glanced worriedly at Joy.

"He's been trying to get with Sana to piss off Beth."

That last tidbit came from Jae.

"How do you know that? And why would it piss off Beth? I thought they had an understanding." I tried not to let the last word drip with sarcasm, but wasn't sure how successful I was.

Jae shrugged. "Because she told me. I don't really know Sana, but Beth seems to have some weird rivalry with her."

"I did notice the tension between them. But Sana didn't go for it, did she? She seemed to find Rob as big a creep as I did."

Ninang Mae leaned forward. "I saw them together not too long ago. I wouldn't say they looked romantic, but they were pretty chummy. If they weren't having an affair, he was definitely pushing for one. I know when a man is trying to woo a woman. Plus, I hear he paid her a huge retainer to do group coaching for the women higher-ups in his company."

"If that's true, that's gotta be part of why Beth is so salty about her. She's not the kind of person who takes kindly to people telling her what to do or acting like they know more than she does." Jae frowned. "She's also the type to see other women as competition, so be careful around her, Lila. If she thinks you're challenging her or getting in her way, she could make life very difficult for you."

I grimaced. "She sure sounds lovely. Thanks for the heads-up, though."

Jae shrugged. "I know how it sounds, but she's really upfront about who she is and what she wants. It's kind of refreshing, actually."

I wasn't sure how, but that was definitely a dig at me.

Amir nodded at what Jae said. "He's right. Beth Thompson is not exactly a sweetheart, but in all of my dealings with her, she's been transparent and professional."

"So that means she's incapable of murder?"

"I didn't say that, Lila. Right now, we have very little to work with, so building character profiles on everyone involved seems like the best move forward." Amir dipped his skewer of fish balls into the spicy, sweet sauce in the center of the table and took a big bite. "Wow, these are great. Did you try a new recipe, Auntie?"

Tita Rosie beamed at him. "I did! Thank you for noticing. What do you think about—"

Lola Flor waved her hand. "Ay, that's not important. Is this Beth woman a viable suspect? If not, who is?"

"I didn't think you'd care about the investigation, Lola Flor," I said. When everything was going down a few months ago, all she cared about was the restaurant. She never joined in the gossiping, clue-finding, or overall investigation.

"I don't. As long as Bernie doesn't go to jail, I don't care what happened to that man. I just don't like when people go off on tangents. You're all here to help Bernie."

"They're also guests and friends who we're happy to have over so we can all eat and enjoy each other's company, Nay. They don't have to be 'useful' to be here." As if to put her words into action, my aunt started heaping more food onto everyone's plates.

My grandmother *tsk*ed and stood up, taking her empty plate to the kitchen. Everybody ate quietly until we heard her banging around in there, hopefully assembling dessert, and collectively decided it was safe to speak again.

"When's the next pageant meeting?" Ninang Mae asked.

I groaned. "Tomorrow. A photographer from the *Shady Palms News* is going to accompany us while we visit the girls at their volunteer sites."

"Aren't there over thirty contestants? You're going to visit all of them in one day?" Jae asked.

"No, we spread it over the week. Made it easier since there were so many, and also because their schedules have them working specific days and times. And there're only twenty contestants now since quite a few were eliminated after the group interviews." I swiped the last kwek-kwek from the plate, the thought of all the work ahead of me making me crave the deep-fried, protein-filled comfort. "Still going to be a pain since this means most of my week is dedicated to this. Plus we have the sportswear designer event this week, and there's also Rob's memorial, which I think we should all go to."

The Calendar Crew exchanged glances and nodded as one. "We'll be in the audience for all the open events, trying to get more information. People love to talk, especially with something as juicy as a murder, so we'll let you know what we hear."

Detective Park frowned. "I wouldn't use the word 'juicy' to describe something as horrific as murder."

"I'm not saying it isn't tragic, Detective. I'm just saying it makes good gossip." Ninang Mae shrugged. "Besides, Rob was far from innocent. I'd bet anything that his behavior finally went too far and someone decided to do something about it."

"Doesn't mean he deserved to die."

"Well, that depends on his crime, doesn't it?"

"No."

"Guess we'll have to agree to disagree, Detective." Ninang Mae winked at him. "Ah, dessert! Perfect timing."

Lola Flor set out bowls of shaved ice as well as the various halo-halo toppings, and I got up to fetch the nondairy milks from the fridge to serve alongside the usual evaporated milk.

Jae eyed the rainbow spread with interest. "What is this? It looks like pat bing soo, but with more stuff."

I laughed. "Yeah, pretty much. We call it halo-halo. Getting to mix and match the ingredients is the best part. If it's your first time, I suggest sampling a little bit of everything. Eventually, you'll figure out what works best for you."

Everybody served themselves, and I piled my bowl high with my favorite nata de coco, kaong, and sweet jellies. Coconut milk wasn't traditional, but I'd already indulged in more dairy than my stomach could handle these last few days. I didn't want to deal with the aftermath of an unhappy tummy around this crowd, especially with Jae and Amir right there. Once everybody was happily digging into their bowls, Detective Park brought the conversation back on track.

"Let's circle back. Beth had a rivalry going with Sana Williams, professionally and personally. What do we know about Ms. Williams?"

"She's a life coach and fitness instructor. Valerie seems to rely on her a lot," I said, spooning some caramelized saba bananas into my bowl.

Amir frowned. "Adeena has gotten pretty close to her as well. She seems like a nice woman, but I could swear I've met her before."

"Before she moved to Shady Palms, you mean?" Detective Park asked.

Amir nodded. "I wonder if my firm represented her or her former employer? Or maybe I saw her at a fundraiser?"

"Sana did say she volunteered with a nonprofit for a while, but she didn't say where. If it was in Chicago, it could be possible. I'm not sure where she's from though, and she's been here for a few years. If this was before her move, how can you be sure it was her?" I asked.

"I'm not sure and that's what's bothering me." Amir was always sure about everything. "But she's a striking woman. It's not likely I'd forget her. Uh, because I never forget a client! Or anyone work-related."

Mr. Smooth was fumbling big-time trying to cover up that last bit. I should've been annoyed by that, but I wasn't. Not the way I was with Jae and Beth, anyway. "I like Sana, but there's something evasive in the way she talks about herself. Maybe you could dig up a little more about her past?"

Amir had tensed up, likely expecting the same interrogation I'd given Jae. When he saw I not only wasn't mad but wanted him to look into Sana further, he smiled and helped himself to more of the halo-halo on the table. "I'd be happy to! Anything to help out."

He shot Jae a smug look, clearly thinking he'd come out the victor in this situation. "So, Doctor, when will you next see Beth? I think it'd be best before the will reading to see if you can figure out whether or not she thinks she's receiving an inheritance. If you wait till after, she'll have time to temper her reaction."

Jae glanced at me, then his brother. "If it'll help Lila."

Bernadette let out an exasperated sigh and set down her dessert spoon way harder than necessary. "How is my freedom at stake and everything is still all about Lila?"

I froze, my own dessert spoon halfway to my mouth. "What? The only reason we're all gathered here tonight is for you. You're the one who asked me to investigate."

"Yes, to help *me*. And instead you're twisting it into some quest your beloved suitors need to fulfill in order to win you over. Spoiler alert, Lila: Nobody likes love triangles. *Nobody*."

OK, first of all, how dare she come for love triangles, one of my most beloved romance tropes. I didn't care that it was on so many people's loathe lists, I ate that stuff up. The tension! The drama. The *angst*. Second, count on her to call out the elephant in the room. I wasn't insensitive to the fact that both Amir and Jae were serious about me—I just couldn't handle that right now. I not only had recently broken off my engagement, but the events of the past few months had put me in a weird place. Focusing on myself and the cafe came first. Though I was messing things up with Adeena and Elena as badly as I was with Jae and Amir. The fact that they'd declined to come to this dinner was proof of that. I'd been honest with Jae and Amir from the beginning. I didn't believe in stringing people along, and they'd both assured me no matter what I chose, they'd always be my friend. I couldn't help that they still cared about me, and it was wrong of Bernadette to embarrass them and put us all on the spot like this.

But before I could let out this tirade, Ninang June stepped in and made everything worse. "Ay, Bernie, she can't help it. She's just like her mother. Cecilia was always papansin, diba? These Macapagal women, always wanting more and more attention, and then complaining when they get it. Like with the judging. It should've been you. And instead—"

"Tama na!" My grandmother slammed her hand on the table, making everything on it rattle. "You insult my family? In my home? Get out."

Ninang June and Bernadette exchanged glances, as if just now realizing we had been privy to what would usually be their private, petty conversation. Ninang June tried to apologize, at a loss for words for the first time since I'd known her. "Ay, Tita Flor, no. You misunderstand me. I didn't mean to—"

"So on top of insulting my family, you now insult my intelligence?" Lola Flor stood up. "Get out. Don't you dare come by the restaurant. Your daughter's so smart, so good? She can get herself out of trouble."

Bernadette went over to her. "I'm so sorry, Lola. I—"

Lola Flor brushed her aside and pointed toward the door. "Lila, you want to stay with that pageant, that's your business. But you're done with this investigation. I won't have you putting yourself at risk for these ungrateful . . ." And here she let out a string of Tagalog curse words. Several of the people around the table had no idea what she was saying, but we all winced at the vehemence in her voice—her feelings were clear, no translation necessary.

Ninang June and Bernadette left without another word, and the dinner party broke up soon after that. Detective Park took me aside before he and Jae left together.

"Lila, I think your grandmother's right. I was foolish to get you involved, especially so soon after your previous trauma. The SPPD can handle this. You just focus on your new business, OK?"

I bristled, not just at the notion that I should follow my grandmother's command, but at the way he referred to that past event as a trauma. I was doing just fine, thank you very much.

"Sure, Detective. Whatever you say."

He knew not to believe me, but let it go for now. There'd been enough drama for one night. Or so I thought.

Joy lingered near the table, wringing her hands. "Um, Ate Lila? Could you give me a ride home? I was supposed to ride with Ate Bernie, but . . ."

I'd completely forgotten she was there. She was so good at making herself small and fading into the background. The whole thing must've been so awkward for her, poor girl. Torn between her mentor and her employer. "Of course, Joy. Let's get you home before your parents start to worry."

Joy smiled sadly. "That won't be a problem."

My heart twinged at those words, a feeling that was becoming more familiar the more time I spent around Joy and the other pageant girls. I decided to let Longganisa ride with us, both to cheer us up and to make up for having her shut in my room all night. We completed the short drive in silence, Joy stroking Longganisa's short fur and hugging the little chonk against herself.

Before she got out of the car, Joy turned to face me, eyes glistening with tears. "It's my fault Ate Bernie is in trouble. I never should've said anything."

I turned off the car and faced her. "How is it your fault? You did nothing wrong."

"I told her what Rob was saying to me. About how uncomfortable he made me. If I hadn't, she wouldn't have confronted him and this whole mess might never have happened."

I pulled Joy into a swift hug, crushing Longganisa between us, who was licking away Joy's tears. "You did nothing wrong, do you hear me? Rob was the one at fault in that situation. Never ever blame yourself for how someone mistreats you. Especially when it's an adult in a position of power. He knew what he was doing. And we know Ate Bernie would never kill anyone, so let's just trust Detective Park to do his job."

Joy pulled away and the look in her eyes broke my heart. "You can't give up on her, Ate Lila. Please. Please help her."

I sighed. For better or worse, Bernadette was family. And the Macapagals didn't give up on family, even when they were being jerks. "I'll do what I can, Joy. I promise."

But Ninang June and Bernadette owed me and my mother an apology. And once I solved this case, they'd better believe I'd come collecting.

Chapter Twelve

I swung by the Brew-ha Cafe early the next day—I not only needed a huge amount of caffeine to get through everything, I'd promised Adeena and Elena I'd stop by to do my baking for the day before my pageant duties. Considering how precarious our relationship had been lately, I didn't want to do anything that made it seem like I was shirking responsibility to the cafe. Though I would've loved to have slept in a bit after the night I'd had.

I arrived at the shop before them and got straight to work mixing up the muffin batter, scooping out the cookie dough, and decided to make up a couple batches of salabat-spiced banana bread while I was at it. I hadn't gone grocery shopping yet, so this was the best I could do with the ingredients we had available. Should be plenty to keep our small clientele happy though.

"Lila, is that you back there?" Adeena called from the cafe. The chugging of the espresso machine kicked in, and I could hear her rattling around out front as she got her various flavor syrups all lined up.

I pulled the last batch of banana bread from the oven and set it on the cooling rack before heading out to greet her. She was prepping a pot of herbal tea for Elena and her mom, who were both seated at the counter. A crateful of zucchini was on the floor next to them.

"Good morning, Tía! How are you? It's been a while." I went over to hug the newest addition to my growing group of aunties, who was not only the woman behind Shady Palms's premier Mexican restaurant, El Gato Negro, but also kindly provided us with all the plants and herbs we wanted for free.

"I'm doing great, nena. Business is good, my plants are thriving, and I'm loving the energy in your new space." Mrs. Torres poured a cup of mint tea, passed it to her daughter, and then poured another for herself. "Would you care for some tea? You look like you could do with a pick-me-up."

"No thanks. I have a long day ahead of me, so I need something stronger." Without a word, Adeena plunked a large Brew-ha #1 in front of me, the drink she created especially for me in one of the reusable branded cups we ordered for the shop. I took a long, slow sip before thanking her. "You know just what I need. By the way, all the baking for the day is done and cooling on the racks. If we run out, there's more cookie dough in the fridge. What's with all the zucchini though?"

"We had more than we needed for the restaurant, so I thought you might be able to use it in a recipe. Zucchini bread is a thing, right?" Elena said, sipping at her tea.

As I pondered a Filipino twist on zucchini bread, Adeena disappeared into the back and returned with slices of banana bread, which she set in front of us. She poured herself a cup of coffee and leaned against the counter to enjoy her breakfast. "So what happened last night? Find out anything interesting?"

I recounted the events of the previous night, taking some comfort in the fact that she'd asked about the case. Maybe she wasn't as mad at me as I'd thought. I left out what Ninang June said about my mom as well as the comments Bernadette made about my love life.

Adeena knew me well enough to sense when I wasn't giving her the full story. "And that's it? That's all that happened last night?"

I nodded, taking another sip of my coffee so I wouldn't have to meet her gaze.

"So that's how it's going to be? I know something's bugging you. How many times do I have to tell you this? Ask for help when you need it. Tell people how you feel," Adeena said, clapping to emphasize each word in that last statement.

"Mami, why don't we go look at the altar I'm working on? It feels like something's missing, maybe you can help me out." Elena tugged her mother away from me and Adeena to give us some privacy.

I had nothing left to say though, so I followed them to the back space Elena had slowly been transforming. A richly patterned cloth covered a small table littered with dried herbs, a vase of fresh flowers, an old pair of golden rings, and several candles positioned in front of framed photos. I recognized Elena's father, from previous pictures she'd shown me, and Adeena's maternal grandparents. Mrs. Torres lit the candle in front of her husband's photo, her lips moving in a silent prayer or conversation.

When she was finished, she turned to me. "This is a wonderful space, but there doesn't seem to be anything of yours here, Lila. Don't you want to contribute something?"

"I don't think Tita Rosie or Lola Flor would like that. They're very Catholic, you know. They might find it sacrilegious." It wasn't exactly a lie, but I also knew they lit candles every week at Mass for my parents and grandfather and kept framed photos of them in the restaurant office. Maybe they would've liked having a special space like this to remember them. Not that I was going to bother asking them.

Mrs. Torres gave me a knowing smile, reminding me that she, too, had been raised Catholic in conjunction with her other spiritual beliefs. But she didn't push it. She just said, "I created the most wonderful jasmine tea blend last week. I'll make sure to have Elena bring some for the shop—I think you'd really like it. Lovely aroma. Something about it reminds me of you."

Did . . . did she know that my mother always wore jasmine perfume? Sampaguita, more specifically, the national flower of the Philippines. I loved the scent but avoided it as much as possible—my sense of smell was too strong and the memories it evoked were better kept in the past.

I forced a smile. "Thanks, Tía. I'm sure our customers will love it. Gotta get ready for my pageant duties though. Adeena," I called out. "I'm going to pack up some snacks for Jae and his staff as well as the other judges. Can you prepare two to-go boxes of coffee with cups and charge everything to the pageant account? I'm going to pop next door real quick."

As I hustled out of the cafe a few minutes later, I couldn't shake off the feeling that all three women knew me better than I knew myself. Bruhas, indeed.

I'd woken up earlier that morning with my mind its usual swirl of confusion, but one thing stuck out clearly—I needed to apologize to Jae. Remembering how I'd lashed out at him just because I was jealous of his friendship with Beth had me cringing as I'd gotten ready for the day, taking extra care with my appearance as I French-braided my hair and wore a particularly flattering summer dress. A fresh slick of lip gloss as well as the caffeine and treats I'd prepared for Jae and his staff gave me the courage I needed to push through the dental clinic's door and greet his receptionist.

"Good morning, Millie! I've got a little something for you and Dr. Jae. Is he in yet?"

Millie Barnes had been trying to pat down her humidity-enhanced curls, her reddish-brown hair forming a huge halo around her head, but abandoned the task when she saw I'd brought breakfast. "Caffeine! Lila, you angel. And yeah, the boss man is in back, but I think he's with a patient. If you're not in a hurry, feel free to keep me company while I eat. I'm sure he'd be sad to miss his favorite patient."

I busied myself setting everything out so I wouldn't have to meet her teasing eyes. "I brought a little bit of every baked good we're offering, as well as Adeena's house blend. I would've brought you her awesome cold brew, but knowing how Jae blasts that AC . . ."

Millie groaned and pulled the knee-length cardigan she was wearing more tightly around herself. "I'd say it's 'cause he's so hot, but my husband also keeps our house at subarctic temperatures, so it must be a guy thing. Men," she muttered, clutching her steaming cup of coffee close to her chest.

"Men," I agreed in an equally grieved tone.

"What did we do now? I mean, other than the usual," Jae asked, coming out from his back office. "Ooh, coffee! Thanks, Lila."

He grinned before scarfing down an ube cookie and filling the *Star Wars*–themed coffee mug I'd gotten him for his birthday. It had a picture of Baby Yoda on it and it said "Yoda Best Dentist," which matched his love of *Stars Wars* and dentistry with my love of puns. Truly the most perfect of mugs. "So to what do we owe the pleasure? You're not experiencing any pain, are you?"

The worry creased between his eyebrows lightened my heart considerably. He wasn't mad at me. My life had become such a cliché that I actually let out a breath I hadn't realized I'd been holding. "Jae, I just wanted to—"

The sound of a flushing toilet cut me off and all the relief I'd been feeling quickly turned to irritation when Bernadette stepped out from the clinic's bathroom. "Thanks for listening, Jae. I—Lila? What are you doing here?"

I crossed my arms. "I wanted to apologize to Jae for my behavior last night. Unlike a certain someone, I admit when I'm wrong."

She *tsk*ed and rolled her eyes before helping herself to some banana bread. I glared at her for a few seconds before realizing I had never actually apologized. "Oh, right. As I was saying . . . I'm sorry, Jae. I shouldn't have treated you the way I did last night, and I'll do my best to not let my frustration with this case spill over to you."

Jae poured a cup of coffee and added a large glug of coconut creamer to it before handing it over to me. "I appreciate you coming over to properly apologize. I don't like it when we're not OK."

I accepted the cup and blew on it before taking a grateful sip. "As long as you're not mad at me, we are definitely OK. Though I might have questions for you again since you're the only person I know who's friends with Beth."

"As you said, Beth is my friend and I'm not comfortable gossiping about her. But if it helps us find out who killed her husband, I'm happy to help." He poured another cup of coffee and offered it to Bernadette. "You're my friend too, Bernadette. Let me know what you need."

She looked taken aback by the gesture but accepted the cup. "Thanks, Jae. You're a real sweetheart." She sipped at the black coffee and smiled her appreciation. "Adeena just gets better and better. And these calamansi muffins are great. Can't wait till you officially open, Lila."

Bernadette smiled at me as she said this, all buddy-buddy. What, did she think by complimenting the cafe suddenly we'd be OK? Heck, those weren't even compliments, they were just facts.

I crossed my arms. "What are you doing here?"

"I needed to talk to Jae."

"What about?"

"You've really got to do something about that jealous streak, Lila. It's very unbecoming."

I counted to ten in my head before unclenching my teeth. "Jae, Millie, it was lovely seeing you this morning. If you'll excuse me, I need to get to my pageant duties."

"Already? I feel like I never see you anymore." Millie sighed. "Ah well, I guess it's to be expected. Responsibilities of a winner and all, am I right?"

At that, Bernadette threw her paper cup in the trash and stalked out, the door shutting heavily behind her. Millie raised her eyebrows. "Well, someone's in a snit."

Jae rubbed his right temple. "Millie, could you please prep Room One for Mrs. Delaney? She should be here soon."

"Of course, Dr. Jae. I'll let you say goodbye to your lady friend. Maybe convince her to stop by with lunch sometime soon?" she said as she hurried off to carry out Jae's instructions.

Jae waited until she'd disappeared into the room before turning to me. "Bernadette came here about you, actually. You and the case. She admitted her mom was out of line, but didn't know what to say to you."

"I mean, she could start with apologizing."

"And you find it so easy to apologize to her when you're in the wrong?" The look on his face said, *You can lie to yourself, but you know you can't lie to me.*

"OK, I wouldn't say it's easy, but I've done it. Way back when that Derek mess happened, I know I apologized to her when I messed up. She's older than me, shouldn't she be the mature one here?"

"Look, all I'm saying is that she's really freaked out right now. She's still not allowed back at work and there hasn't been much movement in the case despite the aunties doing their best to gather info. She should apologize, of course. But you might want to cut her some slack right now. It's not always about who's right."

When I didn't respond, he said, "Anyway, I'm having dinner with Beth later tonight, so I'll let you know if I learn anything. You free tomorrow? It's been too long since I've had one of Akio's specials."

Akio, the amazing head chef at Sushi-ya, was Naoko's dad and Yuki's husband. I hadn't satisfied my sashimi craving in a while, and it'd be nice to see Yuki in a non-pageant setting. "I'm not sure how long my pageant duties will take tomorrow, but I'd love to meet up. We can swap info, stuff our faces, and maybe get Yuki to join us after for some karaoke. What do you say?"

Jae grinned. "I promise to bring a full report on Beth as well as my guitar."

The arrival of Jae's first patient reminded me of the time. As I called out my goodbye to Millie, who was emerging from the back room, and hurried to the door, Jae's fingers around my wrist stopped me. "Be careful out there, Lila. If anything happens, you can call me. Call me or my brother and we'll be there. OK?"

Jae's sweetness had succeeded in unraveling the tension that had settled into my shoulders and stomach, but at his warning, I could feel the familiar pressure return. Jae and I might be OK now, but I'd be foolish to ignore the larger issue: There was another murderer loose in Shady Palms. And none of us would be OK until they were caught.

Chapter Thirteen

"Well, that was certainly enlightening," Valerie said after we'd wrapped up our last volunteer visit.

The committee had told us to clear our afternoons for the week to tackle these volunteer visits, but half of the contestants hadn't met the requirements—not enough hours, not on the approved organization list, and in one notable case, hadn't even started yet—so we were able to knock out the volunteer portion of the pageant in just two days. Which was great, since it meant I had more time for the cafe and sleuthing. However, we were now down to ten contestants. If we kept dropping participants in such high numbers, we'd have no one left come the Founder's Day Festival.

"Don't worry," Valerie said after catching the worried look on my face. "I know this is different from how things were when you competed, but I specifically designed the interview and volunteer portions to go first so we could eliminate the girls who weren't taking this seriously. I'm confident that the ones who remain would all make a wonderful Miss Teen Shady Palms, so there are no more elimination rounds until the final event. From now on, it's a point system."

Which I'd read in the judges' packet and totally forgotten about. In my defense, she was changing up things a lot and the guidelines she'd sent were longer and more thorough than the orientation packet I'd received when starting university. So maybe I'd glazed over a detail here and there.

"Now that that's over with, I'm looking forward to seeing what the girls have designed for the athleisure wear event," Valerie continued.

Despite the fact that she wasn't a judge, Valerie had insisted on accompanying me, Beth, and Sana on all our volunteer visits, something that Beth was not happy about and made no secret of covering up.

"Yes, as the new head of the Thompson Family, I can't wait to see if they've produced anything good enough for our new line," Beth said, her words as pointed as the four-inch stiletto heels she wore everywhere, the red soles flashing like a warning sign.

Valerie's sudden intake of breath was the only sign that Beth's words had scored a direct hit. Continuing on as if she hadn't heard Beth, she said, "Now that the Thompson Family Company has taken a huge blow, I need to be sure that nothing mucks up my family's legacy."

Sana and I hurried to our cars as Valerie and Beth continued their slightly passive and increasingly aggressive snipes at each other. "We finished way earlier than planned, so want to hang out for a bit? I need to decompress and ward off all that bad juju," Sana said, as she unlocked her silver Prius.

I was supposed to meet up with Adeena and Elena later to debrief them on the volunteer visits, but figured they'd be cool with me inviting Sana along. They were already friends with her and we could save any sleuthing talk for later. Besides, I needed to get closer to Sana to see if she was connected to Rob's death in any way.

"I'd like that. I'm meeting Adeena and Elena to go over possible menu additions and you can join us."

"Can I come too?" Valerie popped up next to us, making both me and Sana jump. "Please? I really need something to do after dealing with *her*."

Sana looked at me, eyebrows raised as if to say, *What do you think?*

I held in a sigh. It was going to be a lot less fun and relaxing with Valerie there, but what the heck. She clearly needed the company, and it would be good for me to get to know her better, too. She was still a suspect after all.

"Yeah, of course. We wanted to add some gluten-free treats to the menu, so you'd be the perfect taste tester."

Valerie grinned. "Great! See you there."

I finally figured out what to do with all that zucchini!"

I set out a loaf of zucchini-pandan bread, the green coloring from the extract adding an interesting tinge to the crumb. The grassy, floral taste complemented the neutral flavor of the zucchini well, and the turbinado sugar I'd sprinkled on top added a delicious crunch.

Adeena, Elena, and Sana all reached out to help themselves to slices, but I had to stop Valerie. "Your special dessert isn't ready yet. I had to source a few ingredients from my aunt's restaurant first, so you get to try Adeena's ice candy while you wait for my dessert to come out of the oven."

"Oh, this is just like an Indian dessert I had before, but in ice pop form! How fun," Valerie said, a great big smile on her face. Nothing like a yummy ice pop to have even the most serious of adults grinning like a little kid. Seeing her delight made the somewhat fiddly process of constructing the ice candy totally worth it.

Glancing over at Adeena and Elena chattering happily with Sana,

I realized this was the chance I'd been waiting for. But if I wanted info from Valerie, it was probably best to butter her up first. "Hey, so I've been meaning to tell you how much I love the changes you've made to the pageant. So much better than when I was a kid."

"Really? You mean that? I mean, of course you do. Those were good changes I made. Really good changes," she said, as if convincing herself.

I didn't know what to say in response, so I just nodded in agreement and sipped at my drink, hoping I looked properly encouraging and sympathetic.

She smiled self-consciously. "Sorry, that must've sounded strange. Those dinosaurs on the committee and board are afraid of change, so I'm not used to being praised for my ideas. More likely to be accused of meddling, as if I were a child with no sense."

"Was it hard convincing them to change the rules and events?"

She snorted and threw her empty ice candy wrapper in the trash. "'Hard' is an understatement. They didn't care that I had all these studies and interviews prepared as evidence of why the pageant needed to change if it was going to stay relevant."

I handed her another ice candy. "So what changed their mind?"

"Rob. He told them they had to do it my way, or the Thompson family wouldn't fund it. You should've seen the mayor practically falling over himself to congratulate Rob on being so 'progressive' and taking the pageant to the next level." She shook her head, staring into her still-full cup of coffee. "So as usual, he got all the praise and I got all the blame. Not what he was trying to do, mind you. But still."

The bitterness in her voice was stronger than the dark roast in her cup. I knew I had to keep her talking, but I felt awful poking at her sore spots. "Did that happen often?"

"All the time. No one ever takes me seriously." She lifted the mug quickly to her mouth, but not before I saw her lips quirk as if holding back her words. Or tears.

Behind me, I could hear Adeena and Elena laughing with Sana, completely at odds with the gloomy vibes in our corner. I yearned to join them, but knew I had to keep pushing. "Why? You're an intelligent, educated woman from a well-respected family. It doesn't make sense."

"I told you what my value was to my parents. And if I didn't have my parents' favor, then there was no need to pay attention to me, at least in the minds of everyone else in the company. They look at me and see some frail older woman, but I'll show them."

Adeena came at the tail end of that statement, but other than a quick glance at me, she showed no sign that she'd overheard us. "Either of you need a refill? Lila, is that gluten-free treat ready yet? Jae just texted me saying to expect company, so if you've got anything else to prep, now's the time."

I excused myself and hurried to the kitchen. Jae had truly excellent timing—the ube butter mochi was just about done, which allowed me enough time to toss more cookies in the oven while it cooled. By the time I had the ube butter mochi cut up in cute triangles and diamonds, the cookies were done and on the cooling racks and Jae had arrived with his entourage: Beth and most of the momtestants whose daughters were still in the running. No Yuki or Winnie, which was a shame. Those two were at least fun to talk to and way more interesting than the PTA Squad.

I couldn't complain though. Not only was Jae bringing us a ton of customers, but all people I needed to pump for information about the case? I could've kissed him—figuratively speaking, of course.

"Welcome to the Brew-ha Cafe! As we're a new business, we'd like to hear what you like best and what you think we should add to the menu," Elena said as she guided the group to the counter. "If you have any questions about the plants or beauty products we have on offer, feel free to ask me. I'm going to let Adeena and Lila tell you about our drinks and sweets."

While Adeena talked to the group about all the beverages she had on tap, I brought Valerie a serving of the ube butter mochi. "Here, before the pack descends on the treats, I wanted you to try this. I remembered you liked my ube chocolate chip cookies and mentioned a dessert you loved in Hawaii, so I thought I'd put my spin on their classic butter mochi."

Valerie's eyes lit up at the treat, and she seemed touched that I'd remembered her anecdote. "That is so thoughtful. I'm not used to people . . . Anyway, thank you." She paused to take a bite of the dessert, and I chewed on my lower lip. I'd never had butter mochi before, but it had seemed easy enough when I'd looked up the basic recipe. It was made of ingredients that either I or Tita Rosie always had on hand, was naturally gluten-free, and seemed to fit with my Fil-Am fusion style, so I hoped it'd go over well.

I needn't have worried since Valerie said, "This is one of the best desserts I've ever had! Most are too sweet for me, but this is perfect. And what is this chewy texture? I love it!"

The momtestants heard her exclamations and came over to see what we were talking about. I passed out the rest of the ube butter mochi as free samples, explaining it was a gluten-free treat the Brew-ha Cafe was thinking of offering.

"Oh, you have to keep it on the menu! I'd come every day just for this. Not that the coffee isn't amazing as well," Valerie hastened to add. "But this is something you can't get anywhere else in Shady Palms, you know?"

"Your little shop is so cute," Mary Ann Randall cooed, as she helped herself to another ube butter mochi. "Love seeing what you've done with the place. So much more personality than the previous cafe."

She wouldn't . . . not even Mary Ann Randall would be so tactless as to talk about what happened in the previous cafe, would she? Luckily, I was saved from finding out when Beth materialized next to us, her eyes dancing with delight as she took in the space.

"I would never have imagined finding a place like this in Shady Palms. I love it! The vibes! The snacks! The fantastic drinks," she said, sipping at Adeena's special of the day, a lavender chai latte. "Would you be able to provide the drinks for Rob's memorial? I know it's short notice, but the food is already taken care of so you don't need to worry about that."

I glanced over at Adeena, who was nodding so hard she looked like a bobblehead. "Sure, Beth. We're honored that you'd hire us for such an important event. Do you have time now to talk over the details or—"

"Oh no, I'm much too busy now. I have another meeting with the board tonight and need time to freshen up. I'm sure we can chat after the event tomorrow, and if not, here's my card." We exchanged business cards, the quality and design of hers as expensive and elegant as its owner, and then she left the shop, not bothering to say goodbye to anyone, not even Jae.

"What an ice queen. You'd think she'd at least pretend to be sad about her husband," one of the momtestants said, not bothering to lower her voice.

Mary Ann laughed. "Yeah right. She must be thrilled he's gone. Leaves her free to find a new boy toy, after all."

If I hadn't already been looking at Valerie, I would've missed the exact moment Mary Ann had pushed too far. One second, Valerie was enjoying her dessert and seemingly ignoring the momtestants, the next she was on her feet and in Mary Ann's face.

"That's my family you're talking about," Valerie said, wobbling for a moment before her mobility device steadied her. "So I'd be careful about what you say in such a public place. As Beth mentioned, we have another event soon. Maybe I should talk to the rest of the committee about the slander I heard here."

The momtestants all looked at each other in a panic, and Mary Ann rushed over to Valerie, who strode toward the door at amazing speed after her speech. Mary Ann reached for the door, but Valerie knocked her hands away. "I may have poor coordination, but I'm more than strong enough to open my own door."

Valerie flung the door open with such vehemence, Mary Ann jumped back so as not to get hit by it.

Sana sighed and stood up. "I'd better make sure she's OK. Thanks for your hospitality. I'll see you all again soon."

"I don't see how she gets off acting all wounded like that. As if she hasn't been scheming to break up Rob's marriage and take over her brother's position for years," Mary Ann said, her chin thrust out as she attempted to save face in front of all the momtestants.

Her second-in-command (I'd already forgotten her name) picked up the thread. "She doesn't know that we know that she was the one who pushed Rob into seducing Oskar Weinman's wife. All so she could kick Oskar off the judges' panel and make Rob look bad in the process."

"Why would she want to do that?" I asked. As much as I hated it, this gossipfest was exactly what I'd been looking for. Well, I hated the source of it, but the gossip itself was juicy AF.

"To convince the Thompson Family board that Rob was unfit to lead the company, of course. Why else would she be coming up with so many initiatives and taking lessons from Sana? She's an instructor at Shelbyville Community College, you think she needs high-priced business coaching?" Mary Ann said.

Throughout this exchange, Adeena and Elena played the perfect role of the solicitous-but-otherwise-invisible server. Adeena went around topping up drinks, while Elena held out trays of baked goods and her herbal teas as free samples to our valuable customers. Even Jae played his part, making a big show of browsing the wares and piling bags of Adeena's hand-roasted coffee beans and Elena's scented bath salts next to the register, loudly proclaiming he couldn't wait to get home for a nice soak once he was done with his last patient.

As if on cue, the momtestants started milling around the shop, studying our products in earnest as Elena did the hard sell. Jae grinned at me and waved before calling out his goodbyes.

I watched him for a moment, and the gratitude for everything he'd just done—bringing the women to the cafe to help me with the case as well as the cafe's bottom line—brought flutters to my stomach. I shook it off and hurried over to join the horde of women I hoped to make my loyal customers. I had work to do.

Chapter Fourteen

"All right, everyone, get in close!" the *Shady Palms News* photographer called out.

Naoko was standing front and center, showing off her winning design. The athleisure wear design event went off without a hitch. Naoko went so above and beyond with her entry, that Beth and Valerie couldn't even pretend to argue with the results of the unanimous decision. The budding young artist had not only created an entire lookbook filled with designs for the Thompson Family line, she was also wearing a prototype of one of the outfits, her signature rainbow explosion of colors making her the obvious standout. Yuki was fussing over her outfit, straightening it just so for the camera even though it was already perfect.

"Mom, please stop," Naoko said, the embarrassment straining her voice as Yuki moved from fixing her daughter's outfit to rearranging Naoko's bangs.

Yuki laughed and backed away, hands in the air. "OK, I'm sorry. I'm just so proud of you. I hope you know that."

Naoko flushed and ducked her head, but not before letting a grin peek out, showing how much she actually enjoyed the attention. A lump formed in my throat as I watched their interaction, a lump I couldn't explain until Yuki joined me.

"I always said I would never become my mother, yet look at me, hovering around and fussing over Naoko the way she used to." My friend laughed. "Guess I never realized that was her way of showing love. She sure never said it."

Memories of my mother buzzing around me, always adjusting one thing or another on me until I passed inspection, flooded my mind. And not just before a pageant or performance, either—she'd do this everywhere. Parties. The grocery store. At Tita Rosie's Kitchen. Picking me up from school. Like Naoko, I was embarrassed by all the attention. Unlike her, I resented it. Her constant fixing made me feel like there was something wrong with me, that I wasn't good enough the way I was. My hand went to my chest, seeking the familiar comfort of my necklace, but even that provided no relief because the chain caught in my hair and I had to ask Yuki to help me untangle it.

After twisting up my humidity-heavy hair in a messy chic bun, I went over to give Naoko a high five and pose with the other judges for the congratulatory photo. Valerie had already left, after conceding that Beth's choice was the right one, so we didn't have to deal with her trying to insert herself in all the pictures.

After we got a couple of group shots, Beth reminded the contestants that their essays were due at the end of the week and everyone split up to enjoy the rest of their day. I was shoving the pageant folder into my oversize Brew-ha Cafe–branded tote bag when Wilson

Philipps, the jerk head reporter from the *Shady Palms News*, approached me. He'd printed the most ridiculous articles about me and my family a few months ago, and it seemed like he was back to dig up more sensational trash to print.

"So, Lila, I hear you're at it again."

I hitched my heavy bag higher on my shoulder. "Excuse me?"

"Investigating another murder tied to your family. I heard your cousin Bernadette Arroyo is the main suspect in the case. Care to comment?"

I rolled my eyes. "I don't know who your source is, but you continue to be as wrong as ever. And no, I'm not interested in any follow-up questions," I said, cutting him off before he could lob any other insults my way.

I turned and marched toward the exit, but before I got more than a few steps away, a hand shot out and gripped my upper arm like a vise, holding me in place. The sense memory of the last time someone put their hands on me like that—tried to hurt me—kicked in and I screamed as I fought off my attacker.

"Let me go! Let me go!" I swung my bag wildly and was rewarded with an "Oof!" when it connected, but I couldn't let my guard down. I kept swinging and swinging until the hand gripping me finally released me.

I heard Bernadette's voice floating above me as I sank to the floor. "Didn't you hear her? She said to let her go! Now get out of here."

Through the hazy edges of my vision, I saw Bernadette confronting the reporter. What was she doing here? I didn't remember her being in the crowd earlier.

Wilson held his hands up. "Hey, I just wanted to ask her another question! She's the one that attacked me. And aren't you wanted for murder, anyway? This wouldn't have happened if she'd just answered my questions about you."

Beth and Sana joined Bernadette and they all stared Wilson down. "We all saw you put your hands on her and you were the one who refused to let go when she asked. Now get out of here. You're not welcome to any more of the pageant events and your editor will be hearing about this." Beth turned away, dismissing him, and Bernadette helped Sana pick me up off the floor and ease me onto a chair.

My breaths were coming in short gasps and I couldn't get my heart to slow down—it's like my body couldn't register that I wasn't in danger anymore. It wasn't until I heard Detective Park's voice that I came back to myself. Bernadette was surprising enough, but when did he get here? He was pressing a bottle of water into my hands and speaking in a soothing voice, the same kind you'd use if you were talking to an injured animal.

"Hey, Lila, it's OK, it's just me. Now I want you to focus on me. Good. Now name five things that you can see."

I was too muddled to question him or his sudden appearance, so I followed his odd directive. "Uh, a water bottle. You. Beth's shoes." I paused, my hand moving toward my chest. "My jade necklace."

"That's good, just one more thing. You're doing a great job."

My eyes focused on Bernadette next to him. "Ate Bernie? What are you doing here?"

Detective Park waved my attention back to him. "Perfect! That's five things. How do you feel now? And yes, that's Bernadette. She's the one who called me."

"Called you for what?"

"Bernadette said there was a problem at the pageant and you needed help. Right after that, Mr. Philipps called to say you assaulted him. I'd like to hear your side of the story."

"I was walking away and he—he grabbed me. Only I didn't know it was him. I just felt his hand on my arm, and it was gripping me so tight, and I . . ." I trailed off as the memory made me shudder.

"And you just reacted?" Detective Park guessed.

I nodded. "Next thing I know, I heard Bernadette yelling at him. I'm not sure what happened."

Sana spoke up. "Bernadette did some sort of pressure-point grip to his shoulder and he let go of you. Then Beth kicked him out and said he was banned from future events."

I looked around to thank Beth but she was nowhere to be found. "Where'd she go?"

"She left after the reporter. I stayed behind to make sure you were OK," Sana said. "Do you still want to come to class? I understand if you want a rain check."

That's right, I'd promised to go to one of her fitness classes. That wasn't happening now. I managed a weak smile. "A rain check sounds good. Thanks, Sana. And thanks for sticking around."

"Don't mention it." She returned the smile before leaving me with Detective Park and Bernadette.

"So what are you doing here?" I asked Bernadette. My mind was finally clearing, and more than the anger I felt toward her and her mother's behavior the other night, I was also embarrassed. Of all the people to see me have a breakdown. Was this going to be fodder for our next argument? My recent panic attacks had all taken place when I was alone, so I didn't have to deal with people fussing over me. Now I was completely exposed in front of the man who wanted to send me to a shrink and the woman who'd been looking to exploit my weaknesses all our lives.

Bernadette didn't answer, just grabbed my wrist and looked at her watch. "Hm, your blood pressure is elevated, but you don't seem to be at risk. Is this your first time having a panic attack?"

I snatched my wrist away. "I asked you what you were doing here."

She put her hands on her hips. "I wanted to cheer on Joy, of course."

"Don't you have a job?"

Bernadette refused to meet my eyes. "They still don't want me coming in to work. Thought I might as well make myself useful and be there for Joy."

That's right, Jae had mentioned that the other day. That job meant everything to her. Still, I refused to let myself be taken in by her when she hadn't even apologized for the night before. "Hmm, that's a shame. Good luck with the investigation."

"Lila . . ." Bernadette rocked back and forth slightly, as if preparing to jump off a high dive. "What my mom said . . . she didn't mean it. About Tita Cecilia. We loved your mom, you know that."

I hefted my bag higher up on my shoulder and crossed my arms. "Is this supposed to be an apology? Because it kinda sounds like one, yet you're missing a super important part. Two little words?"

Bernadette sighed and rolled her eyes, but said what I wanted to hear. "I'm sorry."

"For?"

"Um, my mom talking bad about your mom?"

"You know that's not the only thing you have to apologize for, right?"

She threw up her hands. "Look, Lila, this is hard for me. You know how dysfunctional our moms' relationship was. You know I'm not the only one who had to deal with their mom's unrealistic expectations. Can't you cut me some slack here? I mean, your mom messed you up too, you know."

I reached into my bag to pull out my keys. "You know what, forget it. If you can't even apologize when you're clearly in the wrong, that's on you. I don't have time for this."

"Lila!" Bernadette called after me, but I ran out to the parking lot and she was smart enough to not come after me.

Detective Park had exited before me and was waiting in the lot, his car parked right next to mine. "Do you need me to give you a ride home?" he asked.

"I think I'm good. Just need a minute." I took a few gulps from the water bottle he'd given me earlier and the angry buzzing of Bernadette's words began to fade. "Feeling better already."

"Do you want to talk about what happened?"

"What do you mean? I just told you what happened. And the Bernadette thing is family business, not yours."

Detective Park nodded. "Understood. But I meant your reaction to the reporter, Lila. That's a classic symptom of PTSD."

"I'm fine."

"Have you called Dr. Kang yet?" He paused. "Look, I don't want to pry, but Rosie told me a bit about your mom and your connection to these pageants. I wouldn't want this investigation to trigger—"

"I said I was fine, Detective! Now if you'll excuse me, I need to go lie down for a bit."

He sighed, but let it go. "I'm going to follow you home to make sure you get there OK. I don't want you blacking out along the way. And I wouldn't put it past Mr. Philipps to be waiting for you at your house."

There was no point in arguing, so we got into our cars and I took extra care to drive home just under the speed limit—any slower and that would've been suspicious. I guess he didn't trust me to make it the ten steps it took from my driveway to the door, so he sat in his car and watched me even after I'd parked. I made a big show of unlocking my front door and opening it with a flourish.

"See, Detective? Made it here all on my own. You can go back to solving crimes, or whatever it is you do when you're not hounding me."

Detective Park kept his expression blank as he nodded at me through his open window. "Take care of yourself, Lila."

"I always do, Detective."

Chapter Fifteen

I'd fallen asleep shortly after getting home, cuddling Longganisa while listening to *Their Greatest Hits* by the Eagles on repeat. The Eagles were in the middle of their second rotation when a loud, insistent buzzing woke me up. Thinking it was my phone alarm, I slammed my hand on it, trying to dismiss the alarm, but it wouldn't shut up. I grabbed my phone, the bright screen blinding me as I struggled to figure out what was going on without dropping it on my face.

Oh. Adeena and Elena were blowing up my phone in the Brew-ha Cafe group chat. Probably because I was supposed to come over hours ago and hadn't told them there'd been a change of plans. I groaned and dropped the phone back on my bedside table, too tired to deal with them just now. Longganisa had been lying on her own pillow on my bed, but moved over and snuggled next to me, sensing my need for comfort. I was just drifting off again when a knock at my door roused Longganisa and set her off barking.

"Anak." Tita Rosie knocked on my door again, but I didn't bother getting up.

"What?" I called from my bed.

"Can I come in?"

I sighed, but quietly so she wouldn't hear me. No need to take out my bad mood on Tita Rosie. "I guess."

Didn't stop me from being a brat though.

Tita Rosie entered the room with a plate of barbecue chicken, the savory sweetness filling the space. My stomach rumbled and suddenly I couldn't remember the last time I'd eaten. I sat up, ready to thank my aunt, when my brain finally registered the oddly familiar scent.

I knew this aroma. It had been almost twenty years since I last smelled it, but there was no denying the dish in my aunt's hands.

"Is that . . . is that Mommy's chicken?" I choked, trying to get the words out.

Tita Rosie set the plate on my desk and handed me an old, stained slip of paper, likely torn off a sticky pad grocery list since it had a fruit-and-vegetable pattern decorating its borders. "I was going through some old boxes and found this."

She sat on the edge of my bed. "I know you're having a hard time right now. With the cafe. With the pageant. With a lot of things, honestly. And I know it's partly because of her. I thought tasting this dish would remind you of the good parts of her, not just the bad."

My mom hated cooking. As the oldest child of a large, poor family in Tondo, preparing meals for everyone had been her responsibility. Her distaste for the task meant she wasn't a particularly skilled cook, but that didn't excuse her from doing her part to take care of the family. Winning the pageant and moving to the U.S. made it so that she had enough money to support them without having to work with her hands anymore. But marrying into a family of cooks was equal parts a blessing and a curse.

She was happy to always have delicious food and not have to worry about cooking to feed her family. But Lola Flor had very different ideas of what would make a good daughter-in-law and wasn't shy about letting her know. My grandmother got sick of my mom feeding me cereal and instant noodles after school, so she took over all my meals. My mom resented the fact that Lola Flor considered her an inadequate wife and mother since she wouldn't cook proper meals. So, she perfected this one simple chicken dish for me and I ate it as my afterschool snack every day until she died.

Memories of my excitement at coming home to that plastic container, one that'd originally housed margarine or ice cream or some other product that my family had consumed, leaving behind the vessel for us to reuse until it fell apart, filled my mind. She would usually leave a note as well, reminding me to do my homework or practice my walk or daily singing lesson. I'd carelessly thrown away those notes every day, not realizing how precious they'd be in the coming years.

Looking at the recipe now, written out in her lovely, studied script, I wondered at how she'd packed such delicious childhood memories into such a short ingredient list. The only items on the sheet were chicken legs, soy sauce, and brown sugar. The ingredient list to the tangible example of my mother's love.

I grinned as I dug into my favorite childhood food. Memories of this dish had carried me through some rough patches, and I waited for the explosion of salty-sweet comfort that had lived on in my memory.

It didn't come.

Had my palate changed that much since I was a kid? Or did my taste buds hold false memories, overhyping this dish that meant so much to me because it was one of the few happy things I remembered about my mom?

I put down my fork.

"What's wrong, anak?" My aunt came over and speared a piece of chicken for herself. She chewed it slowly, either experiencing her own sense memories or trying to dissect the flavor.

"It's not how I remembered it." My heart clenched so hard, I withdrew into myself, as if tasting that chicken had caused me physical pain.

Tita Rosie put the fork down. "You're right. Something's missing."

"So it's not just me? I'm not remembering things incorrectly?"

She shook her head, studying the handwritten recipe card she'd put on my bedside table. "You know, your mom was so proud of this recipe. It was the one dish she insisted on preparing instead of me or your lola. Maybe this recipe is incomplete."

I unfurled from my cramped position, an idea blossoming in my head. "I think you're right. She was always jealous of you. Maybe she purposely left out some of the ingredients."

Tita Rosie smiled sadly at that but chose not to comment. "You're so good at analyzing food to figure out what's in it. Maybe you can piece together Cecilia's recipe from memory."

She hadn't even finished her sentence before I was out of my chair and heading to the kitchen. Luckily, we always had chicken legs in the fridge and plenty of soy sauce and brown sugar. But what else was in it? The salty sweetness was the dominant flavor, but it was more well-rounded than that. There was a depth and brightness.

Calamansi! My eyes alit on the bottle of citrus juice we kept on hand when we couldn't find the fresh fruit. That must've been what she used. And what else . . .

I closed my eyes, picturing myself at this kitchen table, the fragrant chicken piled on top of a steaming bowl of white rice, a tiny dribble of dark sauce squiggled across.

I smiled and opened my eyes. Garlic. Of course.

I whisked the marinade together and added the chicken legs, then put it all back in the fridge to marinate for a couple of hours. I washed my hands and prepared a bowl of halo-halo to enjoy while waiting for the chicken to be ready.

As I took my first icy bite, ideas for more recipes popped into my head.

Halo-halo ice candy! That would be my signature ice pop at the Brew-ha Cafe.

But what if I got even more experimental with the format? Halo-halo donuts! And cupcakes! And cookies!

Maybe even a halo-halo-inspired chia parfait for health nuts like Elena and Sana. I'd seen Sana eating chia pudding topped with fruit yesterday and it was so pretty, I knew it'd do well on our menu.

I grabbed my bujo to scribble all these ideas down, jumping up a few times to see what ingredients we had in stock. I didn't have the right plastic bags or donut trays, so the halo-halo ice candy and donuts would have to wait. Cookies were my go-to, but I couldn't figure out a flavor combination that would bake well in cookie form. Too much moisture. I tabled that recipe for now, figuring I'd come back to it after letting the idea percolate. Halo-halo cupcakes would be a little labor-intensive, but I did have a few hours to kill while the chicken marinated . . .

While I filled page after page with my ideas, my phone buzzed again. Thinking it was Adeena calling to curse me out for ignoring her, I answered without checking the screen. "Before you scream at me, I can explain."

"Uh . . . I wasn't going to scream at you. I was just calling to see if you still wanted to go out for dinner tonight. My brother told me what happened earlier. Are you OK?"

It was Jae. I groaned and leaned back in my chair. I forgot that I'd also had plans with him. "I'm so sorry, Jae, I thought you were Adeena. I was supposed to meet her and Elena at the cafe earlier, but yeah. Guess your brother told you."

"He sure did. And it's fine, I let them know what had happened when I stopped by for coffee. They're not angry, just worried. If you're not up for going out, I can swing by with takeout. Or if you don't want company, I can just drop off the tea blend that Elena prepared for you. Whatever you need."

Whatever I needed . . . how sad that this simple gesture of friendship was sweeter than any romantic overture I'd received in the past. Derek, my old high school sweetheart, was a bit of a bro and we often ended up just hanging out with friends or watching sports. Sam, my ex-fiancé, was a little rich boy and I'd often go along with whatever he wanted since I didn't want him to think I didn't belong in his world. Even Amir, a close friend and one of the best men in the world, was so used to thinking he knew best that his "suggestions" were really pronouncements. He was smart and conscientious, so he was often right, but I chafed at the lack of agency. Was it so wrong to want to make my own choices, even if they were the wrong ones? I already had Lola Flor and the rest of my family telling me what to do, I didn't need my romantic partner doing the same.

"Actually, I could do with a bit of company. I've got some chicken marinating in the fridge and a new cupcake recipe I'm working on. Care to be my guinea pig?"

"Absolutely! Let me just shower real quick and I'll be right over. I have this awesome coconut porter I want you to try, but is there anything else you want me to pick up?"

I told him to bring some of Adeena's cold brew to enjoy with the cupcakes and hung up with a smile. Time to get to work.

I started with a simple white cake base, added a bit of custard powder to echo the leche flan flavor, and mixed in well-drained sweet red beans, macapuno, and jackfruit. Scooped the mixture into lined cupcake tins and slid them into a 350-degree oven.

Now on to the frosting. As I whipped up the condensed milk frosting, adding a teaspoon of ube extract for flavor and that gorgeous violet color, my mind wandered back to the case. I loved baking because the simple, rhythmic movements put me in a meditative state, and I found that my best thinking occurred when mixing up cookie dough or rolling out scones.

My initial instincts were that the killer had to be a man or a fit woman like Sana or Beth since they needed to be stronger than Rob to hold him underwater long enough to drown. But Detective Park had said Rob was not only drunk, he had a head wound. One of those alone would've weakened Rob, but together? Valerie had mobility issues, but that didn't affect her upper-body strength. Even someone as slight as Joy might've been able to pull it off.

Not that she had anything to do with it, of course, but maybe it was time to redirect my attention to the contestants and momtestants.

I stuck the frosting to chill in the fridge, then pulled out the cupcakes and set them on racks to cool before frosting them. As I flipped to an empty page to document what I'd done, I came across my suspect mind map. The lines crisscrossed the page so much, I worried I'd have to resort to a corkboard and red strings to map things out. But then I noticed a bubble that stood alone. Winnie Pang. She was friendly with the other moms but didn't seem to belong to any of the cliques. Yet her work at the salon probably meant she was privy to tons of gossip. I tapped my pen on my notebook, trying to come up with a good excuse to pump her for information.

My timer went off and I got up to finish the cupcakes. As I piped the ube condensed milk frosting on top of the cooled cakes, I realized these cupcakes were the perfect way to not only apologize to Adeena and Elena for standing them up, but also a way to grease the wheels at the salon. If I offered to pay for their manicures, I could enlist their help to eavesdrop on the salon customers while also advertising the shop. My godmothers would've been the more effective choice, but I'd rather down a quart of whole milk and deal with the lactose-intolerant consequences than allow them a chance to comment on my appearance and style choices—more than they already did anyway. Plus, I still wasn't speaking to Ninang June.

The doorbell rang and I put the finished cupcakes in the fridge to let the frosting set before hurrying to let Jae in.

"I come bearing brews and treats for Longganisa. There was a gourmet pet store by the restaurant I went to last night and the salesperson promised these treats were both delicious and diet-friendly." Jae held up a four-pack of beer, a bottle of Adeena's cold brew, a bag of Elena's calming tea blend, and a box of organic dog treats. "Where should I put them?"

I led him into the kitchen, where Longganisa lay in wait. As soon as he stepped in the room, she pounced on his legs, barking and nudging him until he'd set down everything and stooped down to pet her. "Hey there, Longganisa. I missed you, too." He held out a treat and she went still. "Son jooseyo." She put a chubby paw in his hand and received a treat in return.

I laughed to myself at this scene as I washed my hands and got dinner ready. Jae had taken Nisa out one day when I was sick, and his mom had taught my dog the command for "paw" in Korean. Which was adorable in itself, but it wasn't until Jae translated and explained his mom had been politely asking my dog to "please give me your hand" that I melted.

While Jae entertained Nisa, I finished up our dinner. After pan-frying the chicken pieces in a bit of oil, I added one of the juicy legs to a steaming bowl of freshly made white rice and steamed broccoli drizzled with toyomansi and sesame oil. I inhaled the rising fragrance and grinned. Before I even tasted it, I knew this was it. This was Mommy's chicken.

Jae washed his hands and popped the top on the coconut porter he'd brought, toasting me with the can. "This smells amazing! I didn't know you could cook. I thought baking was your thing."

I clinked my can against his, then savored a large bite—which confirmed that yes, I'd gotten the recipe right—before responding. "I'm an OK cook, but it's not really my thing. Tita Rosie's food is amazing, so I never really had to learn. I usually only cook if I'm craving something other than Filipino food, like pasta or whatever. But there's always so much food in this house it feels wasteful to make anything else."

I took a sip of the beer he brought and the notes of coconut, coffee, dark chocolate, and brown sugar coated my tongue. "Oh my gulay, this is amazing!"

Jae grinned. "I knew you'd like it. I tried it last night at this Hawaiian restaurant I went to with Beth and had to get some for you. It's almost like a dessert, isn't it?"

So while out with Beth, he not only bought treats for my dog but me as well? That had to be a good sign, right?

"I bet we could make ice cream floats with this at the Brew-ha Cafe. Ugh, I wish we could afford an ice cream maker. But I'm sure we'll figure something out. Maybe for the Founder's Day celebration." I speared a piece of broccoli. "So did Beth tell you anything about how the case is going?"

Jae took a swig of his beer. "She spent the first twenty minutes of dinner complaining about the lawyers involved with his will reading, which I guess happens tomorrow. Then she complained about the incompetency of the SPPD, considering no one has been taken into custody yet. She rounded out the night by complaining about Valerie all through the dessert, then leaving early when she got a call."

"Sounds like a fun night," I said, getting up to refill his bowl.

"Oh yeah, just so much fun. Pretty sure I was able to fit in five words all night. At least I satisfied my poke bowl craving and found this beer. Silver linings and all that."

"Did she say anything specific about the will or Valerie that could be helpful?" I asked, placing his replenished bowl in front of him and moving my empty one to the sink. I took the halo-halo cupcakes out of the fridge to take the chill off them before serving.

I was so busy wondering how to garnish them, I almost missed it when Jae said, "Valerie told her that if Rob left everything to her, she planned on contesting the will. Made some snide remark about Beth being nothing without the Thompson family's generosity, and that Beth never would've gotten her hooks into Rob if her parents were still alive. Valerie's parents, that is. I think Valerie might've run a background check on Beth, too."

I nearly dropped the bag of pinipig I was sprinkling on the cupcakes. "A background check? Did she actually say that?"

Jae drained the last of his beer and tossed the can in the recycling bin. "She didn't come out and say it, but it was definitely hinted at. I guess it's typical for the Thompsons to run background checks on anyone entering the family, but Rob didn't do one for Beth."

Interesting. If Valerie ran a background check on Beth, what would she find? The reason behind Rob's murder? Or would it just show that Beth was the tough businesswoman she seemed to be? Considering her job was to clean up messes and make the company look good, it was hard to say who the real Beth was. "Satisfied" from *Hamilton* started playing in my head—from what Jae said about her at that dinner, Beth was a real Angelica Schuyler type.

"Are those ready?" Jae's voice brought me back to the moment. I'd been standing and staring at the finished cupcakes for who knew how long before he spoke up.

I handed him a cupcake and chewed my lower lip as I watched him take a bite. His eyes widened and he smiled at me, his own lower lip covered in frosting. "These are amazing! Not only is the flavor unique but it's got great texture, too."

His tongue teased out to lick the bit of frosting covering his lips. I looked away and drained the last of my beer, the room suddenly way too hot. I poured us both some of Adeena's cold brew and helped myself to a cupcake as well.

They were as good as Jae said, and we smiled goofily at each other as we made our way through our treats. Euphoria coursed through me as I helped myself to another cupcake.

I'd figured out Mommy's recipe.

I'd come up with a fantastic new offering for the cafe.

I'd gotten my friendship with Jae back on track and received some great info in return.

I'd even devised the next step in my investigation that would also help repair my relationship with Adeena and Elena.

Things were finally looking up.

Chapter Sixteen

"What's the game plan?"

Adeena stared into the Honeybee Salon, taking in the multiple packed stations. "If everyone's busy getting their hair and nails done, I don't think they're going to want to get messy eating cupcakes. Also, did you make appointments for us?"

When I'd called Adeena and Elena last night to explain why I'd stood them up and my general plan for the investigation, I told them I was treating them to mani-pedis and bringing along the cupcakes as free samples for the cafe. I did not, however, remember to call the salon and see if there were any openings. I hadn't been to a salon since I'd left Chicago and had forgotten this very basic etiquette.

I grinned at them as we stood in front of the packed salon, projecting confidence and "Don't worry, I got this" energy. "It's fine. Even if we have to wait awhile, this'll give us a chance to talk to the other customers. Get some gossip, ferret out clues, advertise the cafe. It'll be fun."

Adeena and Elena exchanged looks and shrugged, willing to see how this would all play out.

"I'm not one to turn down a free foot massage and you still owe us, so let's do this." Adeena led the way into the shop with coupons and flyers for the Brew-ha Cafe while Elena and I, carrying the cupcakes, trailed behind her.

Katie greeted us at the reception desk. "Hey, everyone! What's going on?" Her eyes zeroed in on the cupcakes. "Are those for us? They look SO GOOD."

I swelled with pride as she squealed over my gorgeous creations. "Hey, Katie! I came up with a new recipe last night and thought I'd bring them by the salon so that people waiting for their treatments could help themselves to a free sample, maybe post pics on social media . . . Is that cool?"

"Absolutely! We serve coffee, wine, and mimosas on Thursdays so these will go great with the drinks." Katie helped herself to a cupcake and posed it carefully with one of our flyers before snapping a picture. She then took a big bite of the cupcake, wiping away the ube frosting that coated her lips and reapplying her lip gloss before taking a smiling selfie with it.

"Do these cupcakes have a special name? I'm about to post these pics online."

"They're called halo-halo cupcakes," I spelled it out for her, "a brand-new offering at the Brew-ha Cafe. Please make sure to tag us in your post."

"No problem." Her fingers flew across her phone as she added a cute description and a ton of hashtags in the comments. I took a quick glance at her profile on my phone and was amazed by the amount of engagement she had—maybe I should have her or Joy help with the restaurant's and cafe's social media pages. I thought I'd been doing a good job, but I was clearly an amateur compared to these teens.

Once she was done, she looked up and said, "Is that all? I don't remember seeing your names on the schedule." She glanced at the computer to see if she was mistaken.

"No, I totally forgot to make an appointment. Do you think you could fit in three mani-pedis today?"

Katie clicked through the day's schedule. "Hmm, we can fit in two mani-pedis but it'll be at least a half-hour wait, possibly more."

Before Adeena or Elena could complain, I said, "That's fine. Put these two down for those slots. Nothing for me though?"

She gnawed on her lower lip as she scrolled through the options, occasionally studying me out of the corner of her eye. "Umm, you could probably do with a good eyebrow wax and hair treatment. My mom's six o'clock just canceled. Would that work for you?" Ignoring that slight against my appearance—at least the Calendar Crew weren't here to add their opinions to that remark—I agreed. She wasn't wrong, and this was the perfect chance to speak to Winnie. Here's hoping she loved to talk while working—I usually dreaded getting a chatty stylist, but I would gladly give her one heck of a tip if she gave me the information I needed.

I waved at Adeena and Elena as Katie led me to the shampoo station, nodding my head toward the other women in the waiting area so they could start gathering information.

"Lila, I'm so glad you finally made an appointment with me! I've been dying to get my hands on your gorgeous hair." Winnie ran her hands through it, then picked up a lock to examine my split ends. "Hmm, let's get you washed and conditioned, then we can discuss style options."

Winnie sat me down, draped a towel around my neck and a black cape around my front to protect my clothes. "Now lean back. Just like that, yes."

She turned on the hose and ran it over my scalp. "How's the water? Too hot?"

"No, it's perfect."

After she soaked my hair, she worked in some shampoo, her strong hands and the cherry almond scent of the cleanser making me sink into the chair in bliss. "Oh my gulay, that feels so good."

She laughed. "I have clients that love my head massages so much, they come in weekly just for a shampoo and blow-dry. Let me know if you're interested, we can work something out."

Paying someone to wash my hair every week sounded ridiculously decadent, but if it made me feel this good, maybe it was time to fit it into my budget. Self-care and all that.

After she'd rinsed out the shampoo and conditioned the bottom half of my hair, she wrapped a towel around my sopping wet strands and led me to her workstation.

"So what are you in for today? Cut? Color? Conditioning? All of the above?" Winnie asked as she combed out the tangles in my waist-length hair.

I took a deep breath as I realized why I'd really come there that day. What I needed to do. "I'm thinking a major chop. Maybe up to here?" I said, indicating my collarbone.

She held up a lock of hair and inspected it. "Have you been straightening your hair this whole time?"

I nodded. "My mom used to straighten it every day for me as a kid. Guess I got used to it."

She grinned. "Considering all the heat-styling, I can't believe it's so healthy. Would you mind donating it? I'd be happy to send it to Locks of Love or a similar organization for you."

I smiled, glad my beloved hair was going to a good cause. "I'd love that. Thanks for the suggestion."

Winnie braided my hair, humming as she did so. Before she picked up her scissors she said, "This is a big cut. Are you sure you want to do this?"

I squeezed my eyes tight and nodded. "It's time."

"All right, I'm just going to cut straight across first and then clean up the style after. Any idea what you want other than the length?"

Since I was already making such a big change, why not go all the way with it? "How about adding a couple highlights? Nothing too colorful, but something to really contrast against the black."

She whistled as she ran her hands through my hair. "You're really going for it, huh? I know just the style for you. Will you trust me?"

Absolutely not, I wanted to scream. "Uh, sure."

"Close your eyes. This is going to be so much fun!"

I obeyed her instructions, stomach churning at giving up so much control, and as she got to work, I racked my brain for how to lead the conversation in the direction I wanted.

The chemical scent of bleach and hair dye filled my nose as I heard Winnie opening bottles and mixing the concoction she was going to paint on my hair. "So how've you been? Got a lot going on with your new shop and pageant duties and everything else."

She hesitated over that last part, giving me the perfect in.

"Yeah, it's definitely been a stressful couple of weeks, that's for sure. I mean, opening my own business is hectic enough but this thing with Rob is . . . I don't even know."

Her hands stilled and I heard her take a deep breath before she resumed applying the dye on the hair framing my face. "It's scary, that's what it is. If Katie didn't need that scholarship so badly, I'd pull her out of the pageant. Not that she'd let me. She loves it, even begged me to let her continue."

"I'm glad you have your daughter's safety in mind. Really hoping it was just a one-off thing though. I'd hate to think anyone was targeting the pageant, you know?"

Winnie laughed. "I'm a single mother. Everything I do is with Katie in mind. She's not going to end up like me, that's for sure."

I started to gesture around the salon, then realized excessive movements when someone was wielding scissors and hair dye around me was a bad idea. "You seem to be doing pretty well for yourself. This place is way nicer than the salon I remember back in high school."

She wrapped foil around the dye-covered hair and swiveled the chair around. "You can open your eyes now. I'm going to grab the heat lamp and you'll need to sit under it for about thirty minutes. Be right back."

She switched her soiled gloves for clean ones, then hurried to the back and came out dragging what looked like a bunch of spotlights glued together. She plugged it in and directed all the lights at my hair. "Better make yourself nice and comfortable, Lila. Do you want a drink while you wait? We got coffee, tea, wine, and mimosas."

Might as well go full-on Treat Yo' Self. "I'll have a mimosa, please."

"Coming right up. Katie!" she called. "We need a mimosa over here."

"Isn't Katie underage? You let her serve the alcohol?"

She shrugged. "Not like she's drinking it. Besides, you think the cops care?"

From her tone, they clearly did not. It's like every time I thought the Shady Palms PD couldn't get any lazier, they were like, *Hold my beer!* But in this case, they were saying it to a minor.

Katie appeared a few minutes later with an icy champagne flute. "Here you go, Lila. Mom, Mr. Weinman is here again. Says he needs to talk to you."

Winnie groaned. "You think he'd get a clue. Sorry, Lila, this'll only take a minute."

I held up my mimosa. "No worries. I got my drink and another twenty minutes to go under this heat lamp."

"And I'll stay here to keep her company," Katie said.

"See, I'm in good hands."

Winnie smiled at that and went out in the parking lot to talk to Mr. Weinman.

"So, he comes by a lot?" I asked, sipping my drink. Wow, it was made with fresh-squeezed orange juice. Way better than I thought it'd be. Must remember to do this self-care thing more often.

Katie shrugged. "He's always had a crush on Mom, and now that his wife left, he seems to think this is his chance. Poor guy."

"She's not interested?"

Katie shook her head. "If she wanted another man in her life, he'd have to be able to take care of both of us. Like, with money or whatever. Mr. Weinman can barely keep that store open, so he's a waste of time, in her mind."

"I wouldn't think money was the most important thing in a relationship."

"Love doesn't last. Security is what's important. That's what Mom says anyway." Katie frowned. "It sucks but it's true. All the relationships I've seen end pretty fast. It's not like in the movies."

I laughed. "Nothing's ever like it is in the movies. They're not meant to reflect real life."

"Then what's the point?"

"Other than entertainment?" She nodded. I thought a moment before responding. "A sense of hope, I guess. That you can move past this. That good things are waiting for you."

She rolled her eyes. "Doubt it."

"Katie, not to be that person, but you're only sixteen. I'm almost ten years older than you and even I still have so much to look forward to. High school isn't all there is to life."

Katie studied me. "I guess that's why Joy likes you."

"What do you mean?"

"I think she kinda sees you as a sign of hope. That she can get out of Shady Palms. And that even if she comes back, it'll be OK."

It hit me then: These girls saw me as a role model. I knew Valerie had gone on about me and Sana being inspirations in her opening speech, but I thought she was being pompous. That there was no way someone would look at me and see anything but failure. It's what I saw every time I looked in the mirror lately. Which was why I needed the Brew-ha Cafe to be a success. I needed to prove to myself that I'd finally made it, despite having to come back home. Despite having to go into business with partners instead of flourishing on my own.

Despite never achieving the things my mother wanted me to achieve.

"Is that why you entered the pageant? To get away from Shady Palms?" I asked.

She nodded. "Mom said there's nothing for me here. I think she secretly hopes I'll marry a rich guy and make it easier on all of us, but I don't want to live like that."

"Married to a rich guy?" I thought of all the Cinderella story–esque romances I used to read (oh, who was I kidding? I still read them) and imagined all the ways I'd expand the cafe if I had a rich spouse to foot the bills.

"Waiting around for a guy with enough money to take care of me. I want to be able to take care of myself," Katie said, showing more integrity than I could muster as I daydreamed about a professional-grade mixer, maybe even a blast chiller and soft-serve machine.

"That's the goal, Katie," Winnie said, appearing behind Katie and tossing an envelope on her workstation.

Katie hopped out of the seat next to me. "Mom! How much did you hear?"

"Enough." Winnie frowned at her daughter. "When I told you to use your looks to get ahead, I didn't mean so you can go off to college and get your Mrs. I meant beautiful people have special advantages and you should use them. Never rely solely on a man."

"But you said—"

"I said money helps. But don't get invested or plan your life around a guy. They don't stick around." Winnie's voice was matter-of-fact, but I caught the bitterness that swept across her face before she sighed and kissed her daughter's head.

Katie eyed the envelope on the table. "So, what did he want?"

"The usual. There are tickets to a concert in Shelbyville in there for both of us. He's trying to butter me up by including you."

"Eww, he wants me to come along on your date? No thanks."

At the look her mother gave her, Katie said, "Oops, I think I'm needed in the front. Talk to you later, Lila!"

After her daughter left, Winnie started unwrapping the foil pieces around my face. "Let's see how we're doing . . . Yes, I think it's ready. Let's go wash this out and we can finish your cut."

"Ooh, another head massage?"

She laughed. "Just a quick one. To get all the gunk out of your hair. No peeking!"

I finished out the rest of the cut with my eyes squeezed shut as she snipped and shaped my hair. "All right, just a quick blow-dry and we're done."

The firm bristles of a diffuser scraped against my scalp as she ran the blow-dryer and I tried not to fall asleep. The calming pressure of the bristles combined with the heat from the dryer was oddly soothing.

The hum of the dryer stopped, and before I could open my eyes, I heard Elena say, "Oh, Lila, you look wonderful!"

My eyes flew open as I took in my appearance. The right side of my hair grazed my collarbone as I'd asked, but the left was above my shoulder, cut in an asymmetrical bob. Streaks of white so brilliant it was almost silver highlighted my hair, somehow striking and understated at the same time, adding depth to the dark color.

But the biggest change of all (at least to me), was that Winnie hadn't straightened my hair. I was wearing my natural hair for the first time since . . . since my very first beauty pageant. I was five years old. My mom had straightened my hair for it and said I was "so much prettier" that she continued doing it. After she died, Tita Rosie helped me straighten it till I was old enough to wield a flat iron on my own.

All these years, it had never occurred to me to wear my hair in its natural, curly state. Why would I? People constantly complimented my long, smooth "straight" hair, so much so that having "nice" hair felt like it was part of my identity. Never mind that I'd never questioned what they meant by "nice." My glossy curls framed my face, so different, but somehow so *me*. I couldn't explain it. "Wow" was all I could say for like, five minutes, trying not to run my fingers through my hair and failing.

Elena slapped my hand. "No touching! You have no idea how to care for curly hair, do you?" I shook my head and she sighed. "Looks like you have a mix of 2C and 3A curls like me. We'll work on your new haircare routine together."

Adeena was too busy admiring my highlights to get into the curl-care talk. "I think you outdid yourself, Winnie. Maybe it's time to update my look?" She ran her hands through her undercut, magenta-streaked waves and eyed the color book lying open on Winnie's station.

Winnie winked at me. "Glad you all like it. Is that cupcake for me?"

Adeena handed it to her. "Sure is. Thanks for letting us advertise in your salon."

"Small-business owners have to look out for each other, especially women like us. And I do love free food." Winnie took a huge bite. "This is so good! I haven't had sweet red bean in years. Is this a limited-edition item or a regular part of your menu?"

"Great question. I'm developing a line of cupcakes based on traditional Filipino desserts, and am trying to figure out which ones should be regulars and which are specials that rotate in. These are pretty labor-intensive, so likely a special." Whoa, where had I pulled that from? Still, that gave me a great base to work from. Cupcakes may be passé, but Shady Palms citizens would be all over them.

She took another bite. "Then I better savor these. Can't wait till you all officially open."

Winnie followed us all to the front and watched me pay and leave a huge tip. "Guess I just found my new favorite customer. Come in a week from now and I'll give you a free wash and blow-dry."

"Wow, thanks!"

"Of course! Just remember that come judging time." She grinned and waved us off, completely killing the good vibes she'd cultivated up to now.

I waited till we were all in the car before asking Adeena and Elena what they'd managed to dig up. Adeena showed me pictures she'd managed to take of some of the letters Mr. Weinman had sent Winnie. "They were just lying on a side table next to some magazine, so it's not like they were private, right?"

The letters were written in a surprisingly neat script, but it took me a minute to decipher the cursive. Nothing particularly illuminating or even juicy—they weren't love letters so much as written invitations to various cultural events in Shelbyville. Mr. Weinman didn't seem like an arts-and-culture type of guy, so I had to assume he was proposing these places to impress Winnie. Poor guy.

"Anything else?" I asked after having Adeena send me the photos.

"A couple of the moms whose daughters were eliminated were complaining about all the changes Valerie made to the competition. Said she was power-hungry and overstepping her bounds, both with the pageant and the Thompson Family Company," Elena said, tapping her newly polished nails on the dashboard as she thought. "Mentioned something about the mayor hating her, too."

Adeena and Elena continued on like that, sharing all the tidbits they'd gathered, and were in the middle of reciting the millionth momtestant complaint when my phone rang. I glanced at it. "Sorry, it's Amir. I should probably take this."

I answered the phone, trying to keep my tone cheery and bright. "Hey, Amir! What's up?"

"Lila, I've got that information you asked for." His tone was brusque and no-nonsense, which was typical for him, but not when it came to me.

I tried not to let him know I'd noticed. "That's great. Should I have everyone over for dinner again so you can tell us what you've learned?"

Though considering how the last one ended, maybe we should hold off on dinnertime investigation. Then again, if Amir's info was good enough to help Bernadette, maybe we could use it to force Ninang June to apologize and reconcile with my grandmother.

"I think we should try to keep this as private as possible. Is anyone at the cafe?"

Amir was always a little uptight, but the tension in his voice was off the charts. I tried to lighten the mood with a joke.

"Let me guess, you already solved the case for us? Mr. Golden Boy Detective swoops in to save the day yet again?"

He sighed. "After all this time, that's still how you see me? Adeena's perfect older brother who can't mind his own business? Who always tries to, as you put it, 'swoop in to save the day'?"

Something told me that "yes" was not the answer he was looking for, so all I said was, "Um, I'm with your sister and Elena and you're on speakerphone, so if you have confidential information—"

He cut me off. "If they're with you, it's probably best I tell you all together anyway. See you at the cafe in fifteen?"

"Sure. And Amir . . ." I trailed off, knowing there was nothing I could say to get us back to the way we were. "Thanks. See you soon."

He hung up without saying goodbye.

Chapter Seventeen

When I pulled into the parking lot in front of the shop, Amir was already there, leaning against his car, hands in his pockets. It was eighty-plus degrees outside and yet the only concession to the heat he'd made was that his suit jacket was draped over his arm and his shirtsleeves were rolled up. He'd also loosened his tie ever so slightly, which was the closest to casual dress I'd seen on him in a while. My stomach lurched the way it always did when I saw him. Guess it didn't matter how awkward the two of us had become, my body still reacted when I was around him.

After I'd parked, he came around to the driver's side, opened the door for me, and helped me out. Even when he was pissed at me, he was still a gentleman. It was both comforting and annoying, which perfectly described our relationship.

"Oh, that's cool, just going to ignore your sister back here?" Adeena said as she slid out the back door of my old SUV.

Amir raised his hand in greeting but kept his attention on me. "Thanks for coming to meet me."

"Thanks for getting that information for me. But why so secretive?"

He gestured at the coffee shop. "We should talk inside."

I let us in and flicked on the lights, while Adeena moved to the freezer behind the counter to grab us all ice candy. "Amir Bhai, you wanna try mine or Elena's signature ice candy?"

"You choose."

She handed him hers to see if he'd recognize her flavor inspiration. "Oh my—is this kulfi? It's so good!" Nothing like an ice pop to transform even the stuffiest person into a little kid. "I haven't had this since Nani Jaan passed away. She used to make this all the time when we were kids," he explained to me and Elena.

"It's so good, right? Just the perfect amount of rose, unlike that floral monstrosity Adeena made me drink months ago," I said. "Elena's is arroz con leche, or rice pudding. Try some." I held out the ice candy and he took a large bite, wincing against the cold.

"That's great, too. You girls are really hitting it out of the park with your offerings. So what's your signature flavor, Lila?"

I glanced over at Adeena and Elena, whose eyes were boring into me to see if I could finally answer this simple question. "I figured since Lola Flor's halo-halo was so popular, I'd put my own spin on it for my ice candy."

"That's a great idea!" Adeena clapped and squealed over this. She'd been mainlining cups of our restaurant's halo-halo every day since summer started, so it made sense she was excited about my decision. Maybe this was the obvious choice all along.

Amir smiled at me, his warmth slowly returning. "That does sound great. Can I try it?"

"Oh, uh, it's not ready yet."

"Why not?"

I shrugged. "Still in development. So that information?"

"Oh, right. So the reason that Sana looks so familiar to me? She was a rising star at one of the biggest law firms in Chicago until she got into an accident and killed somebody."

My stomach clenched at the implication. I almost didn't want to know, but I had to ask. "Drunk driving?"

He shook his head. "She fell asleep at the wheel. Her car veered into a bus shelter and killed an old man who was waiting for the bus. Vehicular manslaughter. She was sentenced to three years in prison but was let out after two for good behavior."

Adeena said, "I can see why she'd want to keep this private. Sana's worked really hard to get to where she is and she probably doesn't want her history spread all over town. Thanks for letting us know."

I was thinking the same thing, except what Adeena saw as a matter of privacy, I saw as a motive for murder. Did Rob know about her record? Threaten to let the people of Shady Palms know if she didn't do what he asked?

Amir frowned. "Well, it's all a matter of public record so I don't feel bad telling you all. But having the usual crowd around feels too much like gossip and the details of the case are rather sordid."

"More than just the manslaughter?" Elena had kept to the background, watering her plants and minding her business, but even she couldn't ignore the draw of "sordid details."

He nodded. "Seems she was married to the son of the head of her old law firm. Not only did her father-in-law fire her, but he pushed his son into divorcing her while she was in jail. That's why it took me so long to connect the dots. She's using her maiden name now, but I'd heard of her case back when she was still using her ex-husband's name."

"That's awful. I mean, I get that she killed somebody and had to serve her time, but why sever all ties with her? You said she wasn't drunk."

Amir raised his eyebrows. "Come on, Lila, you know why. To save face."

The Brew-has and I all sighed. It always came to that, didn't it? What everyone else thought of you. Your precious image.

Amir pulled a folder out of his briefcase. "By all accounts, she did her time and tried to make up for her mistakes. Volunteered with a local legal organization, doing pro bono work for nonprofits in underdeveloped neighborhoods for a while. I'm not sure what brought her to Shady Palms, but I'm guessing we're the only ones who know the full details of her past. Well, except for . . ."

After he paused for a beat too long, Adeena rolled her eyes. "Oh come on, Amir Bhai. You know dramatic pauses are my thing. It's not cute when you do it. So spill, who knew about her past?" Realization lit up her expression. "It was Rob Thompson, wasn't it?"

He hesitated. "You know I hate gossip. But someone at my firm told me they'd seen Rob and Sana out on an alleged date a few days before he died. Only it didn't seem all that romantic. It seemed like he was threatening her."

"How so?"

"Rob put a manila envelope on the table and said something to her. She must not have liked whatever was in there, because after she looked at the contents, she threw a glass of water in his face and left."

I frowned. "You think he was blackmailing her?"

"Most likely."

"I don't get it. If he blackmailed her, why would she agree to judge the pageant with him?" Elena asked, setting down her watering can. "She's great, but I don't think 'suck it up and do it for the kids' applies here."

"The judges were chosen ages ago. I only joined because one of the original members left, remember?" I said. "And if this happened just a few days before he died, she couldn't drop out without bringing more attention to herself."

Adeena frowned. "Which gives her a motive for murder. She's built up a successful business and peaceful new life here and he was threatening that."

I swore under my breath. "Ugh, this is so messed up. What Rob did was disgusting but that doesn't mean he deserved to die."

"I know Sana is your friend," Amir said, looking at Adeena and Elena before shifting his focus back to me. "And that you and Sana were getting close, so I wanted to warn you all. I'm not saying she did it. I'm just saying maybe you shouldn't be alone with her anymore. She must know you've been looking at the case. She's a highly intelligent woman."

Thinking that the kind and vibrant woman I'd been getting to know might've been pushed to murder was bad enough, but then I remembered something else. "Valerie! She relies on Sana for everything. I think she might be her only friend. What happens if Sana is the killer? That the person she trusted the most murdered her last remaining family member?"

Amir held out his hand, likely trying to look authoritative but it was hard to take someone seriously when their hands were covered in ice candy drips. "You're getting ahead of yourself. Watch her closely during your pageant events, keep your ear to the ground, and don't hang out with her alone. That's it. You don't have to concoct all these wild theories about what might happen."

"Wild theories? I'm just thinking about the possibilities. Isn't that what you're always telling me? Look at situations from multiple angles?" I glared at my arroz con leche ice candy as if it were the ice pop's fault Amir was being condescending.

"Yes, so that you don't get hung up on one idea. I gave you information that hints at just one possibility. Do you know if Sana has an alibi for the time of Rob's death?"

I scowled. "I don't even know his time of death, so how would I know who does or doesn't have an alibi?"

"What time did you find his body?"

"Around one in the afternoon."

"Witnesses at the bar report him leaving alone a little after midnight, and the coroner's report puts his death shortly after that."

"Why do people remember the time he left so clearly?" Elena asked, wiping up the drips Amir and I were leaving behind, then handed me a kulfi ice candy to enjoy as well. I smiled my thanks at her.

"After the fight with Bernadette, people were watching him to see if anything else interesting would happen."

"And did it?" Adeena asked. She handed her brother a wet napkin to clean his hands and raised her eyebrows at the mess he'd made.

He smiled sheepishly and cleaned up after himself before nodding. "Valerie and Sana were there, too. After Bernadette left, a drunk Valerie chewed him out. Something about not wanting a repeat of last time. He laughed and she threw a drink in his face." He let out an unamused laugh. "That seemed to happen to him a lot."

"It must feel so satisfying. I've always wanted to do that." I grinned before remembering I threw a pot of hot coffee in someone's face to save my life a few months ago. The image became a lot less amusing then.

I took a few deep breaths to steady myself. "What happened after that?"

"The bartender kicked Valerie out and Sana left with her. Not sure about anything else."

I eyed him. "You sure know a lot about this case for someone who's not involved."

"Excuse me, I need to go wash my hands." He walked away and

Adeena and I followed him to the sink behind the counter. Elena stayed out of it, either because she didn't know him well enough to hound him or because she was way better at minding her own business than me and Adeena.

"Amir. What are you not telling us?" I gasped, like the melodramatic person I was. "Has Bernadette been charged? Are you officially representing her?"

"She hasn't been charged. But it seems things have progressed enough that Detective Park advised her to officially seek legal counsel." Amir dried his hands on a dish towel and looked over at me. "Look, I know the other night didn't end well, but if you care about your cousin, it doesn't matter who's right. She needs your help, whether she admits it or not."

Excuse me? It didn't matter who was right?! In what world?

As I formulated a way to tell him just how very, very wrong he was, Adeena stepped in. "Lila, I don't know what happened, but he's got a point. Don't look at me like that, Amir Bhai. You have, on occasion, been correct about things. Don't make a big deal out of it."

Amir covered up his smile and turned to pour himself a glass of water. I crossed my arms. "You can say that because you weren't there. Bernadette said that I was making the case all about me."

Adeena made a noise in her throat, her *But was she wrong though?* noise that I was very familiar with, so I said, "And they insulted my mom."

Adeena stopped making that noise and straightened up. "Oh, so Bernadette wants to fight. That's what you're telling me."

Elena finally joined in the conversation. "I don't know what's going on, but if someone's talking about your mom and we need to throw hands, I'm in. You don't mess with the ancestors."

I probably shouldn't have been so happy that my best friends were threatening my cousin with bodily harm, but just knowing they had my back filled me up with the warm fuzzies. "Aww, thanks, you two. Bernadette would absolutely destroy me in a physical fight, but good to know I have seconds if it ever comes down to a duel."

I briefly filled them in on what had happened at dinner and Elena gasped. "She is totally your Aaron Burr! Super jealous of you and blaming anything that goes wrong in her life on you."

Adeena laughed. "And Lila as Hamilton totally works, because she's also a workaholic who's full of herself, strings people along, and thinks she can only make it on her own." She grinned, nodding her head. "I'm really into this comparison. Babe, let's watch *Hamilton* again later tonight so we can continue making fun of Lila and Bernadette."

"OK, but then you have to watch *Hadestown* with me and learn 'Wait for Me' for our next karaoke night."

Adeena shook her head. "You and your musicals. Fine, but you have to bring home mushroom quesadillas and those awesome beans from El Gato Negro next time you're there. And you still owe me a mezcal cocktail for the menu, so I'm expecting a tasting soon."

"It's a date, mi amor." Elena gave her a quick kiss that managed to linger just long enough to make my heart twinge.

I didn't appreciate all their jabs, but they were so freakin' cute together. Why didn't I have someone to watch musicals with and supply me with tasty Mexican food and cocktails? I glanced over at Amir, who was watching his sister and her girlfriend with the saddest expression on his face.

Ah. Right.

I cleared my throat. "So, uh, what do you all think my next move should be? I need to talk to Bernadette, obviously. I wonder if I can get the Calendar Crew together without Lola Flor throwing them out of our house."

Amir looked at his watch. "It's almost closing time for Auntie, right? Maybe if you get them all together at the restaurant after your customers are gone, Grandma Flor would be more interested in their money than being petty."

If he thought my grandmother kicking Ninang June out of our house was pettier than the disrespect Ninang June showed our family, then he did not need to be at this dinner. Adeena met my eyes and the line connecting us, the understanding that flowed between our gazes, gave me the support I needed.

"I'll contact the aunties and Bernadette. Tita Rosie's Kitchen doesn't close for another hour, so that should be plenty of notice." I drew my shoulders back and gestured Amir toward the door. "Anyway, we have some work to do here. Thanks for the update."

Taking his cue, Amir picked up his briefcase and headed to the door. "The ice candies were great. Can't wait to try yours, Lila. Stay out of trouble, you three."

Elena wrinkled her nose, but waited till he was gone before speaking. "Lila, I know that man is fine as hell," she glanced at Adeena to say, "Sorry, babe," before turning her attention back to me, "but you can do better. Every time he opens his mouth, he sounds like the precursor to a 'Why are men' meme."

Adeena sighed. "He's always thought he was right, but he never used to be condescending. He's good at admitting he's wrong, but I do worry that he's changing for the worse."

Glad to see I wasn't the only one who'd noticed. "I wonder what's going on with him. Like you said, he could be overbearing, but he was never an out-and-out jerk. I was half expecting him to pet me on the head before he left."

"I think he's under a lot of pressure at work. He's been spending a lot more time in Chicago trying to fit in with the good ol' boys at the head of the firm." Adeena frowned. "He got passed over for a promotion and he thinks it's because he doesn't socialize with the other lawyers enough. Apparently the guy they chose over him is big on schmoozing."

Amir worked for a fairly prestigious law firm in Chicago and had arranged his schedule so that he could spend half the week working from Shady Palms, only traveling to Chicago to meet new clients and attend court. It seemed exhausting, but he didn't like being away from his family. He also didn't drink alcohol, which probably made those nights out with his fellow lawyers a little awkward.

"Is he thinking of moving to Chicago full-time?" I asked, not knowing what I'd prefer. Even though I'd only been back home a short time, I couldn't imagine him not being around all the time. He was a good friend who'd come through for me and my family time and again. But things between us had gotten so weird, and I of all people understood doing what you could to advance in your career. I'd hate for him to feel as stuck in Shady Palms as I used to.

"I think that depends on you, actually."

"Excuse me?"

She sighed. "I know I wasn't supportive of you two from the beginning, but I'm OK with it now. You being all hot and cold toward him is really confusing. For all of us. He wants to be with you and is willing to stay in Shady Palms if it means you can finally be together. So if you'd rather be with Jae, let my brother know. And soon. He's being a jerk, but you're not innocent in this, either. He doesn't deserve to be kept hanging like this. And I'm not choosing sides!" she added, putting her hands up to ward off my protests. "I love you both and you both kinda suck right now, so I'm hoping you two figure things out before it's too late."

It was amazing how many times I had to hear that very same advice before I actually took it. Nettie Bishop had said something similar to me a few months ago, back when Adeena and I were feuding. I cared about Amir. Bernadette was family. I'd managed to fix things with Jae, so I knew I could do it. Time to begin the Lila Macapagal Apology Tour.

Pushing down my anxiety about what I was going to do, I pulled out my phone. I had some calls to make.

Chapter Eighteen

"What's this all about, Lila?" Lola Flor settled into her usual place, exerting enough authority that it was obvious she sat at the head of the table, even though the table was round and that should've been impossible. Ordinarily, she and the aunties would've made a big fuss over my hair since they loved commenting on my appearance, but this was no ordinary dinner. Lola Flor surveyed the food my aunt was bringing out, a wicked smile spreading across her face as she took in Ninang June's reaction to the spread—Lola Flor had purposely chosen Ninang June's least favorite dishes for this meal.

Lola Flor may not have gotten along with my mother, but my mom was still a member of the Macapagals, and the woman could hold a grudge when you messed with her family. If avoidance was my Olympic event, pettiness was Lola Flor's. The purpose of this meal was a reconciliation, but I couldn't help but admire this pro-level shade disguised as hospitality. My grandmother and I were both Scorpios, and game couldn't help but recognize game.

I tried to arrange my expression to a more neutral one because this wasn't going to work if Ninang June and Bernadette saw how much I was enjoying this. "Our last dinner didn't end well, and I think we need to have it out so we can focus on what's important: helping Ate Bernie and keeping the pageant girls safe."

Ninang June sniffed, eyeing the platter Joy had just set in front of her. A stir-fry of shrimp and ampalaya. Next to that was a plate of tortang talong, or eggplant omelet. Bitter gourd and eggplant were her most hated foods, and to cap it all off, Tita Rosie proudly set down a plate of chicken adobo with liver. She rarely served this dish since it wasn't popular with the general public, but it was one of her absolute favorites. It was rich, tasty, and relatively healthy due to all the iron and vitamins it provided. Unfortunately, Ninang June didn't like liver either, and while Tita Rosie might not have realized what Lola Flor was doing when she requested these dishes, Ninang June definitely did.

"If this is your idea of an apology, I don't accept. It's bad enough that you insult my daughter, but now you try to serve me this? This slap in the face?" Ninang June shoved her plate away.

Tita Rosie's face crumbled. "What's wrong, June? I wanted us to all be OK again, so I took extra care when preparing the food. What did I . . ." Her voice trailed off as she took stock of the dishes and realized what her mother had done. "Nay! How could you!" My aunt turned to my godmother. "We have other food prepared in the kitchen. I'll get you something else to eat, something you like."

"Rosie, sit down. This woman insulted us in our home and now she's insulting us in our restaurant. If she wants to apologize for the disrespect she's shown to all of us, she will eat the food she's given. It's poor manners to turn down the food your host has prepared." Lola Flor turned to Bernadette. "You. Say grace."

Bernadette started, glancing guiltily at her mother before crossing herself and leading us in a brief prayer. After we all said, "Amen," we helped ourselves to the food in the middle of the table. First my grandmother, then Ninang Mae and April, then finally me and Joy. Tita Rosie always served herself last, so she looked at Ninang June and Bernadette in anxious anticipation.

Bernadette took a deep breath and helped herself to large portions of all the different foods—from what I remembered, she actually liked these dishes, so she probably didn't want to drag on a fight that her mother had started. Besides, for all her faults, she would never purposely hurt Tita Rosie and she knew that if she refused to eat, it would break Tita Rosie's heart. She scooped up a large spoonful of omelet and rice, and after she chewed and swallowed, she turned a big smile toward my aunt. "This is delicious, Tita Rosie! Thank you for this meal."

Bernadette nudged her mother, who still hadn't served herself any food. Ninang June sighed and spooned small portions of everything alongside a heaping plate of rice. She separated the pieces of liver from the chicken, brought the spoon slowly to her mouth, and chewed hesitantly. Once she swallowed, she admitted, "This tastes better than I remember. Thank you for your hospitality, Rosie. And . . . I'm sorry."

The table let out a collective sigh and we all turned to our meals, eating and chattering as usual. Once we'd all cleaned our plates (several times), Joy helped my aunt clear the table and they brought out the usual bowls of halo-halo. Desserts in front of us, it was time to get down to business.

Ninang April pulled out a small spiral notepad and flipped through the pages until she got to the one she wanted. "OK, so we've checked up on all the past contestants that are still in Shady Palms.

The only ones that seem to have a connection to the current pageant are Mary Ann Randall, Helen Kowalski,"—it took me a minute to realize that was the name of the second-in-command of the PTA Squad, mother to Sharon Randall's best friend, Leslie—"and Barbara Jennings. However, they all have alibis at that time, and, with the exception of Barbara, their daughters have all made it to the final round."

Ninang April paused to turn the page and Ninang Mae jumped in. "We tried to find out more about the contestant who was obsessed with Rob, but she seems to have left town. It's also possible she married and changed her name, but we haven't been able to track her the way we did with some of the other contestants, so it's unlikely. We also looked into some of his rumored affairs, but the only one that seemed to have any blowback recently was the Weinmans. Sources close to them say that they saw the divorce coming a mile away and Rob just gave them a reason to make it official. Mrs. Weinman is using this as an opportunity to pursue her graduate degree and is perfectly happy. Seems the Rob affair was a onetime thing. Oskar Weinman had his pride hurt, and that's about it. From what we hear, he's busy trying to get in good with that woman who owns the Honeybee Salon."

I was ready to jump in with my info at that point, but the aunties weren't done yet. "Mayor Gunderson and William Acevedo are in the clear. Both wives said that all four of them were together having dinner at the Acevedo household, and a third party can confirm that." Ninang April flipped another page. "Rob's will reading was yesterday. From what we've heard, Beth and his sister got almost nothing. The majority of his wealth went into the Thompson Family Company."

Bernadette leaned forward. "So does that mean both of them have motive? Or does it clear them? They could've killed him because they were mad he wasn't giving them any money. Or maybe he died so one of them could become the head of the company."

Ninang June shook her head. "They would've had to know the contents of the will ahead of time. The Thompson family lawyer said no one else had seen the contents before the reading."

"How do you know that?" Lola Flor asked.

Ninang June shrugged. "I know people."

Lola Flor bristled at that response, so I cut in before another argument could break out. "Were any of you able to find out if Beth really is the new head of the company, or is it being passed down to Valerie?"

"The board voted the same day as the will reading. Beth is officially the leader of the company. They didn't think Valerie had the head for business or vision for the company that Beth has."

Ouch, that had to hurt. Bad enough that her family had kept her out of the company most of her adult life, but to have the entire board agree with that decision when you were the only blood-related Thompson left? I made a note to reach out to Valerie soon. She'd displayed a level of vulnerability that I hadn't expected that day at the cafe, and I figured I should check in on her. As long as I wasn't alone with her or Sana, it would be a good opportunity for more sleuthing and bonding.

"I guess that means Beth and Valerie are in the clear. It's unlikely that either woman would've killed him over the will if they didn't know what was in it, right?" Bernadette asked.

Ninang June said, "Really? I thought the opposite. If they didn't know what was in the will, wouldn't it be natural to assume they'd get money or power? If they knew he wasn't leaving them anything, wouldn't they have just let him live? What would be the point of killing him?"

"They could've killed him for other reasons though. We need to look at the four *L*'s of motives: Love, Lust, Loathing, and Loot," Ninang Mae said.

"Where did you hear that?" I asked.

"I wanted to know the main motivations for murder, so I Googled it and that's what it said. It was really very helpful," my godmother said, as if that were a perfectly normal thing to Google. Good on her for doing her own research, I guess. Just hoped she didn't end up on some FBI watch list. Something told me "amateur sleuthing" wouldn't go over all that well if she had to explain her search history.

"I researched it, too, and found a fascinating article that said men and women kill for different reasons. Although men tend to commit the most murders for a wide variety of motives, the main two reasons were concealment and jealousy. For women, it was love or personal gain," Ninang April said, reading off a page from her notebook.

Which still fit all our remaining suspects. Mr. Weinman could've killed Rob out of jealousy. Valerie and Beth for personal gain. And we had to figure in that there were unknown suspects that we hadn't been able to connect to the case yet. So in other words . . . we were right back where we started.

The restaurant phone rang and Tita Rosie got up to answer it. The rest of us sat quietly, plowing our way through our bowls of shaved ice, which Joy silently replenished whenever we ran low. She was always quiet, but at least had shown interest in our previous conversations. Today, she seemed subdued, her actions a little stiff as if she ran on autopilot. Maybe she was just stressed over the pageant, but I made a note to talk to her later, just in case.

The tinkling of our door chimes cut through the silence, and we all turned toward the door to see Tita Rosie and Detective Park coming to join us. The set of his shoulders and grim expression on his face told me this wasn't a social visit.

"Is everything OK, Detective? Nobody . . . I mean, there hasn't been any . . ." I fumbled over my words as I tried to find out whether he was here to arrest Bernadette or if somebody else was dead.

He held up an envelope. "Nobody's in trouble. Yet. We received another letter threatening the pageant. I already checked for prints and it's no one in our system, so I figured it wouldn't hurt to see if you had any theories. No one else at the station is bothering," he added bitterly.

The aunties and I all raised our eyebrows. Detective Park had always maintained a professional attitude toward his colleagues, even when their ineptitude had caused him problems. I guess their lack of interest in this case was finally getting to him. He wasn't even supposed to be a regular employee, just a consultant, but since there were no detectives on the force, he got called in whenever a big enough case came in. After all, Sheriff Lamb had to at least pretend he cared, especially when the mayor got involved.

Detective Park handed me the envelope and everyone, except for Lola Flor, scooched closer to inspect it. It had the red and blue markings around the edges that designated it for international mail use. WARNING was written in scratchy-looking capital letters. I pulled out the letter, which had been written on a yellow legal pad and contained a single sentence.

I hadn't paid much attention to the first note he'd shown me, so I made sure to take my time looking over this one. The first thing I noted was that it was written in cursive, probably using a black fountain pen, based on the style. My eyes struggled to decipher the script so I could read the letter out loud, but Ninang April got impatient and took it from me.

Shut down the pageant before someone else gets hurt

She lowered the page. "That's it? They couldn't be more original with their threats?"

It wasn't the phrasing that stuck out to me, but the trappings. I'd seen that envelope and script before. "Oh my gulay, I know who's been sending these letters!"

I ran to my aunt's office to grab my bag and riffled through it till I found my phone (Lola Flor wasn't a fan of phones at the table, so I always left it in another room so I wouldn't be tempted). "Mr. Weinman has been writing letters to Winnie Pang to try and woo her, I guess. He dropped off an envelope when I was at her salon and the other salon customers said he does it all the time. There were a few lying open in the waiting area and Adeena got a picture of them."

I went to the Brew-ha group chat and pulled up the photo to show the detective. The aunties crowded around him to look at the screen—you didn't have to be a handwriting analyst to see the notes were written by the same person.

"Send me that picture, Lila. I think it's time I had a talk with Oskar Weinman. Thanks for the tip. This is some good work." Detective Park handed me back my phone and nodded at me. He didn't smile or say anything else, but that was high praise coming from him and I reveled in the validation. Nice to see that I was good at something. I mean OK, it was Adeena's quick thinking that got the photos, but I was the one that put it all together. That had to count for something.

"Does that mean I'm off the hook?" Bernadette asked. She'd been hanging back at the table with Joy, her posture curled in small as if she didn't want anyone to notice her. The exact opposite of how she usually carried herself. Any other day, she'd be crowded around with the aunties giving her own opinion on the situation, but she must've been too uncomfortable to approach the detective since he still considered her a suspect.

Detective Park must've noticed as well because he tempered his voice before addressing her. "Mr. Weinman is a person of interest and it's too early for me to say anything definite. However, I'm hoping this is the breakthrough we need to clear you of suspicion and bring closure to this case."

That was the closest he'd get to admitting he didn't consider her a real suspect, so it would have to do. And if Mr. Weinman really did it, that meant it was safe to hang out at Sana's again. A way to try to fix my and Bernadette's relationship came to me. "Hey, do you want to join me and the girls for one of Sana's classes? I'm thinking of taking up yoga."

Bernadette's eyes gleamed. "I love Sana's studio! I've been going there all the time now that they cut my hours at the hospital. But we're not doing yoga. You have to join me for one of her Zumba classes. They're the best!"

I groaned inwardly. Bernadette was the dancer in our group. I was a good singer, but somehow suffered in the rhythm department. Bernadette, meanwhile, had been in several dance crews in high school and college and had an entire wall full of trophies to show how good she was. She probably could've gone pro if her mother had let her. In fact, there's a better than average chance that she would've won the crown the year we competed together, but she'd injured herself while practicing her dance routine for the talent portion. She still performed, but it was obvious she couldn't put 100 percent into it. I wondered how differently things would've gone for us if we'd both been able to compete at top form.

Before I could go down the rabbit hole of what-ifs, my aunt nudged me and I realized I hadn't given Bernadette an answer. "Oh! Sure, Ate Bernie. But no making fun of my dance moves! And you have to come do karaoke with me sometime as well."

I make a fool of myself on the dance floor for her, she embarrasses herself at the mic for me. Equivalent exchange. We shook hands on it, signaling the end of the dinner party. Everyone packed up leftovers to take home—even Ninang June, proving the power of Tita Rosie's cooking—and left as a group, chattering happily now that the fear of Bernadette getting arrested was gone. Now that we knew who sent those threatening letters, it was only a matter of time till he confessed to killing Rob. I helped my family clean up and we went home filled with the pleasure of a job well done.

I snuggled up to Longganisa and had the most peaceful night's sleep that I'd had in months.

Chapter Nineteen

Who knew exercise could be fun? I went jogging all the time, but that's because the slow, rhythmic pace helped me think and was good for Longganisa's health. But here I was dancing and sweating up a storm—in public!—and I didn't mind at all. In fact, it was the perfect way to shake off the bad vibes from that day's pageant event.

It had been quick and uneventful—well, if you ignored all the sniping between Valerie and Beth. Those two were in terrible moods and didn't bother hiding it. I could understand Valerie acting out. The one-two punch of losing her brother and her family's company/money would have anyone screaming because someone talked to them before they'd had their first cup of coffee (the poor contestant had just asked her to pass the sugar). Beth's behavior was surprising though. Not only was she usually the picture of poise, but she still had power over the Thompson Family Company, if not direct access to the fortune. Yet not only did she ignore me when I offered her a muffin and snub a momtestant who asked her a question, she purposely knocked over a full coffee cup onto a stack of Valerie's papers when Valerie interjected her opinion for the fifth time.

After a brief meeting to go over the scores for the girls' essays, we'd handed the essays back to the contestants, told them their scores, and Beth dismissed everyone with little fanfare. She had her sunglasses on and was halfway out the door with her keys in hand before most of the girls even finished reading the comments we'd left them.

After that unceremonious dismissal, Sana had suggested a group Zumba class for everyone gathered so the day wouldn't feel like a total waste. I'd tried to back out, saying I hadn't packed any workout gear (which was true), but Bernadette had just grinned at me.

"Don't worry, Lila, I'm sure Sana's cool with giving everyone time to change since we don't want anyone injuring themselves. Sana, should we meet you at your studio?"

Sana nodded. "Absolutely. Make sure to wear shoes with good support because there are some high-impact moves in Zumba. Try not to wear running shoes though. They have too much grip and you need something with a little slip to perform some of the moves. See you all in half an hour!"

"Great job, everyone! We're done for the day, so make sure to hydrate. If you liked the class, I teach Zumba every Monday, Wednesday, and Friday afternoon, with advanced classes on the weekend."

Sana stood at the head of the class, hands on her hips, a faint sheen of sweat giving her a nice healthy glow. I knew I didn't look nearly so blissful as I gulped down water from my reusable bottle, muscles I didn't remember even having throbbing and letting me know I'd feel it tomorrow, but I'd be lying if I said I hadn't enjoyed it all. Great way to take my mind off everything that'd been going on.

Bernadette was still on the floor, stretching out her bad ankle, but otherwise looking as radiant as Sana. Feeling my eyes on her, she quickly got up and grabbed her own water bottle. "So?"

"OK, I guess maybe this is something I could fit into my busy schedule." Bernadette rolled her eyes at that, so I added, "Now that I held up my end of the bargain, when are we having our karaoke party?"

"Karaoke? That sounds like fun! I didn't know they had karaoke places in Shady Palms," Katie said as she walked up with her mom and Joy.

"There aren't. My aunt's restaurant will have karaoke nights and sometimes we have karaoke parties at people's houses. It's usually a low-key kind of thing, but lots of fun." And usually lots of alcohol, but she didn't need to know that. "Sometimes people will bring their instruments and it's almost like an open mic night."

That was a new development, and had started when Jae asked if he could bring his guitar. He wasn't much of a singer, but was happy to accompany anyone on the guitar as long as he knew the song.

"I still haven't been to one of Tita Rosie's karaoke parties. We should have one soon! How did it get started?" Joy asked.

"Lila's mom started it as a way to get more business for the restaurant. It worked really well since she was a great singer and loved showing off, two traits she passed on to her daughter." Bernadette winked at me, to show she was joking probably. I still didn't appreciate it.

"Anyway—"

I turned and walked away from her while she was still midsentence and went to join Sana and several members of the PTA Squad. That's right, I was so annoyed that I willingly went to join a group of the worst momtestants. I instantly regretted it when one of them spotted me walking up and said, "Lila! Just who I was looking for. I was about to show Sana something, and I think you'd be interested in it, too."

I couldn't help noticing the nasty grin on her face and wondered what it could be. If I wasn't mistaken, her daughter had already been eliminated from the competition, so whatever was putting that smile on her face couldn't have been good.

When I saw the *Shady Palms News* article she'd pulled up on her phone, I knew I was right. The headline read:

PAGEANT JUDGE'S DARK PAST REVEALED!

The article detailed everything Amir had told me about Sana's history, with added bits of editorializing and speculation thrown in. Wilson Philipps (because of course it was him) ended the story with the rumor that Sana was one of Rob's spurned lovers and she'd killed him when he refused to leave his wife.

The moms all stared at Sana (who stood frozen, eyes still fixed on the woman's phone) in horror before hurrying off to their daughters. "I knew something wasn't right about you!" Mary Ann Randall said as she shoved her daughter toward the door. "I'm going to talk to the mayor right now! You have no business being on the judges' panel." She'd been yelling this over her shoulder while still hustling toward the exit and bumped right into Detective Park. "Oh good, you're here. You must be here to arrest Sana, right? Because she killed Rob Thompson?"

That snapped Sana out of her stupor—she put her hands on her hips and glared at Mary Ann. "How dare you! I did no such thing."

"I . . . what?" It took a lot to throw Detective Park off his game, but he clearly wasn't expecting that. "Those are serious accusations. What makes you think I'm here to arrest her?"

In response, all the moms held up their phones, the Philipps article on their screens.

"Ah. I see. Ms. Williams, I suggest talking to your lawyer about libel, but I have nothing else to say about the unprofessional speculation at the end of the article." He looked around the room. "I actually need to talk to Ms. Williams, Ms. Macapagal, and Ms. Arroyo in private, so if you'll excuse us . . ." He gestured for everyone else to leave.

"Wait, what about Joy? I'm her ride," Bernadette said.

"Don't worry, she can come hang out at our house for a bit and then we'll take her home. Is that OK, Joy? I'm sure Katie will appreciate the company since I need to get back to work," Winnie said. Joy agreed, and the trio left together.

When it was just the four of us and Sana had locked the door to ensure privacy, Detective Park got down to the reason for his visit. "Lila and Bernadette, can you wait for me in that room over there?" He pointed toward the changing room. "I need to speak to Ms. Williams first, but there's something I need to talk to you about."

Bernadette and I obeyed. The changing room was too far away from where he and Sana were talking to eavesdrop, so Bernadette and I had to speculate on what was happening.

"Do you think he's here about the newspaper article?" I asked, chewing on a nail. I thought I'd kicked this habit but guess not. I should visit Winnie's salon again. If I kept my nails pretty, maybe I'd be less inclined to gnaw on them.

"Has to be. Why else would he want to talk to her? I wonder what he wants from us." Bernadette cracked open the changing room door and peeked out a bit. "You don't think . . . It couldn't be her, right? I really don't want it to be her."

"It can't be her. Mr. Weinman's the one sending those notes."

"She could still be Rob's killer though. I mean, obviously I hope not, but you never know." Bernadette pulled out her phone to look over the newspaper article. "I wonder who leaked the info?"

I pulled out my own phone to reread the article, maybe get an idea of who could've given the *Shady Palms News* the story. "Who else knew about this? Amir would never do anything like this and neither would Adeena and Elena."

"Wait, you knew?" Bernadette looked up at me, eyes wide.

"Amir told me and the girls the night before that dinner at Tita Rosie's Kitchen. He thought it might have bearing on the case, but he didn't want word to spread since, you know, sensitive nature and all."

Bernadette looked hurt I hadn't told her, but just asked, "Well, do you think anyone else knew about it?"

"Rob did. We think he was blackmailing Sana, which Amir considered a motive."

"So then—"

"Oh my gulay, do you think it was Beth who leaked the story? If Rob knew about Sana's past, it's possible that Beth did, too."

"True . . . but I'm pretty sure you're just saying that because you're jealous about her and Jae."

"Shut up! Not every choice I make has to be about my love life!" And whether or not I was jealous, which I wasn't, it all made a sick kind of sense if this was her way of lashing out about everything that had been going on. Jae already said Beth saw Sana as competition. Couple that with the fact she wasn't getting any money from Rob's estate, the antagonism between her and Valerie aggravating the situation, and, you know, her husband's murder, and she was bound to implode. "Anyway, it makes more sense that Beth did it than—"

Detective Park suddenly opened the door, causing me to shriek and Bernadette to stumble over since she was still peering through the crack. He sighed.

"I'm going to let it go this one time, but I don't want to catch you trying to eavesdrop on another one of my conversations. Are we clear?"

We both nodded, and the look on Bernadette's face told me she was thinking the same thing as me: We were in the clear as long as he didn't actually catch us in the act.

"Moving on, the reason I asked you to stay is because of these." He pulled on a pair of gloves before showing us a clear evidence bag holding two envelopes. He handed them to us and said, "I came here to talk to Sana and saw these two envelopes on your car windshields out in front. Considering what's been going on, I wanted you two to open them in front of me."

Bernadette and I looked at each other, then opened the envelopes at the same time, pulling out the paper to compare. Same envelope, same handwriting, same message.

Mind your business. Curiosity killed the cat, remember?

Mr. Weinman must've found out we'd tipped off the police about him. But why include Bernadette in this? I looked over at her and asked as much. She gave me one of her *Are you for real?* looks, the one that let me know I had just asked something completely thoughtless.

"Did you honestly think you were the only one investigating? The only one asking questions? Just because I asked for your help didn't mean I was sitting at home watching K-dramas while waiting for you to get results. Someone must've let it slip I was asking about him."

Detective Park glared at us. "I thought I told you to stay out of this. Do you not remember how dangerous it was last time?" He held out his gloved hand for the notes and we handed them back. "These were definitely sent by the same person as the other notes. I'm just waiting on results from the fingerprints. One of the other officers is handling that and is supposed to let me know once they're in. I can't bring in Oskar Weinman until we have that final bit of evidence, unfortunately, but with this new evidence against him, I can push to expedite the process."

"So that's it? We just sit around and wait and hope he doesn't come after us until those results come in?" I asked.

"I have officers watching both your houses, as well as the cafe and restaurant during working hours. As long as you both stay vigilant and stick together, I'm sure we'll get our man." At our skeptical looks he added, "I'm sorry, but until all the proper paperwork is in order, we can't make a move. We can't afford to make any mistakes on such a high-profile case. But I promise you, I'm doing all I can to keep you two safe. Now are you ready to head out? I'll escort you home."

As Bernadette and I grabbed our bags, Detective Park said, "By the way, Lila, Dr. Kang says you still haven't called her. I think talking to her will help you with this waiting period, so you don't fret too much. I—where are you going?"

"I just remembered I needed to talk to Sana about something. You two go on. I can have her drop me at home."

Before he could stop me, I hurried out of the studio and up the stairs to Sana's apartment. I pounded on the door, glancing behind me to make sure he wasn't following me, and slipped inside once she opened the door.

"Lila? Can I help you?" Sana stood at the open door and glanced down to see the detective staring up at us and Bernadette on the landing. "Oh, hi, Detective. Don't worry, I'll make sure they get home OK," she called down the stairs before moving aside to let Bernadette in and shutting the door.

"Thank you so, so much. Sorry for just bursting in on you like this, but I couldn't deal with being around him anymore," I said. "Ate Bernie, you should probably get going. I bet your mom's worried about you."

Bernadette snorted. "And Tita Rosie and Lola Flor won't be? We can call our families later. What's going on with you?"

"Yeah, Lila, are you OK? Is he . . . Are you . . ." Sana hesitated, not sure which delicate question to ask first.

"No, it's nothing like that. I'm just annoyed with him right now. He won't shut up about this therapist he wants me to talk to. But I'm fine."

Bernadette said, "You are *not* fine," at the same time that Sana said, "Are you sure? I know that we only met recently, but even I can tell that some of your behavior has been a little . . . erratic lately."

I scoffed. "Erratic how?"

Bernadette raised an eyebrow. "Lila, you had a panic attack and punched that reporter when he grabbed your arm."

"Yeah, well, he shouldn't have touched me without my consent."

Sana nodded. "True, but I'm guessing that there's more to it than that?"

I focused on taking off my shoes so I didn't have to look at her. "What did Detective Park want to talk to you about?"

"If you want me to open up, I expect you to do the same."

I crossed my arms. "I'm fine. It's just that sometimes little things happen that remind me of what happened a few months ago."

Her face took on a sympathetic look and she gestured to her couch. After I sat down and Bernadette settled herself on the floor, Sana poured us each a glass of cold-pressed juice and joined me on the couch. "I'm guessing you mean your ex-boyfriend's murder?"

I flinched. "Yeah. Detective Park kept it out of the papers, but I almost died. Adeena, too. How do I just move on from that? How do

I just pretend that everything's the same as before? The killer held Adeena hostage and she's still kicking butt and taking names. Why am I the only one who can't move on?"

Months and months of frustration and guilt and shame just poured out of me, a catharsis I hadn't realized I'd needed. Sana and Bernadette just sat there and listened, not butting in, not offering their opinion, and from what I could tell, not judging me. Was this what it was like to talk to a therapist?

As if reading my mind, Sana said, "Why haven't you seen a therapist about this? It seems like Detective Park has done a lot of research to find someone willing to help you. Is it the cost? I know it's not cheap."

I shook my head. "You wouldn't understand. Asians do *not* go to therapy. We don't even acknowledge that mental health issues exist. It's considered a sign of weakness, that we couldn't work things out for ourselves. And a sign of shame, that we even needed help in the first place. Tita Rosie is the kindest, most loving person I've ever met and even she believes in not airing your dirty laundry for other people to see. She's very much an 'It's in God's hands' type person. Bahala na, you know? And my grandmother?" I laughed. "She'll just tell me I'm lazy like my mother. To keep my mouth shut and get to work."

Sana frowned. "Why do you act like this is specifically a race thing? As if this society doesn't push this mental health stigma on everyone? You think Black families love having relatives who are in therapy? That hasn't stopped me."

"You're in therapy?" I blurted out, then clapped my hand over my mouth like a kid. "That was so rude and invasive, I'm sorry. You don't owe me an explanation."

"To be fair, I asked you first. I'm not ashamed of it. Therapy was the best decision I've ever made, and it sounds like you could benefit from it as well." She took a deep breath and eyed me and Bernadette warily. "You know about my past."

It wasn't a question.

"It, uh, might have come up at one point, even before that article."

"And you also know that Rob was trying to blackmail me into sleeping with him. So that nobody else would find out."

"Punyeta!" Juice sloshed out of Bernadette's glass as that curse burst out of her. If Rob Thompson wasn't already dead, I would've been worried about what'd happen to him if Bernadette got her hands on him.

I knew he was shady AF but had no idea he'd stoop that low. I wasn't happy he was dead, but let's just say my lack of sympathy over his death was growing by the minute. "I didn't realize that's what he wanted in return from you. How did he even know about it?"

She grimaced. "I told him. I thought he was my friend. Like I mentioned with Valerie, I work hard to keep my coach-client relationships professional. It's extremely difficult to separate the lines between coach, therapist, and friend, and I wanted to have clear boundaries from the beginning. But that meant cutting out a lot of possible friendships. I didn't know anyone when I first moved here and didn't have to worry about that separation with Rob. When he wasn't busy being led around by what was in his pants, he was a funny, charming, and intelligent person."

I swirled the juice in my glass. "Did you have feelings for him?"

"Not romantic ones. Rob and Beth's relationship wasn't healthy, but not because it was an open relationship. True polyamory involves openness and communication. It's not meant to be manipulative. I've been through enough that I wasn't about to let myself become a pawn in a rich man's game. He entertained me, but he didn't manage to charm me. Thank God," she added under her breath.

I must've looked like one of those shoving-popcorn-in-mouth

GIFs as I leaned forward, eager to learn more about this sordid tale. "So, what happened when he blackmailed you?"

Sana laughed. "What do you think happened? Friendship over. On my side, from the betrayal. On his part because the Thompsons are used to getting what they want. I mean, he still played the flirt when he was in public. Whether to save face or because he thought I'd change my mind, I don't know. But he was mad that his threats held no weight. My past isn't a secret so he couldn't use it against me."

"It's not? No offense, but I got arrested for something I didn't even do back in Chicago and I still tried to hide it from everyone. With the way those women acted at the studio, I wouldn't blame you for wanting to keep it a secret. Your past is . . ."

She straightened her back. "A horrible experience that I don't expect forgiveness for. But it'd be shameful if I tried to pretend that it never happened. That man had people who loved him, I can't just pretend he never existed. I've learned from it and strive to do better every day, but it's something I'll be atoning for my whole life. It's what led me to my current profession."

"Coaching and fitness?" I could understand her going into counseling or nonprofit work but didn't really see the connection here.

"It's important to take care of the body and the mind. To nurture and build self-confidence. Which is something I learned through intense therapy and, oddly, the weekly volunteer-led yoga sessions in prison." She stared into her cup, as if trying to divine her life's meaning the way Elena read tea leaves. "A man lost his life because of me. Unintentionally, but he's gone all the same. That knowledge almost broke me, but to hide it would dishonor his memory and all the work I've done to make things better. I would never have let myself be blackmailed over this. And I would *never* want blood on my hands again. I don't miss Rob, but I didn't kill him."

"I know."

I hadn't meant to say it, but once I did, I knew it was true. Maybe it was Elena's influence since she talked about intuition all the time, but I felt the truth in Sana's words.

"To get back to my point, I have an idea of what you're going through. I had massive panic attacks when I first got to jail. Not because of where I was but because of the knowledge of what I'd done. They finally had to send me to the prison counselor, who was not great but did a good enough job to convince me I needed help. My lawyer was able to find me a great therapist who I still see to this day." Sana put her hand on my arm. "It doesn't go away completely, Lila. This is just something we both have to live with. But it helps. You don't need your family's approval to seek help, you know. In fact, I'd say they lie at the root of your more harmful coping mechanisms."

"What do you mean?"

She hesitated. "You said your grandmother considers you lazy like your mother. And I've seen the way you react when Bernadette brings her up."

I avoided her eyes but shot a glance at Bernadette, who'd been silently listening this whole time. "She knows she's not supposed to talk about her."

"Why? She was saying nice things. They sounded like lovely memories, in fact. I'm surprised you have such a strong aversion to them."

I twisted my necklace around my finger. "She's been gone a long time. I don't really like thinking about it. It's just easier to move on."

Bernadette finally spoke up. "But you haven't moved on. You're just avoiding thinking about her in the hopes that it'll all go away. Just like you're doing with your memories of what happened a few months ago. When will you learn that hiding from your problems doesn't magically make things better?"

Sana refilled my glass. "She's right. After your parents passed, how did you cope? Did your aunt and grandmother help you grieve? Maybe take you to talk to your priest friend?"

I shook my head. "I wanted to talk about them, but it made my aunt sad and grandmother angry. So I knew that topic was off-limits. As for coping . . . I don't know. We worked, I guess. That was when I started helping out at the restaurant."

"So your family taught you to not talk about your problems and throw yourself into your work to avoid dealing with them? Does that sound healthy to you?"

I shrugged. "It's what we do."

"But it doesn't have to be what *you* do. You can choose to seek help if you want it, you know. It's not up to them."

"She's right, you know. Besides, I don't think you give Tita Rosie and Lola Flor enough credit. Have you even broached the topic with them, or did you decide they were against it all on your own? I bet anything you built this all up in your head. And if they're not cool with it?" Bernadette shrugged. "You're grown. It's none of their business anyway."

And there it was. Despite fighting against my family's expectations most of my life, I still craved their approval. Even Lola Flor, who I pretended to brush off but whose voice was always the loudest in my head, held more sway over my decisions than I did sometimes. Most of the big choices in my life had me working either for or against their wishes—rarely did I center myself in my decision-making. Even my more selfish decisions were more about rebellion than anything else. So why was I fighting the idea of therapy so hard? Why not accept the help so many people were trying to give me?

"Thanks, you two. You've given me a lot to think about. And I'm sorry for being suspicious of you, Sana."

Sana shook her head. "It's understandable, considering the circumstances. Don't be so quick to dismiss someone because you like them or think they're not capable of it. My time in prison taught me a lot of things, including this: Everyone is capable of murder."

The mood was way too serious, so I tried to lighten it with a joke. "Even me?"

She looked me in the eye. "Considering all the love and loyalty you seem to have for your family and friends? Absolutely."

Chapter Twenty

The usual crew gathered at Tita Rosie's Kitchen for our morning meeting: me, my aunt and grandmother, my godmothers, Bernadette, and Joy. My aunt had also convinced Adeena and Elena to come join ("We never see you anymore! You're getting so thin, please eat with us!") and we all built up our silog platters, this time with the addition of fried tofu and bangus for my vegetarian/pescatarian friends. I had to admit, it was nice to see them chattering with everyone and stuffing their faces with my aunt's excellent cooking again. I hadn't realized how lonely I'd been feeling lately considering that I was the one who kept pushing them away.

After filling everyone in on what happened yesterday, Bernadette passed her phone around the table so everyone could see the picture of the notes she'd snapped the day before.

"Oh yeah, that's definitely Mr. Weinman's handwriting. I haven't seen the first pageant letters, but I saw the ones he sent to Winnie and it's a match. I'd recognize that old-fashioned handwriting anywhere," Adeena said once the phone reached her.

"And the detective said they can't do anything until they get the fingerprint results back?" Ninang June asked her daughter. Bernadette nodded and Ninang June scowled. "What a waste of time. I understand the need to do things properly, but with a town this small, how long could it possibly take to run those prints?"

As if in answer to her question, the door chimed and Detective Park walked in. He didn't waste time with pleasantries.

"The results came in this morning. Oskar Weinman admitted that he sent those notes, both the pageant ones as well as the ones on your car the other day. Said he didn't appreciate you poking into his personal business during such a sensitive time," here he gestured to me and Bernadette, "and he was humiliated after he got kicked off the judging panel even though it was Rob Thompson who did him wrong. He'd hoped the threats would be enough to derail the pageant, but seems like Shady Palms's parents weren't going to be put off by something as small as threatening letters." Detective Park did a good job of keeping the censure out of his voice, but I knew it was there all the same. He continued, "Anyway, it's good that you figured it out when you did. We searched his home and found that he was planning to escalate. Stage schematics and scribbled notes lead us to believe he planned on sabotaging the final event, possibly causing harm to all the people onstage. Good work."

I shook my head. "I can't believe Mr. Weinman would go that far just because he couldn't be a judge in this ridiculous contest. What was he hoping to gain from all this?"

Ninang April said, "Even though it wasn't publicly announced, most of the town knows Rob slept with his wife and got him kicked off the panel. On top of that, his business is struggling and that position would've come with free advertisement and other perks. He probably wanted to ruin something he knew Rob cared about."

What a sad thought. "You said he confessed to the notes, but what about Rob's murder?"

Detective Park frowned. "No, he says he had nothing to do with it. Claimed he was on a date with Winnie Pang when the murder happened."

"Really? Did she, what's the word . . . validate? No, corroborate? Whatever, did she back up his claims?" She'd given me the impression that she'd wanted nothing to do with him, but maybe she was seeing him on the low and was too embarrassed to say something. He was quite a bit older than her after all, and she'd made such a big deal about not relying on a man. Maybe she didn't want to look like a hypocrite.

Detective Park nodded. "She said he was telling the truth, but asked me not to spread that information around. So again, this is confidential and I better not hear this making the rounds. Is that clear?"

He directed his stare at the aunties, who rolled their eyes but agreed. "It's fine. Oskar Weinman admitting to the notes and attacks on the judges is more than enough to keep us busy. For now," Ninang Mae added.

"So what does this mean? Are you still looking for Rob's killer?" I asked, trying not to glance toward Bernadette.

"The sheriff seems to think that Mr. Weinman did it. He admitted to the threats because we had evidence against him, but thinks he can fight us in court over the murder."

"That's not really an answer, Detective."

He sighed. "As far as the mayor and SPPD are concerned, we've got our man and it's only a matter of time until he confesses. He's out on bail now, but he'll have his day in court. Case officially closed."

"That's great!" Bernadette said. "Now I can go back to work without dealing with my patients thinking I'm a killer. And once he's behind bars, we'll all be safe."

Detective Park didn't seem to agree, but he smiled and said, "I'm glad you don't have to worry about it anymore. This must have been very stressful for you."

Before she could respond, his phone rang. He excused himself and moved away from our group, but we could still hear his conversation. "Who found him? I see. And there's a note? Well. That just wraps everything up in a neat little package, doesn't it? No, I won't watch my tone. Seems my job is done here. Goodbye, Sheriff."

We all looked at one another. I wasn't sure about the others, but I was too afraid to ask what that conversation meant. It was Tita Rosie who finally spoke up. "Jonathan? Is that . . . Did something happen?"

He studied the group for a moment, his hesitation signaling that bad news was coming. But I still wasn't prepared for what he was about to tell us.

"Oskar Weinman is dead. Suicide, apparently. His wife had stopped by the house to pick up the divorce papers and found the body. There's a note, too. Confessing to Rob Thompson's death."

He flinched, as if anticipating a barrage of questions or hysteria, but he'd managed to shock us all to silence. What a feat.

"I can't believe it," Bernadette said. "So it's over?"

Detective Park shrugged. "Like I said, guess everything's wrapped up nice and neat now."

"You don't believe this was a suicide?" I asked.

"Hard to say without inspecting the crime scene. But I'm off the case now." He tried to smile. "And so life in Shady Palms moves on. Now we can all focus on what's really important, like the Founder's Day Festival. If you'll excuse me, ladies."

He left without looking back, even after Tita Rosie called after him.

"Is it bad that I'm kind of relieved things wrapped up so nice and neat?" Bernadette asked, voicing what I was thinking. "I mean, I really wish that things had turned out differently. But now I can finally feel safe and not have to check my car for a killer hiding in the backseat."

Ninang June moved to comfort her daughter. "He's just acting like that because he wasn't the one to solve the case. And I'm sure he's upset about the loss of another life. You shouldn't feel guilty about our community being safe again. Closing this case is good for all of us."

The other aunties all nodded their heads, and even Lola Flor agreed. "You girls are all safe. That's what matters right now. Anything that happens after this is not our business. Best to get back to work."

And that was that. We still had Rob's memorial to get through the next day, not to mention dress rehearsals later in the week, but still, we were in the home stretch. Thank goodness the Founder's Day Festival was less than a week away. I couldn't wait to put this all behind us.

Chapter Twenty-one

"I have to give it to Beth, she really knows how to put together a memorial service," Ninang June said, looking around the large viewing room at the Johannsen Funeral Home. Noticing my and my aunt's looks, she said, "What? You never know what to expect with rich people. I thought it'd be flashy and full of important people giving boring speeches, but everything is tasteful, and with the right touch of solemn. She used local restaurants to cater instead of some fancy big-city chef, had Lila's cafe provide the drinks, insisted on people donating to the Shady Palms Agricultural Grant Foundation instead of giving flowers, and even managed to keep Mayor Gunderson's speech under five minutes. Very impressive."

She actually reached out to rub the tablecloth and nodded her approval at the quality of the linen. I shook my head as she also tapped on the cups to see if they were real glass, but had to admit she had a point. The Thompsons were known for being ostentatious, and Beth had kept Rob's importance on display with the photo wall of his various achievements, a thick, leather-bound program that detailed his life and legacy, and a speech from the mayor. But she'd been respectful to the town's more middle-class sensibilities by keeping the decorations high quality yet understated and hiring local people to handle everything. She even kept our pompous, long-winded mayor in check, which was reason enough to raise a glass in her direction.

Beth had been talking to Mr. Acevedo, but that gesture caught her eye and she extricated herself from the conversation to come join us. Jae had been by her side for much of the day—not enough to be scandalous but doting enough to draw attention. It didn't help that they were both quite striking and easily drew your eye—Beth had her beauty and confidence, Jae the handsomeness and warmth he wore so effortlessly. They really would make a beautiful couple and I tried to ignore what seeing them together did to my heart.

"Hello, everyone, how's it going?" Beth paused and let out a tinkling little laugh. "I almost asked if you were having a good time. This feels like a Thompson family cocktail party, with all the required social niceties." She smoothed the skirt of her black, tailored crepe sheath dress before fixing the smile back on her face.

Tita Rosie smiled in support. "How are you doing, Beth? I hope you're enjoying the food we sent you. Let me know if you have any questions about the food or need refills on anything."

"When did you have time to drop off food?" I wasn't surprised she'd prepared food for Beth since that was to be expected—even someone like Beth, who could afford to have a private chef cook all her meals, deserved the comfort of a lovingly prepared meal. She might not look like she was grieving, but she was also the type to not let anyone know if she was. And from the little I knew about her, she sure wasn't the type of person to let people know that she needed help. If something was going to get done, she'd take care of it herself. At least we had that much in common.

"Jae stopped in to eat before going to visit her yesterday, so I sent along a big tray of food with him. I'd already planned on it, but he made it easier for me, telling me her food preferences and delivering it for me. Such a thoughtful boy," Tita Rosie said, gazing at him fondly. In the short time she'd gotten to know him, she'd grown pretty attached. Maybe because he did all the things for her that her jerk son Ronnie never bothered with. Ronnie was my older cousin and he'd run off years ago, just like his good-for-nothing dad. Both men had stayed around just long enough to break Tita Rosie's heart. Having Jae and Detective Park around had done wonders for her. Jae was sweet and the detective was kind—neither of them suffered from the banality of Midwestern "niceness." We were lucky to have the Park men in our lives.

As I thought that, Beth put her hand on Jae's shoulder and murmured something in his ear, making him laugh. I fought down all the dark, jealous thoughts swirling in my head, trying to temper them with kinder, less judgmental ones. *Everyone grieves in different ways, Lila. This doesn't mean anything. You know they're friends, and you know Jae looks out for his friends. You've been over this already. You don't get to judge their relationship. You could never know someone's private grief.* I had just succeeded in reminding myself of that when Jae took Beth's hand and squeezed, looking down at her with the sweetest concern.

"Excuse me, I need something to drink," I said as I attempted to flee from the group. Unfortunately, Amir and the aunties appeared at that moment and boxed me in.

Amir had two glasses in his hand. "I've got seltzer water with lime and sparkling grape juice. Which would you prefer?"

I accepted the seltzer, happy to see him but disappointed I'd lost my chance to escape. "I thought you wouldn't be able to make it. Weren't you working on a case?"

He took a sip of his drink. "We were able to wrap it up quickly since the client didn't need us anymore."

"Oh, that's good," Ninang Mae said. "Was it anyone we knew?"

I brought my hand to my face and massaged my temples. "Ninang Mae, you can't ask him stuff like that. Even if that person is no longer his client, that doesn't mean Amir can just gossip about them."

Ninang April waved her hand. "Mae has no tact. Besides, his client was obviously Oskar Weinman. Isn't that right, Amir?"

I had barely recovered from the fact that Ninang April had the nerve to call Ninang Mae tactless, with a straight face and everything, when Amir choked on his drink.

"Excuse me, this juice is much sweeter than I thought. I'm going to get some water. Does anyone need anything?" Amir looked around the group as if he were taking orders but refused to meet anyone's eyes. Interesting. "Oh, Joy! And, um, Joy's friend. I'm about to get drinks. Do you want anything?"

Joy and Katie had just joined our group. They both blushed and asked for fizzy water, which he hurried to retrieve. Watching him scurry away, I asked the girls, "I didn't think you'd come. How'd you get here?"

"The mayor and Ms. Thompson told all of us in the pageant that we needed to be here to pay our respects. I asked my sister to drop us off on her way to work. Ate Bernie is back on schedule at the hospital and Katie's mom couldn't take us." Joy bit her lip, as she turned to face Beth. "I didn't like Mr. Thompson. At all. But I am sorry for your loss. We both are," Joy added, gesturing at Katie, who looked surprisingly solemn. Her usually lively eyes were dull and ringed with dark circles, and her freckles stood out in sharp relief to her unnaturally pale skin.

"You OK, Katie?" I asked, worried that all that'd been going on was making her sick.

She nodded. "Yeah. I just . . . I've never been to a funeral. Or memorial. Or whatever this is."

"That's understandable. I'm sorry your mom couldn't be with you for this. Is she at work?" I asked. Winnie worked way too much, and I wished she had taken off an hour or so to be here with her daughter. Katie really seemed to be struggling now that she was here.

"I bet she's too busy working and mourning Oskar Weinman," Mary Ann Randall said as she joined our group.

Katie blanched and tears sprang to her eyes as she held back a sob. Before I could tell off Mary Ann, she continued sticking her foot in her mouth by turning to Beth and saying, "You must be relieved that the case is over now."

The statement itself was fine, but she must've also heard something amiss in Mary Ann's tone because Beth narrowed her eyes at the momtestant. "I must be? Why?"

"Well, because your husband's killer was caught. Why else? It's just so convenient, though, don't you think? Because it means now you can move on." Mary Ann raised her eyebrows. "Unless you don't think Oskar was the killer. That would really be something, wouldn't it? Though it seems you've found someone to protect you should that be true. Good of you, managing to move on despite the *very* recent tragedy."

Beth had just looped her arm through Jae's when Mary Ann made that comment. Jae stiffened and tried to move away, but Beth had an iron grip on him. "While I don't like your tone or the implication, of course I'm happy Rob's killer has been brought to justice, and I don't appreciate you trying to spread rumors or fear. I may not have lost a husband in the romantic sense you all seem to go on about, but I did lose my life partner. Because that's what he was to me."

As much as I loved seeing Mary Ann get put in her place, I knew this was directed at me as well. It's like she could hear the inner monologue that constantly ran through my mind when I saw her and Jae together. I shouldn't have been judging anyone's sorrow and yet I'd been doing that since I met Beth. Being petty was one thing, poking at someone's pain was another. Before I could say anything (though honestly, what could I say that wasn't me trying to make myself feel better?), Sana and Valerie came to join us.

"So this is where the party is," Valerie said, taking in the large group of us and either not noticing or hoping to alleviate the tension. "Beth, I just wanted to say you did a fabulous job. Company issues aside, you've done right by my brother and I want to thank you for that."

For possibly the first and only time in her life, Beth was speechless. It might've been because she'd been drinking from a flute of champagne when Valerie complimented her, and she was now too busy coughing up the most expensive champagne Shady Palms Beer & Liquor carried. We all looked away and gave her a moment, knowing she wouldn't want us seeing her do something as undignified as choke on a drink, though Mary Ann did let out a snide laugh.

Jae discreetly handed her a napkin, which she used to dab at her mouth. Despite being painted a lovely shade of coral, her lips managed to stay perfectly done and not a bit of color was transferred to the white napkin. Impressive. Beth found so many ways to show she was not to be trifled with and somehow this was what made the biggest impact on me.

After she regained her composure, Beth said, "Thank you, Valerie. I know the two of you had a complicated relationship, but I also know how important you were to each other. He respected you. I can't think of a higher compliment when it comes to Rob."

Valerie sipped at her glass and cleared her throat several times as if to say something, but she didn't. Sana stepped in to say, "I can't wait for the big event. I have to say, the girls really surprised me. Never realized how hardworking and ambitious their generation is. I'm looking forward to seeing the culmination of everyone's hard work."

"Honestly? Same. The moms are just as ba—um, just as I remembered, but working with these girls is really inspiring. I love how they're not afraid to ask for what they deserve. That they feel like they can just go for it." I smiled at Joy and Katie, who blushed at the praise. "So thanks for insisting that I be one of the judges, Valerie. This experience has been . . . invaluable." I smiled at Valerie, who was still speechless after Beth's compliment.

"Yes, but who do you think is going to bring home the crown?" Mary Ann asked, leaning forward so she was literally the center of our attention.

Beth, still clutching her champagne flute, extended her arm and exerted just enough force to push Mary Ann back, then stepped into the empty space so that Mary Ann was boxed out. Without missing a beat, she turned to Joy and Katie. "Thank you for coming out to pay your respects, girls. I'm sure this must be very awkward for you, considering Rob's unforgivable behavior toward you. I will not try to excuse it, but I do apologize. You never should've been subjected to that, and I hope I've done a better job of keeping you safe since then."

Joy nodded like a bobblehead. "Thank you, I really appreciate you saying something. I—"

"And what have you done to keep us safe? I haven't seen you putting in new rules or even releasing a statement about his behavior." Katie's previously pale face was now flushed bright red. "You could've canceled the pageant at any time when you saw how things were going but you didn't. If anything happens to us, it's your fault. My mom was right, I shouldn't have bothered coming here. Thompsons only care about saving face and taking care of their own."

Katie stalked off, leaving a concerned Joy to run after her. Beth and Valerie watched the teens, thoughtful expressions on their faces.

"Youths," Beth said, shaking her head. "Do they have to be so frightfully earnest all the time?"

"She was right," Valerie said, a hint of sadness in her voice.

Beth snorted. "Of course she was right. The problem is she was right, out loud, in public, and now I actually have to do the right thing as well." She sighed and handed her champagne flute to Jae. "Looks like I'll be drafting a press release later, so I should probably stop drinking now. You're off the hook tonight. But I expect an answer soon. And you deserve one, as well. Don't forget that."

With the barest of glances my way, Beth walked away, leaving a contemplative Jae and my gossiping godmothers behind.

Chapter Twenty-two

"Count on you to bring the entire memorial crowd back with you," Adeena said under her breath, as she squeezed past me to fulfill another drink order.

I hadn't done it on purpose. The Calendar Crew had insisted on staying till the end of the memorial on the grounds that something scandalous and gossip-worthy might happen, what with so many important people around, Rob's less than pristine reputation, and a good amount of champagne. However, they were sorely disappointed when the event went off without a hitch, ending in the early evening for a private ceremony for the family and close family friends. Those who'd stuck around hoping for something interesting to happen followed my suggestion to join us at the Brew-ha Cafe to sample our new cocktail menu and other goodies.

The momtestant crowd was with us again, and you would've thought they'd be on slightly better behavior than last time since the crowd included their children and husbands, but Elena had a notoriously heavy hand when it was her turn to prepare drinks and the ladies' lips were even looser than usual.

"He was trying to get rid of her, you know," one of the moms, a recent divorcée, said. "My maid told me, who heard it from one of the Thompson family maids, that Beth was having a hard time conceiving. Rob was threatening that if she didn't get pregnant soon, he had no use for her." The divorcée drained her cocktail and rattled the glass at Elena to signal for a refill. She continued on, as if she weren't the rudest person in the world. "That's the only reason he married her, you know. She's no fool. I bet she killed him before he could kick her to the curb. I bet . . ."

My phone rang and I dragged myself away to answer it before I could say something I'd regret. I glanced at the screen and frowned. Bernadette? My heart beat in anxiety as I answered, knowing it had to be something big, good or bad, for her to actually call me.

"Lila, I need you to pick me up. Right away. Please," Bernadette said as soon as I answered. I could hear the tears in her voice, and I snapped to attention.

"Where are you?"

"The hospital. I just finished my shift."

"I'll be there in fifteen."

As soon as I pulled up in front of Shady Palms Hospital, Bernadette rushed out to meet me. She must've been keeping watch at the doors since I hadn't had time to alert her to my presence.

"Thanks for coming," she said. "Pinky's still working, and I didn't want to bother my mom."

"It's fine," I said. "Do you want to come back with me to the cafe or should I drop you at home? Some people from the memorial have stopped by and I don't know if you're in a social mood."

Bernadette stared out the window, not answering. I turned off the car and shifted in my seat so I could face her, but she still kept her face pointed at the window. I put my hand on her shoulder and . . .

Bernadette, my fearless cousin Bernadette, who'd broken my cousin Ronnie's nose after he broke her heart. Who was so determined and strong, she'd not only performed an intense dance routine on a fractured ankle for the Miss Teen Shady Palms Pageant, she'd almost won. Who handled crises every day as an ER nurse. *That* Bernadette . . . was trembling with fear and holding back tears.

Terrible possibilities filled my head. "What happened? Did someone do something to you? Say anything while you were working?"

She still wouldn't look at me, but at least replied. "Somebody slashed my tires. Just mine, no one else's. I checked the entire parking lot."

"You checked the entire parking lot? By yourself?" I stared at her, fighting the urge to shake her, to yell at her for being so careless. "What if they were still around? What if they were waiting for you to come out and attack you?"

That finally got her attention and she turned to look at me with scorn. "I can take care of myself." *Unlike you,* was the unspoken implication.

Typical Bernadette bravado. It was all well and good for her to tell me I needed to be honest about my feelings, but heaven forbid anything challenge her tough girl, hyper-competent image. I counted to ten slowly in my head, the way Elena taught me, before saying, "Have you reported it to the police yet? Or at least told the security guard?"

She snorted. "What good would that do? All that trouble over some prank."

I clutched the steering wheel to resist shaking her. "You know it wasn't just some prank! That's it, I'm calling Detective Park."

I started rummaging through my purse, but Bernadette grabbed my hand to stop me. "Let it go, Lila."

There was a warning in her voice. That tone just made me smile and start up the car. She could try and order me around, but she was in my car, at my mercy. Which she came to understand just a few minutes too late when she realized we were heading for my house, where my aunt, grandmother, and the Calendar Crew were sure to be.

Detective Park was there too, as it turned out, which made my job so much easier. Before Bernadette could even think to threaten me to keep my mouth shut, Tita Rosie and Ninang June had surrounded her and forced her into a chair near the detective. Like me, they only had to look at Bernadette to know something was wrong.

"There was no note, but I think it had to do with the case." She looked at Detective Park, who was jotting everything down while watching her carefully. "I know everyone thinks that it's all over now that Mr. Weinman is dead, but it kept bugging me. Case closed or not, everyone is still gossiping about Rob. Talking about all his past scandals and relationships. And it got me thinking . . . That rumor about the contestant who was obsessed with him. People talk as if it were all one-sided, but what if it wasn't? What if he got that girl in trouble?"

"And by trouble you mean . . . ?" Detective Park prodded.

Bernadette sighed. "Pregnant. I heard one of the moms hint at it during one of the events, and wondered if it was more than idle gossip. So I started asking around, tried to look through old maternity ward records. I haven't found anything yet, but I wonder if someone learned about what I was doing."

And by someone, she meant Rob's real killer. If they were still out there, that is. There was no evidence to support that theory. And yet.

And yet, why slash Bernadette's tires? It was a risky move. The sun hadn't quite set yet when I picked her up, so it must've still been daylight when they did it. Yes, the hospital security cameras were usually busted, but there were still security guards on the premises. And yes, Bernadette wasn't like, the nicest girl in town, but she was respected at the hospital and had done nothing to provoke this kind of personal attack. At least not lately. Could it just be a prank, like she'd said in the car?

Detective Park refused to say either way. However, when he got up to escort Bernadette and Ninang June home, he gave us this advice. "I don't want you all taking any more risks. I'm going to do some digging into this, but as far as you're all concerned, the Thompson case is closed. Let it go."

And for once, all of us, me, my aunt, my cousin, and the whole Calendar Crew, were only too happy to follow orders.

Chapter Twenty-three

"It's still not right! William, what are you doing over there?" Mayor Gunderson bellowed at Mr. Acevedo as the screech of microphone feedback made us all wince.

Mr. Acevedo mumbled something under his breath as he fiddled around with switches and knobs for the millionth time. The dress rehearsal progressed in starts and stops as tech issue after tech issue sprang up, reducing the usually cool Mr. Acevedo, who had no trouble presiding over a screaming match at the chamber of commerce, to a foulmouthed, sweaty mess.

Mercury must've been in retrograde, considering the way everything was going wrong. The computer that operated the soundboard wasn't working, and Mr. Acevedo had to use a backup laptop while Mayor Gunderson yelled at his assistant to find a repairperson ASAP. One of the contestants couldn't find her special fire batons for her routine and accused another girl of stealing them. It was only Valerie's quick intervention that stopped it from turning ugly. And to top it all off, Beth swept into the dress rehearsal twenty minutes late, trailed by Jae, who was carrying several shopping bags full of supplies for the rehearsal. No apologies for being late, no explanation to why Jae was there, just a quick head nod to acknowledge us, eyes shaded behind her giant sunglasses.

I averted my eyes from the two of them and focused on refilling my water bottle with the hydrating iced tea blend Elena had concocted—at three o'clock, the worst of the heat had passed, but the humidity clung to me and I needed to stay hydrated if I was going to make it through the rest of this cursed rehearsal.

I sensed his presence before I actually saw him—he didn't wear cologne, but the lemon-lavender scent I associated with him enveloped me, and I took a deep breath before turning around to face him. He held out a Brew-ha #1 in a frosty to-go cup, and I took it from him, his sweetness taking all the fight out of me. No matter what happened, he was my friend. I needed to remember that and curb this ugly jealous streak. A bit of pettiness was fine here and there, but not to the one guy who didn't deserve it.

"Thanks, Jae. How did you know I was in desperate need of caffeine?"

He grinned at me. "You kind of always need caffeine. And I figured you'd be in a bad mood since you'd have to be out in this heat. I would've brought you some halo-halo or ice candy, but it would've melted before I got here."

He looked me over, and I self-consciously tugged at the hem of my dress, which had been clinging to my sweat. One good thing about wearing dark colors in summertime, you couldn't see my gross sweat marks. "Sorry for not saying anything earlier, but I really like your new hairstyle. It suits you."

What did it say about me that that simple compliment made all my aunties' disparaging remarks seem like nothing? "Thanks. The aunties hate it, of course. They preferred my long, straight hair."

Before he could respond, Joy ran up to us, an adorable pink ukulele tucked under her arm. "Hi, Ate Lila! Dr. Jae! How are you?"

Jae reached out for a high five, which she returned. "Hey, I didn't know you played the ukulele! We should jam together sometime."

Joy's eyes lit up. "You play the ukulele, too?"

"Yeah, I taught myself in college. My friend was part of the ukulele club and got me to join since he knew I played the guitar. It was a lot of fun, but I haven't played in a while."

"I taught myself, too! I really wanted to learn piano when I was younger, but we couldn't afford it. So my sister got me this ukulele for my birthday freshman year. Said it reminded her of me." Joy cradled her ukulele, a soft smile on her face as she looked at her beloved instrument.

I was about to ask what song she was playing for her talent portion when Mr. Acevedo beat me to the punch.

"OK, that's great! I think we figured out all the audio stuff. Joy, can you play a quick piece one last time to be sure? And make sure to sing, not just play the instrument. I want to make sure the mic picks up your voice," Mr. Acevedo called out, as he messed around with the soundboard for the stage.

Joy obeyed, stepping up to the microphone stand and strumming her ukulele. She sang the first verse of "Over the Rainbow" in a clear, sweet voice that somehow managed to be equal parts hopeful and nostalgic. Tears sprang to my eyes and I had to fake a sneeze so I could dig a tissue out of my purse to dab at my face. Jae put a hand on my shoulder and squeezed, the light pressure more comforting than I expected. I wasn't even sure why I needed comforting.

The *click* of a camera made both of us jump, and I whirled around to catch Natalie Philipps and Dave, the *Shady Palms News* photographer, grinning at us.

"Sorry, just wanted to make sure my exposure was right. All this sunlight was washing out my photos," Dave said.

"Since it was just a test shot, you'll be deleting that photo, won't you?" Beth came over to us, the smile on her face doing nothing to temper the steel in her voice.

Natalie Philipps hurried to reassure Beth, likely not wanting to be banned from the festivities the way her husband had been. "Of course, Mrs. Thompson! Dave, get rid of it. Now."

Dave grumbled, but complied. "I need to start snapping the final photos of the girls anyway. How did we want to stage this?"

Beth led the way to the giant stage, where a curved staircase rose six feet to the platform the girls would be standing on for the majority of the final event. "Let's get all the group photos out of the way first, then you can move on to individual shots. We need to wrap this up quick while the lighting is still good."

"Lila, can we get a picture of you with all the contestants? You know, a former winner passing on the crown and whatnot," Dave said.

"I don't think—"

"That's a lovely idea! Yes, Lila, go join the girls. It would make a lovely shot," Valerie said. "I'm sure the paper will mention your new cafe as well. You know, local girl makes good?" she added, looking at Mrs. Philipps pointedly.

"Of course, of course! We'd be happy to. We've been enjoying all the little snacks you've been supplying for the various events, after all," the reporter said.

I sighed and trudged toward the stairs. Good thing I was used to walking in heels because the stairs were narrow and it was hard to find good footing as I posed alongside the ten contestants.

"Lila, go further up. Yes, all the way to the top! Now lean back against the railing and spread your arms across it. Try to look natural and inviting," Dave said, taking photo after photo while issuing these instructions.

I squeezed past Katie and tried to follow Dave's instructions, but she was taking up too much room, positioning herself so that she stood above all the other girls. "Katie, could you move down just a—"

Katie turned to look at me midquestion, and the section of railing we were leaning against came loose. We both screamed and I reached out to Katie to try to pull her back onto the stairs, but it was too late. We both tumbled to the ground, and I just barely had time to tuck my head in and cover it with my arms before we hit the stage. I landed on my left side, my hip and ankle taking the brunt of the damage.

Katie sobbed next to me, repeating something over and over as she tried to choke back tears. It took me a minute to realize she was saying, "I'm so sorry." I turned my aching body toward her to reassure her it wasn't her fault, but that simple motion drew a hiss of pain from me and she started crying even harder.

I didn't register the other people in attendance talking and screaming until Bernadette jumped on the stage and began to check Katie over for injuries, Jae and Sana right behind her to provide assistance.

Bernadette swore under her breath. "Looks like a dislocated shoulder. Possible fractures, but we'll need X-rays to confirm that. Can you sit up? An ambulance will be here soon, but I want to make sure you don't have a concussion." She had Sana help Katie up to a sitting position and continued her inspection, noting that other than her arm, she was fine. "Thankfully that's the worst of it."

While Bernadette examined Katie, Jae turned his attention to me, checking me for injuries and having me rotate various body parts to make sure nothing was broken. I yelped when his strong fingers prodded my left ankle, but was able to move it.

"Badly sprained ankle and some bumps and bruises, but overall you should be OK. You'll probably need a mobility device to help you get around for the next week or so, but I'm sure Bernadette can help with that." He brushed a stray curl away from my face. "You scared me. At least you have good instincts. I saw you protect your head, which probably prevented a worse injury."

Beth, Valerie, and Mayor Gunderson all rushed up to us at once. "Oh thank God you're both OK. Who the hell put these stairs together? Because they're about to be out of a job!" Valerie raged. In a rare show of unity, Beth and Mayor Gunderson agreed with her.

"This is terrible! Girls, come down from there! We don't need a repeat of this," Mayor Gunderson called up to the contestants, who had finally stopped screaming but were still frozen to the steps.

There was a moment of calm while the pageant committee passed out water bottles and the parents in the audience comforted their scared children. Jae, Bernadette, Sana, and I huddled around Katie and Joy, the latter doing what she could to console her crying friend. I could already hear the ambulance approaching in the distance, but before it pulled up, Winnie Pang arrived.

"Katie? Katie! What happened?" Winnie ran over to join us onstage. "Joy called me at the salon and said there was an accident. Are you OK, baby?"

"I'm so sorry, Mom. My arm's broken. I can't compete anymore." Katie cradled her injured arm and fought back tears. "I hope you're not disappointed."

"Disappointed? Of course not! And who said you can't compete? Just because you have a broken arm? Where does it say that in the rules?" Winnie turned to Valerie, directing that last question at her.

Valerie held up her hands. "We never said she couldn't! If she feels up to it, we wouldn't keep her out. But it's her choice."

"Of course she wants to compete! Isn't that right, Katie?" Winnie reached out to smooth back Katie's hair.

"I—oh good, the ambulance is here," Katie said, the whine of the siren cutting into their conversation.

Winnie blanched. "We're not paying for an ambulance! Can you walk? I'll take you now. You must be in so much pain. I'm so sorry, baby," she said, gesturing at Mr. Acevedo to help her with Katie. Joy went with them, carrying hers and Katie's bags.

Mayor Gunderson watched the four of them hobble off. "I guess there's no point in continuing. At least we worked out all the audio problems." He paused, his eyes landing on Mrs. Philipps, who was writing furiously in her notebook, and Dave, who'd been snapping photos the whole time. "Great, just what we needed. Beth, Valerie, come with me so we can handle this."

Beth hesitated, looking at me with Jae. "You've got Valerie. Surely you don't need me there, too."

"You're the head of the Thompson Family Company, so your voice carries weight. Now come on!"

She glared at him, but obeyed. "Jae, this will only take a minute."

Jae spared her a glance as he helped me to my feet. "Sorry, Beth, I'll have to take a rain check. I need to get Lila home. There's no way she can drive in her condition."

"But—"

"Thanks for taking such good care of my cuz, Jae! Don't worry about your car, Lila. I'll drop it at your place and Sana can give me a ride back here," Bernadette said, hands out for my keys.

"That's right! We need to talk about the advanced Zumba class she'll be teaching on the weekends anyway," Sana added.

Beth turned away without another word and went to deal with the *Shady Palms News* team.

Well, look at Bernadette conspiring to get me alone with Jae. Didn't think she had it in her. Maybe we really had turned a corner in our relationship. "Thanks, Ate," I said, handing over my keys. "Any medical advice you can give me for a quick recovery?"

"Keep that ankle iced and elevated and stay off it as long as possible. I think we still have Daddy's cane at the house, so I can drop it off later."

It had been years since her dad passed from MS, but I still couldn't believe she was willing to part with something that belonged to him. That simple gesture was enough to bring tears to my eyes, which I pretended was due to the pain in my leg. "Don't worry about it. Pretty sure we still have Lolo's lying around somewhere. But thanks. I appreciate it."

And because she couldn't leave well enough alone, Bernadette said, "Hey, just two more days and this will all be over. Try not to die before the Founder's Day Festival, OK?"

She walked away cackling, but I couldn't laugh at her weak joke. As Jae led me away, I glanced back at the fallen railing one last time. Was it just shoddy workmanship? Or had someone purposely tampered with it to hurt one of our girls?

Chapter Twenty-four

"Are you ready, Joy?"

We were behind the Main Stage, waiting for the final event of the pageant to start. All the other contestants were busy practicing their talent with their mom, or having their makeup adjusted by their mom, or receiving a pep talk from their mom.

Except for Joy. The teen was pacing back and forth by herself, muttering what sounded like algebra equations to me. Or maybe geometry? Math wasn't really my strong point, but she was definitely reciting something math-related.

"Huh? Oh, hi, Ate Lila. I'm fine. I just like reciting formulas when I'm nervous. Focusing on it helps take my mind off things." She smiled shyly. "I know it's weird."

I shifted my weight to my uninjured ankle and reached out with the hand that wasn't gripping my grandfather's old cane. "Hey, whatever works, right? I should probably find my own version. It's like a magic spell—say these words and they'll help you focus or not stress out or whatever."

"That's exactly what it's like! I like using calculus because it's a prereq for my major. It's like I'm studying and stress relieving at the same time."

That was so her. To distract myself from the pain of watching her do this alone while everyone else had a parent with them, I thought about what "magic spell" would work for me and came up blank. Adeena would probably recite coffee varieties and Elena different plants and their properties. Lola Flor would recount all the varieties of kakanin and Tita Rosie would probably just recite the rosary. But what about me?

"Anyway, you know I have to be completely objective in my scoring. But good luck. Give it your all, OK?"

She flashed me a smile and thumbs-up. "I hope it's me or Katie! Have you seen her around?"

I shook my head. "She's probably still getting ready. Anyway, I'll let you get back to it. I should say hi to the other girls, too. Don't want anyone accusing me of favoritism."

"That's OK. Ate Bernie and Ate Pinky will be here soon and they'll keep me company. And Katie, too."

She went off to find her best friend and I made my way over to Naoko and Yuki. "How're you two doing?"

The duo were fussing over a table with various flowers, greenery, and vases laid out over it. Naoko hadn't participated in the talent rehearsal, saying that her talent didn't require any technology checks, and that for her to do her best, her supplies had to be fresh anyway. She planned on doing a modern ikebana demonstration, which I found fascinating.

"What made you choose flower arranging as your talent?" I asked.

"It's the only thing I like doing that would be interesting to watch live. Like, I love making jewelry and sketching outfits, but that's not something I can do onstage in front of people. I wish you'd change those rules. Not everyone's talent can be performed in front of an audience, but it still counts." The girl fiddled with her bracelets as her mom also laid sheets of origami paper and slim twigs next to the greenery. "I'm not going to win, so can you tell that to Ms. Thompson? Maybe then I'll have a chance for next year."

I promised to pass along her feedback. "You never know, though. You racked up quite a few points with your winning design last week. It's still anybody's game."

Naoko perked up and rewarded me with a brilliant smile. "Thanks. I needed that. Um, this is for you. Because you've been so nice to me. And my mom. She didn't really have any friends in town until you came back. She seems really happy now."

She held out a matching set of her signature beaded bracelets and earrings. She'd used nothing but black beads, in keeping with my aesthetic, but when you held them up to the sun, there was a rainbow sheen reflecting off the darkness. They were absolutely lovely and I told her so.

"Thank you, Naoko," I said as I put on the bracelets and switched out my hoops for the dangly earrings. "I'll cherish them. Just like I cherish your mom's friendship. Good luck today."

We said goodbye and I continued wandering around to wish the rest of the girls luck, making slow progress thanks to my injured ankle and the amount of people running around backstage. I finally found Winnie and Katie Pang with Joy at the last makeshift vanity station. Winnie was adjusting Katie's makeup and putting the finishing touches on her hairstyle, and the teen was stunning. She still had her girl-next-door cuteness (no amount of contouring could take away the sweetness of those round cheeks), but the fake lashes and upswept hairdo gave her an air of sophistication.

"Oh Katie, you're so beautiful!" Joy sighed as she looked at her best friend. "How's your arm? Are you feeling OK?"

Katie's forearm was enclosed with a bright green cast, which was already covered with signatures and doodles. She flexed her fingers and glanced at her mom before answering. "Yeah, I'm fine. My hands are free, so I'm still able to perform my talent. You look beautiful too, Joy."

"I'm not very good with makeup, but I tried. You're lucky your mom's so good at it." Joy smiled, but there was no hiding the wistfulness in her voice.

Winnie's eyes met mine, and there was a look I couldn't read there. Was she also wondering about Joy's absentee parents? How anyone could neglect their children, let alone a girl as sweet as Joy?

Winnie broke eye contact to look down at her watch. "You know what, we still have some time. Joy, come here and I'll adjust your makeup. Do you want me to do anything with your hair?"

As they started discussing possible looks, I said my goodbyes and made my way back to the judges' table, passing Ate Bernie and Joy's sister Pinky on the way. I glanced back as they joined the trio chattering away happily as they prepared for the competition. I said a silent prayer for all of them. As long as Joy had that kind of love and support in her life, maybe she'd be OK after all.

The Q&A portion of the pageant, usually the bane of everyone's pageant experience, flew by thanks to Valerie's insightful questions, Mayor Gunderson's skill at the mic (he was really quite charming when he allowed other people to get a word in), and of course, the contestants, who were bringing their A game now that they'd made it to the final round. Even Leslie, Sharon Randall's wallflower friend, excelled during her interview—she seemed to have realized she didn't have to be giggly or bubbly to play the part of a beauty queen, and her quiet thoughtfulness made me see why a girl as vivacious as Sharon Randall was her best friend.

She also showed quite a bit of bravery when asked the last question, "If you could change one thing about the Miss Teen Shady Palms Pageant, what would it be?" (Every contestant was asked this question, so Naoko got to deliver her bit of feedback herself.)

Leslie glanced at Sharon, who was just offstage, before saying, "I want this pageant to be more inclusive. Saying 'anyone who identifies as female' still limits it. I think if you want to create a truly modern pageant, you have to open your mind to all the other possibilities out there. Oh, and I use she/they pronouns, by the way."

Mayor Gunderson said, "I'm not sure I understood all that, but I recognize the courage it took for you to speak your truth. Thank you, Leslie." Leslie waved at the crowd before exiting the stage, and Mayor Gunderson continued, "What a way to wrap up the Q&A! And now for the main event: the talent portion of Miss Teen Shady Palms! Take it away, ladies! Or, um, contestants? Whatever, good luck, everyone!"

Everyone in Shady Palms lived for the talent show, but it was my least favorite part. Yeah, some of the contestants had awesome skills, but it was like Naoko said: Not everyone had a talent they could perform. It was painful to watch these girls, already at such a self-conscious age, fumbling their way through routines they'd obviously learned just for the competition. There were also some wonderfully creative performances that made me proud to be part of the pageant: Sharon Randall displayed amazing athletic ability as well as choreography in her cheerleading routine, Naoko did a traditional ikebana demonstration as well as showed how to create origami blooms that were inexpensive and lasted year-round, and Sara Colon, the teen mom who blew us away during the group interviews, recited some of her own poetry.

Each contestant had to give a brief explanation of why they were performing their chosen talent, and when it was Joy's turn, she held up her ukulele and said, "Music is a great escape. It's something I do only for myself. It's fun. I don't have to be good at it. I don't plan on making a career of it, so it doesn't matter how bad I am or how long it takes me to learn a new song. I might even try writing my own music someday. But I don't want that pressure yet. For now, just the feel of the strings against my fingertips is enough." She strummed the instrument, the pleasure radiating from her face. "Today, I'm performing Israel Kamakawiwoʻole's version of 'Over the Rainbow.' I know it's kind of cliché now, but I'm originally from Hawaii and this song reminds me of home. And for me, home was my grandfather, who taught me to love music. So this is for you, Lolo." Joy's voice would never be called technically perfect, but she sang with her usual sweetness and earnestness, and the emotion of the song made its way into my heart. I didn't even bother hiding the tears streaming down my face this time and was gratified to see that Sana was in a similar state. Beth's eyes remained dry but riveted on the stage, a slight hitch to her breathing the only sign she was equally affected.

When she was finished, Joy quickly bowed and exited the stage to tumultuous applause. It wasn't a standing ovation or anything, but she was clearly the crowd favorite so far. Which made it extra tough when Katie came out to play the piano. Anyone following such a strong performance would've had a hard time, but considering her injured arm and that she'd come on the heels of her best friend, Katie's performance was extremely lackluster. She had the technical skill Joy lacked, but none of the passion—it was like she was just going through the motions. After the last chords of Debussy (I knew enough classical music to recognize the composer if not the song) drifted away, Katie got up and hurried offstage to polite applause, not even acknowledging the crowd or judges' panel.

Once the last contestant completed their really quite decent hip-hop dance routine, Sana and I huddled around Beth with our scorecards. Even though today's events were the showiest, they were no longer the deciding factor for a pageant win. The volunteer portion was worth the most, point-wise, followed by the talent portion, then Q&A, and then the rest of the events. As usual, there were a few who dominated in every category, but there were always some falls from grace and rises to glory at this last event. Because there were only ten girls, the lowest in Shady Palms history, it didn't take long to tabulate the scores. Beth had Sharon Randall in the top spot, followed by Joy, then Sara Colon. Sana had Sara at number one, Joy at number two, and Naoko at number three.

As much as I loved Naoko's energy, she really only excelled at the creative side. She kind of fell flat in other areas for me, but Sana just shrugged when Beth voiced what I was thinking. "She's got entrepreneurial spirit. That always calls out to me."

I had Joy in the top position (Sara had originally been my frontrunner, but Joy's song pushed her to number one), followed by Sara, then (grudgingly) Sharon. Looking at the numbers, I couldn't believe it, but it was there—Joy had won. Bernadette had coached a champion.

Beth called Mayor Gunderson over and handed him the envelope. He glanced over the results, quickly confirmed it with us, and then moved back to the stage.

"Shady Palms! Are you ready to meet this year's Miss Teen Shady Palms?" He paused while everyone cheered. "In third place . . . let's hear it for Miss Sharon Randall!"

Sharon smiled and made her way over to Valerie, who presented her with a lovely bouquet. Over the applause, I could swear I heard Mary Ann Randall scream, "What?!"

Mayor Gunderson continued. "And our runner-up, who will take over as Miss Teen Shady Palms in the event that our winner can no longer carry out the responsibility . . . Miss Sara Colon!"

Happy screams and cheers and blaringly loud air horns greeted this pronouncement, as Sara stepped up to receive her bouquet. She blew a kiss toward the section of the crowd that must've been her family, considering the giant banner they proudly held up. Mayor Gunderson tried shushing them, which only made them cheer louder (not going to lie, this made me cheer along with them).

Once it finally quieted down, the mayor cleared his throat and did his impression of (what was later explained to me by Jae) the announcer calling out the starting lineup to the 90s Chicago Bulls team. "And finally, this year's Miss Teen Shady Palms . . . let's give it up for Joy Munroe!"

Chapter Twenty-five

As soon as Joy's name was called, Katie burst into tears and ran off the stage.

Joy didn't notice because she was too busy having the Miss Teen Shady Palms sash draped over her, so I got up from the judges' table to go talk to Katie backstage. I could understand her disappointment, but I didn't want her ruining this moment for her friend.

The backstage area was bustling with the festival organizers who were preparing for the band that was set to go onstage as soon as the pageant contestants finished their photos. It took me a while, but I finally got someone to point me in Katie's direction. She was hiding out in the VIP area that the band had just vacated.

"Katie? Are you OK? I hope you're not too disappointed." I leaned my cane against a table and held out my arms in case she needed a hug. The teen hurled herself into my arms, sobbing so hard her body shook. "I'm really sorry. I know it's tough. I've lost more than my fair share of competitions. But I hope you don't let this ruin your friendship with Joy."

She pulled away at that, her efforts to stop crying resulting in weird hiccupy gasps. "It's not that. I don't . . . I'm so scared, I—"

"Katie!" Joy ran up to us and hugged her friend. "When I couldn't find you onstage, I got so worried. Are you OK?" She yanked off her tiara and sash, setting them aside on a nearby table. "I'm sorry, I wish we both could've won. You're not mad at me, are you?"

"No, it's not about you, Joy. I could never be mad at you. It's just . . . I wanted out so bad and nothing worked, no matter what I did. And now that I lost, I'm worried what else—I mean, I'm worried how my mom is going to take it."

"Your mom loves you, Katie. That's all that matters."

"Sometimes I worry she loves me too much."

I'd stepped aside to give the two some privacy, but something about Katie's tone caught my attention. "What do you mean? How is that even possible?"

Katie glanced over at me and our eyes met. The pain in them conveyed the truth—it was her mom. Winnie Pang killed Rob Thompson.

I shook my head. No, there was no way she'd do something like that. I was reading too much into her distress. Although . . . if it had something to do with Katie . . .

I put my hand on her arm. "Katie, are you sure? Why do you—"

"There you are, Katie! I've been looking all over for you."

Winnie Pang's voice, as well as the sharp jab of something hard in my ribs, cut me off. Winnie linked arms with me and pulled me close, her right hand buried in her purse to conceal the gun pressed into my side.

"Katie, hold on to Joy. She and Lila are going to walk us to the parking lot. Nice and slow, no drawing attention our way. You just had to come after my daughter, didn't you?" she added under her breath, so only I could hear. "You know what'll happen if you don't cooperate, right?"

Katie hadn't seen the gun or heard her mother's threat, but there was no mistaking the tightness in her voice. Katie knew. Had probably known for a long time. "Mom. Let's just go, OK? It doesn't have to be like this."

"We are going. *Now.*"

"But Mom—"

"Katherine Marie Pang. Everything I've done has been for you. Everything. We are not going to throw it all away, especially over the girl who stole your crown. Now let's go!" Winnie's voice rose higher and higher as she spoke, the last sentence almost a scream. A few people glanced our way, but most were focused on the band and paid us no mind.

Katie flinched. "I'm so sorry, Joy. Just . . . just walk with us and everything will be fine."

Joy turned frightened eyes toward me. "Ate? What's going on?"

Winnie jerked her head toward the exit, signaling them to go first. "Just follow us and keep your mouth shut. You're a sweet girl and I don't want to hurt you. But I will if I have to. Now move!"

The steel in Winnie's voice let Joy know she wasn't messing around. Katie pulled her arm through Joy's and tugged her through the crowd. The parking lot was at the opposite end of the festival, but everyone was too busy stuffing their faces and getting drunk to notice our odd procession down the thoroughfare. Detective Park was nowhere to be seen and the Shady Palms Police Department seemed to be solely congregated around the beer garden, so they were useless as always.

I had to rely on the old villain standby: get her talking. "Katie is Rob's daughter, isn't she?"

Katie's head whipped around at that. "What? That can't be true."

When Winnie didn't say anything, Katie said, "Mom? Please tell me that's not what started this all."

"So when did Rob figure it out? Joy told me Rob put the moves on both of them the night of the potluck, so he couldn't have known before then."

That finally got Winnie's attention. "That pig! I confronted him after Katie told me. I lost my chance at the crown all those years ago because of him and he didn't even remember me. Had no idea that his family had given me money to 'take care of the problem' as they'd put it. I took their hush money, but that was it. I had no plans to force my way into their lives or try to claim Katie's inheritance. All he had to do was keep his hands to himself, but he couldn't. I wasn't going to let him ruin another girl's future the way he did mine."

"Did you tell him who she was?"

"Of course I did. I needed him to know how disgusting he was. And do you know what he did?"

"Laugh at you?"

The hand gripping me shook, but not with fear at what she was doing. "You think my ego is so easily bruised I'd kill over that? No, he threatened to take her away. He'd been trying for an heir for years, but Beth kept miscarrying. So he saw Katie as a way to continue his legacy. He was going to pay me to just hand over my daughter. When I said no . . ."

Her slackened hold caused me to stumble—she'd pulled me away without my cane and I needed her support to move forward. Not only was I out a possible way to defend myself, but the fact I needed her assistance made her death grip on me look natural—friendly, even. Just a kind person helping her injured pal navigate the town festival.

She tightened her hold on me and I knew I had to keep her talking.

"Could he do that? I mean, she's almost an adult. There's no way he could force her to stay after she turned eighteen."

"Yeah, but she's only sixteen now. And he's a Thompson. You think the courts would rule in my favor? He wanted to cut me out of her life! Said it'd be better if she went away to some fancy boarding school to finish her education, and I couldn't . . . I couldn't let him take her away. I'd never be able to recover."

"Mom, you thought I'd leave you just because he had money? You think I wouldn't have fought to stay with you? That I would just let him *buy* me? That's really what you think of me?" Katie's eyes watered as she tried to keep a hold on Joy. "I've spent all this time trying to convince you to leave town with me!"

Caught off guard, Winnie jerked to a stop. "What?"

"I knew you killed Rob. I overheard you planning with Mr. Weinman. That's why I kept trying to sabotage the pageant, so you'd leave with me because it wasn't safe. I even had Mr. Weinman help me with all those threatening letters and everything. I could tell that you were losing it, and I was scared. After you slashed Bernadette's tires, I remembered Mr. Weinman's plan to mess with the stage, so I loosened the railing's screws so I'd get hurt. I needed you to snap out of it and get out of Shady Palms so we'd be safe. Why couldn't you do that?"

Winnie made a move as if to hug Katie, but stopped and tightened her hold on me. "I'm sorry, baby. I'm listening now though. And we could still get away. I took care of Oskar when he was starting to crack, and I'll take care of this, too. Just listen to me and nobody else has to get hurt. We could start over in a new town. Wouldn't that be great?"

"Katie, don't do this, please. You can just let us go. You don't need us. You'll be able to get away so much faster without us, don't you think?" Joy pleaded with her best friend.

"She's right, Katie. Joy has nothing to do with this. You don't want her getting hurt, do you? Don't make this worse." There was no way Winnie would let me go, but if I could at least convince them to let Joy get away safely, then that was one less thing for me to worry about.

Katie looked over at her mom, who shook her head. "Let her go so she can inform the police? Go running to their detective buddy who's always hanging around? I don't think so. If I go to jail, what do you think happens to you, Katie? We don't have family. We only have each other. Now let's go."

"I'm sorry," Katie whispered as she pulled Joy along with her.

Joy cast desperate eyes my way, and I did what I could to reassure her. "Don't worry, Joy. Winnie doesn't want any more blood on her hands, isn't that right? Especially not the blood of an innocent young girl with a bright future, who happens to be her daughter's best friend?"

OK, so maybe I was laying it on thick, but now was not the time for subtlety.

"Right, Katie? Joy has always been good to you. You wouldn't hurt her, would you?"

"Never! We're just holding you so we have time to get away. Rob and Mr. Weinman were jerks. She'd never hurt innocent people. Right, Mom?" Katie glanced over at her mother. When Winnie didn't respond, she asked again, "I said, right, Mom? Y-you're not planning on hurting Joy, are you?"

"Not if she listens to what I say and doesn't cause any problems. Because if she does, it's her Ate Lila that's going to feel it. And we don't want that, do we?" Winnie said, jabbing the gun farther into my ribs to make her point.

Katie and Joy both faltered, but sped up when Winnie ordered them to hurry. The two of them speed-walked through the festival area, heads down and avoiding eye contact, as if the sooner they reached the parking lot, the sooner this nightmare would be over. I wasn't quite so optimistic about my chances. Winnie wasn't a monster, and I could feel her tense up when her daughter asked about hurting Joy. There was no way she could do it—Joy was like a daughter to her as well. Me, however? I brought about no such love and my meddling was endangering her life with her daughter.

As if she could hear my thoughts, Winnie said, "It's not like I'm proud of what I've done. If I had to do it over again, I'd find some other way to keep me and Katie together. But it's too late now. You have to understand, Rob was going to ruin everything. I just want a good life for me and my daughter. For the two of us to be together. Is that so much to ask?"

No, it wasn't too much to ask. But a life was too high a price to pay, and she took two. I could only sympathize so far.

She must've sensed this because she decided to go for the jugular with her next words. "Your mother would've done the same, you know. The way you and Bernadette talk about her . . . that was a woman who would've done what it took to make sure you were taken care of. You just don't understand how strong a mother's love could be."

And that . . . that just broke me. Because while I didn't agree with her idea of what a mother's love was, I couldn't deny that for both her and my mom, that was absolutely how they showed their love. That's what their love amounted to. My mother had loved in the way that she knew how. It had never felt like enough. But maybe I needed to either let people love me in the limited way they could or learn to ask for what I needed out of a relationship. And if they couldn't provide it . . . maybe I needed to learn to move on.

Funny how all it took was a gun-toting murderer for me to have an epiphany. Dear Lord, if I got through this, I was going to sign up for all the therapy. Just all the therapy, give it to me. Adeena and Elena would be so proud.

Adeena and Elena! As if the very thought of asking for help conjured them, the Brew-ha Cafe booth came into view and I could see them hard at work serving customers. Longganisa was with them, wearing the shirt emblazoned with the cafe logo I'd ordered especially for her. She started barking and pulling at her leash once she'd noticed me, but it was attached to the table and she couldn't come any closer. All the noise drew Elena's attention, and she smiled and waved, calling out a greeting, which I returned after Winnie nudged me again with her purse gun.

"Give a quick, friendly hi and keep it moving." Winnie's voice wavered a bit as she took in the crowd around us and how much farther it was to the parking lot.

Sensing this, I knew it was now or never to make my move. After her earlier slip, Winnie had been careful to keep a tight hold on me, and I'd been limping along, ignoring the pain, waiting for the right moment. When I saw a small pothole in the street that hadn't been fixed yet, I took my chance.

"Ope!" I yelped, as my foot caught in the hole. I grabbed Katie's injured arm in an attempt to catch myself and succeeded in having her let go of Joy as she started to fall with me. Winnie had to let go of her gun and take her hand out of her purse to catch her daughter. I waited till Winnie's hands were full, then shoved Joy toward Adeena and Elena's table. "Run!"

Winnie cursed and pulled out her gun, pointing it at me as I lay prone on the street. "Get up." She tossed Katie her keys. "Run straight to the car. Don't stop for anybody. Be ready to take off as soon as I get there."

Katie was still rubbing her sore arm and fumbled the catch. Joy, moving faster than I thought possible, snatched the keys off the ground and sprinted toward my aunt and grandmother, who were set up directly across from Adeena and Elena. Winnie's gun arm swung toward Joy, and both Katie and I screamed, "No!"

I launched myself off the ground and tackled Winnie before she could hurt Joy, muscle memory taking over as my body relived this way too familiar situation. Winnie dropped the gun and it skittered away into the screaming crowd, which had finally caught on to what was happening. Unfortunately, that sudden motion put way too much pressure on my already messed up ankle and I could no longer stand up or put any weight on it.

"Katie, get the gun and get out of here!" Winnie screamed as she straddled me to prevent me from reaching the gun myself.

"Mom, stop it! Leave her alone, we need to go!" Katie sobbed, pulling on her mother's arm. But it was too late—someone must've alerted the SPPD, and they were (slowly, so slowly) making their way over to us.

Winnie let out a furious cry. "You ruined everything! Now what's going to happen to Katie?"

Before I could react, she wrapped her hands around my throat. Those hands, as strong and powerful as I remembered from the head massage she gave me mere days ago, squeezed tighter and tighter as they choked the life out of me. I tried to tear her hands away, but she was too strong. I couldn't put enough weight on my feet to try and buck her off. I started to slip into the blackness, Katie's sobs and Longanisa's furious barking the only sounds I could hear . . .

Suddenly, a great weight was lifted from me as Winnie toppled off me with a cry and light crept back into my vision. I coughed, hand to my throat, as I drew in great big gasps of air, the feeling both razor sharp and relieving. As my vision cleared, I saw Bernadette standing over me, the restaurant's electric kettle in her hand. The police were standing watch over a dazed Winnie while Detective Park comforted a hysterical Katie, who was screaming curses at Bernadette.

I blinked up at Bernadette. "What are you doing here?"

That simple question burned my injured throat and caused a coughing fit.

"That's really all you can say to the person who just saved your ridiculous ass?" she said as she eased me into a sitting position and checked me over for injuries. As her fingers probed my throat, I hissed at the sharp pain her ministrations brought. "Hmm, some bruising is likely but nothing serious. You'll probably be sore for the next few days, so try to rest and not speak too much. I know how hard that is for you, but try, OK?" She smiled as she said that, not with the usual sarcasm or venom, but with actual concern.

Tita Rosie hurried over with an ice pack, followed closely by an EMT who wrapped my ankle. Adeena crouched down to help me stand and guided me over to our booth, where Elena handed me a cup of salabat with honey—the hot ginger tea coursed down my throat, bringing its usual relief. With Longganisa on my lap, the cold of the ice on my neck combined with the heat from the tea inside worked its magic and I sighed in relief.

"It's over."

A few days later, my throat had healed enough for me to talk, so Adeena, Elena, and I got together at the Brew-ha Cafe to enjoy bowls of Lola Flor's halo-halo, as well as discuss all that had gone down.

Winnie was in custody and had confessed her crimes, but not before arranging a meeting with Valerie and Beth over Katie's future. The two women talked it over with Winnie and their lawyers (after

Valerie had a paternity test drawn up that confirmed Katie was Rob's daughter), and the three of them decided that until Katie came of age, she would be in the care of the Thompsons. Valerie and Katie would move into the Thompson house, Beth would move into her own condo nearby, and together they'd provide guidance and hopefully love to that confused young woman. My heart went out to her. But Valerie and Beth were both powerhouses in their own way. The fact that they were setting their egos aside long enough to care for this girl together spoke volumes.

Sana realized she'd strayed further than she'd meant to from her nonprofit-loving ways, and partnered with Sara Colon, the runner-up of the pageant, to set up an organization to help teen moms get an education and learn business skills. Since she wasn't a practicing lawyer anymore, she enlisted Amir's help. It wasn't his area of expertise, but he was eager to do his part and helped the organization pro bono. Part of it was his good heart delighting in helping a good cause. Pretty sure the other part was how Sana's eyes lit up when she saw him. Nothing had happened yet, but it was only a matter of time. Good for them. They suited each other perfectly, and I wished them luck.

When I was resting at home, not allowed to speak or do anything but sleep and drink plenty of fluids, Jae came to visit me. He had a sparkly black ukulele and music book with him.

"I noticed your reaction when Joy was playing. I know you won't be able to sing for a while, but maybe you can create music in a different way."

I tried to hold my tears back, but that just made my throat hurt even more, so I let out a sob and threw myself into his arms. He patiently stroked my hair as I let out everything I'd been holding in for the last few days . . . months . . . years. When it was time for him to leave, I grabbed his hand before I could lose my nerve.

"Wait for me." I didn't elaborate—even those few words hurt to force out, but they had to be said. The look in Jae's face changed ever so slightly as he bent over to kiss my forehead.

"OK."

That's all he said. But it was enough. He was willing to wait—he knew I had to heal, in so many different ways, before I was ready to be in a relationship with him. He understood and was willing to let things be for now.

All that was left was making things right with Adeena and Elena. Even though I'd been good about my responsibilities regarding the shop, I knew they could sense my wishy-washy attitude and were annoyed by it. They were my partners. They had just as much riding on the success of the cafe as I did. And it was time to stop acting as if everything were all about me. The icy halo-halo soothed my throat as I listened to my besties chattering about the immense success the Founder's Day Festival had been for the shop—the rather dramatic climax notwithstanding.

"I called Dr. Kang," I said when there was finally a lull in the conversation. "After all that happened at the festival . . . it was time."

"Well, I would've preferred a less life-threatening way for you to have that epiphany, but I'm glad you got there in the end. But now I wonder . . . are you ready to go all in with the business? Once you're healed up, I need to know that I can count on you. That we can count on you," Adeena said, placing one hand on mine and the other on Elena's.

The seriousness of the moment required an honest answer and my full, undivided attention. But before I could respond, the bell above the door sounded, announcing the arrival of a small family.

Their laughs died as they took in the tension in the room and our serious expressions. One of the parents cleared their throat. "Oh, I'm sorry. We loved your booth at the Founder's Day Festival and wanted to check out your shop. But I didn't think to check . . . Are you officially open yet?"

They herded the children closer in case they had to leave, but I made up my mind in that moment. I stood up and said, in a voice that was only a touch shaky, "Yes, actually, we are. Welcome to the Brew-ha Cafe!"

Acknowledgments

Second Book Syndrome is all too real, and I need to thank my agent, Jill Marsal, and my editors, Angela Kim and Michelle Vega, for helping me bring this book to life. There were many times I thought I was never going to finish, or never going to get it right, but you all provided fantastic feedback and support and understanding. Thank you so, so much for that. I also need to thank Vi-An Nguyen for providing me with yet another AMAZING cover that I absolutely adore (Longganisa with that tiara? My heart . . .), and my amazing PR and marketing team for their tireless work in getting my books out there: Dache' Rogers, Jessica Mangicaro, and Natalie Sellars. I'd also like to thank the rest of my Berkley/PRH family: Christine Legon, Liz Gluck, and the ad/promo team.

The past year and a half has been A LOT, so I especially need to shout out the group that helped me keep it together this whole debut journey: my beloved Berkletes. Thanks for providing a safe space to celebrate, commiserate, thirst, and more. Y'all are the best.

Another group that's been there for me this past year is my awesome DnD group, Ye Olden Girls. Real life has gotten in the way and we can't meet as regularly as we used to, but you all have brought so much fun and laughter into my life. Thanks so much for your love and support.

Slightly unorthodox, but since we're talking about people who helped me keep it together in 2020 and beyond, I want to thank Alyssa Cole and Talia Hibbert (among many other BIPOC romance authors) for saving my mental health with your joyful portrayals of BIPOC romance. We don't, like, know each other or anything, but your books helped me get through some tough times, and I can't thank you both enough for that. Same for Sherry Thomas, whose Lady Sherlock series I reread over and over and over in the first few months of the pandemic, when I needed the comfort of familiarity as well as excellent storytelling. Books truly can save people.

To all the librarians who've been so supportive, thank you so much! Library work is tough, and I appreciate the wonderful things you all provide to the community. Same goes to all you booksellers out there who are kind enough to not only stock my book but also hand-sell it and include it in your employee picks. It's never not thrilling to see my book out in the wild.

To my readers, thanks so much for your support! To the ones who take the time to message me or post on social media about how my book made them feel seen, you have no idea what that means to me. And to the ones who take the time to educate me when I mess up, thank you. From the bottom of my heart, thank you for letting me know so I could learn and do better. For investing your time and energy in me because you believed I *could* do better. I love you all.

And finally, to James and my family. I love how excited you all get for me over every little thing, and all the ways you try to support and be there for me. I couldn't have done this without you all.

Love love!

Tita Rosie's Grilled Adobo Chicken Wings

Tita Rosie makes this fun summertime spin on chicken adobo for parties and picnics. These are the general proportions that you can scale up or down, depending on how many people you're serving.

Ingredients (per pound of chicken):

1 pound of chicken wings and/or drumsticks per person
1 teaspoon baking powder
½ teaspoon garlic powder
½ teaspoon salt
½ teaspoon black pepper

For the sauce (per pound of chicken):

1 tablespoon butter
1 tablespoon soy sauce

1 tablespoon vinegar (white cane vinegar or apple cider vinegar)
1 teaspoon brown sugar
1 to 2 teaspoons minced garlic
1 bay leaf
Red pepper flakes (to taste)
Black pepper (to taste)

DIRECTIONS:

1. Rinse chicken and pat dry. Mix the baking powder, garlic powder, salt, and black pepper, and coat the wings.

2. Lay the wings flat in baking trays or zippered plastic bags and store in the fridge for at least 6 hours or overnight.

3. Prep your grill and cook the wings over indirect heat for 30 to 40 minutes until the skin is crisp, turning once or twice. You can also bake in a 400°F oven for 40 to 60 minutes, turning every 20 minutes to evenly crisp the skin.

4. While the chicken is cooking, add all the sauce ingredients to a saucepan. Bring to a boil, then lower the heat and simmer uncovered until the liquid reduces to a thin glaze.

5. Toss the grilled chicken wings in the sauce until evenly coated and serve.

Lola Flor's Turon

These sweet, crispy spring rolls are sooo addictive! The recipe below is for the traditional banana and jackfruit filling, but feel free to get creative by swapping in different ingredients, such as cheese (Filipinos love the combination of salty and sweet) or even chocolate.

YIELD: 12 TURON

Ingredients:

1 cup brown sugar

12 square lumpia or spring roll wrappers

6 saba bananas (sliced in half lengthwise) OR 4 large firm-ripe yellow bananas (cut in thirds)

⅓ to ½ cup sliced jackfruit (fresh or canned)

Neutral oil for frying (canola, vegetable, etc.)

DIRECTIONS:

1. Place the brown sugar in a medium-wide bowl and fill a small bowl with warm water.

2. On a clean work surface (cutting board, large plate, etc.), position a lumpia wrapper so it looks like a diamond, with a point facing toward you.

3. Roll the sliced banana in the brown sugar and place horizontally in the middle of the wrapper. Add a strip or two of jackfruit next to the banana.

4. Take the wrapper point closest to you and fold it over the banana-and-jackfruit filling, then tuck the point tightly under the filling.

5. Fold the left point and then the right point over the filling (it'll overlap slightly and look somewhat like an envelope), then use both hands to roll the wrapper tightly away from you until only a 2-inch point at the top is exposed. Dip your finger in the warm water, spread it on the exposed point, then continue rolling until the wrapper's fully sealed. Set the wrapper aside and continue doing this until all the wrappers are filled. Reserve the remaining brown sugar in the bowl.

6. Add ½ to 1 inch of oil to a heavy-bottomed pan (such as cast iron or a Dutch oven) and heat to medium high. You can also use a thermometer for more even cooking, in which case, you want it heated to about 350°F.

7. Add about half the turon to the oil in a single layer and fry until golden brown, about 3 minutes, using tongs to turn the turon over a couple of times. Remove to drain on a wire rack, colander, or on a plate covered with paper towels. Repeat for the rest of the turon.

8. Once all the turon have been fried, raise the heat to high and add the remaining brown sugar (that you reserved in the bowl) to the pan. Spread the sugar out in an even layer using the tongs. Once it's melted and slightly dark, return the turon to the pan, a few at a time, and use the tongs to roll the turon in the caramelized sugar until fully coated. Return the turon to the wire rack/colander/plate (remove the paper towels so they don't stick to them) and let cool until the caramel sets into a crisp coating.

9. Best served while still hot and crisp, though you might be able to reheat in a toaster oven. Enjoy!

Lila's Halo-Halo Ice Candy

These simple ice pops are a little fiddly to put together, but they're fun, delicious, highly customizable, and take up way less space in your freezer than traditional ice pop molds. But if you don't want to bother with the bags, feel free to use molds instead.

YIELD: ABOUT ELEVEN 8 X 2-INCH BAGS

Ingredients:

1 12-ounce can evaporated milk
1 14-ounce can condensed milk
2 tablespoons cornstarch (optional)*
Halo-halo fixings, rinsed and drained (your choice):

Jarred halo-halo mix
Jarred or canned sweet red beans
Jarred sweet garbanzo beans
Jarred nata de coco
Jarred kaong
Jarred macapuno OR dried coconut
Ube halaya (jarred or homemade)
Saba banana, chopped small
Jarred or canned ripe jackfruit

**I've read that cornstarch helps the frozen mixture stay creamy rather than completely icy, but I've seen plenty of recipes without it.*

Equipment:

Blender or large mixing bowl with spout
Thin plastic bags (I use FroZip brand) OR ice pop molds
Chopsticks or long-handled tweezers
Funnel

DIRECTIONS:

1. Add the evaporated milk, condensed milk, and cornstarch to a blender or large mixing bowl with spout. Fill the empty evaporated milk can with water and add to the mixture as well.

2. Blend or mix everything until completely smooth.

3. Taste the mixture to check for sweetness level—the halo-halo fixings will add additional sweetness, so if the milk mixture is too rich or sweet, add another can or two of water to dilute the mixture to your desired level. Freezing dulls the level of sweetness somewhat, but you don't want it sickeningly sweet at this stage.

4. Use chopsticks or long-handled tweezers to insert 1 to 2 teaspoons of your choice of halo-halo fixings into your plastic bags or ice pop molds. Again, the more fixings you add, the sweeter the overall ice candy will be.

5. Using the funnel, pour the milk mixture into the plastic bags or ice pop molds. Make sure to leave room for the mixture to expand in the freezer, about two-thirds of the way. If using the bags, either twist tie or zip them closed.

6. Lay the bags or molds flat in the freezer and allow to freeze at least 6 hours or overnight.

7. Enjoy!

Adeena's Brew-ha #1

(aka The Lila Special)

The Brew-ha #1 is an extra-refreshing spin on iced coffee, diluted with coconut water instead of plain water. It's perfect for those blazing hot days when you could use some extra electrolytes. A baller move—and the way my protagonist, Lila, prefers her drink—is to use both coconut water and coconut milk for a naturally sweetened, lactose-free, and vegan-approved beverage.

YIELD: ROUGHLY 3 CUPS OF CONCENTRATE

Ingredients:

5 to 10 pandan leaves (depending on length), well rinsed

4 cups filtered water

1 cup coarse ground coffee

Coconut water (can be replaced with plain filtered water)

Coconut milk

DIRECTIONS:

1. Blend the pandan leaves with the water, then mix with the ground coffee in a lidded container. Stir so that the grounds are fully saturated.

2. Cover the container and steep for 24 hours at room temperature, then another 24 hours in the fridge.

3. Using a fine mesh strainer or colander lined with coffee filters or cheesecloth, carefully strain the mixture into a clean pitcher or container, pressing down on the grounds and leaves to extract as much liquid as possible. Feel free to strain it a second time for a more grit-free mixture.

4. Now you have pandan cold brew concentrate to use however you like!

5. However, we're making the Brew-ha #1, so fill a glass with ice (if making the iced version) and add the cold brew concentrate, coconut water, and coconut milk in a 1:1:1 ratio. Stir and enjoy!

6. If you'd prefer it hot, heat the concentrate and coconut water together until steaming and pour into a mug. Steam and froth the coconut milk and pour on top, in a fancy pattern if you so please.

Keep reading for a special preview of

Blackmail and Bibingka

Coming soon from Berkley Prime Crime!

Chapter One

"Adeena, can you *please* shut that off? If I have to listen to that Mariah Carey song one more time . . ."

I scratched out the third mistake I'd made while trying to finalize the menu for the annual Shady Palms Holiday Bash. It tied with the Founder's Day Festival as the biggest event in my tiny town of Shady Palms, Illinois (population 18,751), and this was the first year my business—my *dream*—the Brew-ha Cafe would be participating. Considering what a mess the Founder's Day Festival had turned out to be, I really needed to *wow* at this party. Despite obsessing over it for the past month, I had less than two weeks till the big party and hadn't finalized anything.

My best friend and business partner, Adeena Awan, turned the cafe's speaker system down to a decibel that didn't make my ears bleed. "Way to be a humbug, Lila. Ms. Mariah cannot and will not be silenced. Her lambs will make sure of it."

"Hon, you don't even celebrate Christmas. Why do you have all of these?" Elena Torres, Adeena's girlfriend and the third and final member of the Brew-ha Cafe crew (aka our voice of reason), scrolled through the cafe's playlist on Adeena's laptop. It currently had no fewer than ten Christmas music compilations that she'd had on repeat since December first. It was only December fourth, and I was ready to ban her from programming the shop's playlists ever again.

Elena raised her eyebrows at the mix of both religious and secular Christmas songs. "Were you secretly raised in an intensely Catholic family like me and Lila? Because this is a *lot*."

Adeena laughed and handed Elena her morning cup of yerba buena tea. "No, I just like the music. It started as me being rebellious as a kid. Well, as rebellious as you could be in my house. You didn't grow up here, but Shady Palms has a pretty big Muslim and Jewish population, so it was really easy to keep Christmas out of schools. But there were still all the commercials and Christmas specials on TV, so I got kind of obsessed with the holiday. I'm mostly over it now, but I still love the music and movies. And also the parties because Lila's family goes *all in* on the holiday."

Despite my "humbug" response, as Adeena put it, I really did love the holidays. The food, the parties, the gifts, the karaoke, the fantastically cheesy and comfortingly predictable holiday romance movies... What wasn't to love? Though I was finding it hard to get into the holiday spirit ever since my long-lost cousin Ronnie came back into our lives a few days ago. Fifteen years of nothing, only for the prodigal son to show up on our doorstep like nothing had happened, saying he'd bought a winery just outside of town and would be staying in Shady Palms for the foreseeable future.

"Overjoyed" might be an understatement regarding Tita Rosie's reaction to seeing her only child again after more than a decade. If she wasn't filling his plate with third and fourth helpings, she was touching his face and bursting into tears, as if she couldn't believe he was real.

I couldn't believe it, either.

Considering everything he put her through, the kindest thing he did for our family was leave, just like his father before him.

"Let them go," Lola Flor had muttered when I was a kid, as we watched first Tito Jeff and then Ronnie abandon us, Tita Rosie sobbing alone in her room each time. "The Macapagal women will do just fine without them."

My grandmother had been right. Maybe it had taken awhile, but the Macapagal women thrived without them. Tita Rosie's Kitchen, our family restaurant, sat right next door to the Brew-ha Cafe and was now doing so well that people from all over the Midwest came down to Shady Palms just to enjoy my family's food. That's right, our hole-in-the-wall restaurant was now a tourist destination. Thanks to that, we finally had enough money to hire outside help and, get this, my aunt and grandmother could actually take a *whole entire* day off.

My beloved Brew-ha Cafe wasn't quite there yet, but was still on track to turn a profit within the next couple of years. We had a rough start back in the summer, but thanks to Adeena's barista skills, my baking wizardry, and Elena's plant witchery, we'd started to establish ourselves as the hang-out spot for the below-forty crowd. We also appealed to anyone who appreciated quality drinks, Filipino-inspired bakes, and an array of plants and organic bath and beauty products.

As I doodled in the edges of my notebook, trying to figure out what was easy to bake in bulk yet still had enough pizzazz to draw a crowd among the twenty or so tables and stalls that would be at the holiday bash, Adeena came over with a tray holding three small cups filled with a creamy concoction dusted with cinnamon.

"Tasting time!" she said. "This is the atole recipe I plan on serving at the big bash. Elena's mom gave me the recipe and I added my own tweaks. What do you think?"

I picked up a cup and took a big sniff, little curls of steam enveloping my face. Along with the cinnamon, I detected a touch of vanilla and a faint scent that I couldn't immediately place until I took a small sip.

"Corn! Is this thickened with masa harina?" I asked.

Elena nodded. "Yup! It's pretty typical for breakfast, especially around Christmastime. I'd asked Adeena to make champurrado, the chocolate version, but she said there was also a Filipino dish called champorado that was rice-based, and we didn't want the customers to get confused."

"Aww, that's sweet. And a good idea, since I think my family will be serving champorado at the big bash. I love this, Adeena! Are we all set with the beverages?"

"Think so. There's Elena's atole, my chai, and of course the house blend with bags of my hand-roasted coffee beans to sell alongside it. You sure you don't want to include one of your drinks?"

"Three is plenty. Our table's kind of small, so I want to make sure we have enough space for everything." I looked down at my holiday bash planning list and scribbled down Adeena's contribution before checking her off my list. "What about you, Elena?"

She was reeling off the inventory of potted plants, herbs, and other products she'd set aside for the party when the bells above the door tinkled, announcing our visitor: my cousin Ronnie. He was barely average height and had a slight build, but the way he held himself made it seem like he filled the entryway. That air of confidence, plus his carefully styled wavy black hair, golden brown skin, and cocky grin had led to more than one Shady Palms mom showing up on our doorstep, screaming at Tita Rosie because he'd broken another girl's heart—most notably my cousin Bernadette (not a blood relation, don't worry). If I was annoyed by Ronnie's return, Bernadette was *livid*. She hadn't stopped by the restaurant or cafe since he'd arrived, and I missed her.

That, coupled with the old feelings of resentment that always bubbled at the surface whenever I thought of him, and my anxiety about preparing for the holiday party made my voice come out sharper than I'd meant. "What are you doing here?"

The grin didn't leave his face. He was way too smiley for seven in the morning—I didn't trust anyone who smiled that much before the sun had fully risen.

"Good morning to you too, Cuz. And to you, Adeena." He nodded at her before turning his attention to Elena. "Sorry, we haven't met yet. I'm Ronnie Flores, Lila's cousin."

Elena shook his hand. "I thought you were Auntie Rosie's son? Your last names are different."

His smile flickered for a moment before going back to its usual brilliance. "Yeah, it's my dad's last name. My mom went back to her maiden name after he left. Can't blame her."

"Ronnie, what do you want? If you haven't noticed, we were in the middle of a meeting."

He had the grace to glance guiltily at the table strewn with our meeting notes. "Sorry about that. I just came over because Lola Flor said it's breakfast time. She wants you all to come over. Plus I have something for you all."

"What is it?" Not that I wanted anything from him. But the idea of him giving us something when all he'd ever done is take roused my curiosity.

"Guess you'll have to join us for breakfast to find out." He winked at the girls, who gave him grudging smiles.

I couldn't ignore a breakfast summons from our grandmother, but something held me in place. Since he'd arrived, I'd done my best to avoid him. I'd had more than my share of trouble this year and being around Ronnie would increase the chances of more drama a billion times over.

He noticed my hesitation. "Mommy would love it if you could all eat with us."

I sighed. This man was playing dirty and he knew it. You couldn't say no to anything that would make Tita Rosie happy. Not unless you were a monster, anyway. *It was just breakfast,* I told myself. Nothing bad ever happened over breakfast, right?

Chapter Two

"Taste this."

Lola Flor shoved a tray of freshly baked bibingka toward me, the charred banana leaves wrapped around the grilled rice cakes releasing an indescribably intoxicating aroma. There were four different topping choices: the usual butter, sugar, and cheese, plus butter, sugar, and coconut, in addition to the more unusual varieties of salted duck eggs and the works (which was basically all of the above). Tita Rosie cut the bibingka into slivers so we could sample them all while Lola Flor poured us mugs of tsokolate to accompany.

We crowded around the table and took our time tasting each one. Bibingka had a soft and spongy texture, like a chiffon cake, but with a flavor all its own. Modern bibingka was simply baked in an oven, but it's traditionally grilled using charcoal. Lola Flor had a grill behind the restaurant that she used for occasions like this, and her bibingka was miles ahead of any other version I'd tried. My sweet tooth preferred the simplicity of the sugar-topped ones, but the complexity of the salted duck eggs against the other ingredients made me keep reaching for another piece.

"If you're trying to decide which ones to serve this weekend, I'd say combine the sugar, cheese, and coconut toppings for a sweet version and have the salted duck eggs with cheese to tempt our more adventurous eaters," I said.

Lola Flor gave a curt nod, as if I'd passed a test. "What do the rest of you think?"

"The sweet version definitely gets my vote," Adeena said, picking up another piece and dunking it in her hot chocolate. "What do you think, babe?"

Elena had also grabbed another piece, but she chose the salted duck egg. "I think Lila's right about combining the sweet versions, but you should also add coconut to the duck egg and cheese. That hint of sweetness with the salty ingredients is really something."

Lola Flor actually cracked a smile at that. Huh. Couldn't remember the last time she'd smiled so approvingly at me. I glanced at Ronnie out of the corner of my eye and saw him studying Lola Flor's expression with a frown. At least she grudgingly approved of me. She never bothered hiding her dislike of Ronnie.

"Lola, I think—" Ronnie didn't get a chance to finish his sentence because our grandmother turned away while he was talking and walked back to the kitchen.

For just a moment, he let the facade slip and his face crumpled at Lola Flor's rejection. I instinctively moved toward him to . . . what? Comfort him? Why would I bother?

But he must've sensed that small movement, so before I could decide what I wanted to do, he wiped the expression off his face and went back to his practiced nonchalance. "Hey Mommy, what else are you preparing for the weekend?"

She touched his cheek and went into the kitchen without saying anything. The four of us left in the room stood around awkwardly until Ronnie broke the silence.

"They really upgraded the place. It looks way better than I remember. My mom said you had a big hand in it."

I'd been home for almost a year now, and in that time the restaurant had transformed completely. The walls gleamed with a lovely warm terra-cotta shade instead of the dingy white they'd been my whole life. The art prints, fans, and the large wooden-spoon-and-fork set hanging on the walls as well as the woven table runners added a distinct Filipino flair, while the carefully cultivated monstera plants scattered around the room added a lushness and freshness we never would've achieved without Elena's skillful hands. We'd been able to replace the mismatched and scratched up chairs and tables a few months ago and were starting to acquire new tableware as well. Elena's mom was a skilled ceramist, just one of her many talents, and we'd hired her to create special dishware for the restaurant. The only things that hadn't changed were the large painting of the Last Supper hanging above the table in the party area and the karaoke machine tucked in the corner.

"She wouldn't get rid of that painting, huh?" Ronnie asked, smiling knowingly.

I fought the urge to smile back and failed. "Tita Rosie can be surprisingly stubborn when she wants to be. Considering she let me change everything else and get rid of the Santo Niño statue, it wasn't worth fighting about."

He nodded, a contemplative look crossing his face as he stared at the familiar painting. "Look, Lila. I—"

"Hoy, come help your mother with the dishes," Lola Flor said, interrupting whatever Ronnie was about to say.

He obeyed without a word, a first for him, and with his help the table was laid out. Not with the typical meat, fried egg, and garlic rice we'd usually have for breakfast but with what I can only assume were the dishes they'd planned for the holiday bash. They chose dishes that were easy to portion out and still tasted OK when cold: the typical pancit and lumpia (vegetarian and with meat) that you'd see at any fiesta, along with two kinds of siopao, Filipino fruit salad, and champorado.

While we helped ourselves to a little bit of everything (Adeena and Elena sticking to the vegetarian dishes), Lola Flor and Ronnie were locked in another battle, with my grandmother trying to make him eat tuyo with his champorado and Ronnie absolutely refusing:

"These go together."

"I don't like tuyo."

"You're supposed to eat them together."

"Why would I eat dried fish with chocolate porridge? It doesn't make sense!"

"It is traditional! Salty goes with sweet, just eat it!"

This went on for a while before I interrupted their childishness.

"You said you had something for us, Ronnie?" I glanced at the time on my phone to show that we were on a tight schedule.

"Oh yeah! Hold on a sec." He got up and grabbed a tote bag that was over by the hanging coatrack. "I wanted you to try this. It's a few bottles of our signature cabernet sauvignon as well as the lambanog I've developed with our vintner. I know you have a liquor license, so I thought I'd offer you free samples to see if you'd like to stock it at your cafe."

"Lambanog? How're you making coconut wine in Shady Palms?" The traditional Filipino coconut liquor was popular, especially around Christmas, but since my aunt and grandmother didn't drink, I'd only tried it a few times with friends in Chicago.

Ronnie launched into a long story about how he'd met a master lambanog maker in Florida (what had Ronnie been doing in Florida?) and had convinced him to come to Shady Palms so they could introduce the

Midwest to the wonders of Filipino-made wine. He also explained step by tedious step the process of making lambanog—something about collecting coconut sap from flowers. I'd zoned out a few minutes into the explanation, the only thing I could focus on was Ronnie's obvious passion for this subject. I'd never seen him care about anything so much, and that included his own family.

Tita Rosie, meanwhile, was hanging on his every word, smiling and nodding as if she cared about the laborious distilling process and Ronnie's grand plans to put Shady Palms on the map as a purveyor of delicious and unique wines. Which she probably did, since she was nothing if not supportive and loving toward those of us who didn't deserve her.

"Anyway, I was hoping you'd have time to tour the winery with me later today. Mommy's been wanting to see it and I'd love to introduce you all to the Shady Palms Winery team. Our investors are in town and I was hoping we could all show them a good time."

I hadn't realized how much I'd spaced out till I caught the last half of Ronnie's sentence and couldn't for the life of me figure out how we got from me tasting his wine to entertaining his business investors.

"Sorry, can't. We're finalizing the holiday bash menu today and then I'm going into full production mode. Tell them to stop by the cafe though. I'm sure Adeena and I can set something aside for them."

He frowned. "You sure you can't free up an hour or two? I really talked up how our whole family are successful entrepreneurs, and they'd love to meet you. I also bragged about the karaoke parties we have, and they really wanted to attend one. I was hoping we could have one tonight."

My aunt froze. "Oh anak, why didn't you say something sooner? I have time to visit your business, but we're also busy preparing for the party and serving our usual customers. We can't just shut down the restaurant at the last minute to accommodate your party."

I flinched at Tita Rosie's use of the word "anak" for someone who wasn't me. OK, so Ronnie was truly her anak since it means offspring, but she'd been using it to refer to me and only me for over a decade. I didn't appreciate sharing that term of endearment with anyone, especially not someone who left us over a decade ago and was now glaring at my aunt as if she were the one being entirely unreasonable.

"These are my main investors. Without them, I wouldn't even have this business or be back in this town. I owe them everything." Realization at what he just admitted swept over his face, and he clapped his hand over his mouth like a little kid who accidentally said a bad word. "No, Mommy, I didn't mean it like that! I just, of course I would've come back eventually, it's just that I didn't want to return with nothing to show for it, you know? I, uh . . ."

But the damage was done. Both Lola Flor and I stood up and walked to Tita Rosie's side, who was staring at her son as if he'd just insulted her food. The ultimate betrayal.

"If you want to impress your investors, tell them to stop by our table at the holiday party. Now get out of here. Don't you have work to do?" Lola Flor pulled Tita Rosie up and marched her to the kitchen, not allowing her to stop or say anything.

Elena cleared her throat. "Um, it was nice meeting you, Ronnie. Thanks for the wine." She met Adeena's eyes and the two of them left together. I should've followed them, but I had one last thing to tell my dear cousin.

"If you've turned up after all these years just to break Tita Rosie's heart again, I'll kill you. I'm serious. And Ate Bernie will help me hide the body," I said, bringing up his ex-girlfriend and my cousin/friend. "So you better not mess up this time. Tita Rosie may be all forgiving, but Lola Flor and I aren't."

Tita Rosie hurried over with a bag full of takeout boxes, interrupting my threats. "Oh anak, I'm sorry we can't host your business partners tonight, but please take this for their lunch. Let them know they're welcome here anytime as customers, and I look forward to meeting them later. Maybe tomorrow after the lunch rush?"

She held out the bag as a peace offering, and Ronnie met my eyes before taking it and thanking his mom. She smiled before hustling back to the kitchen.

Ronnie watched her, his expression unreadable. "I swear to you, Lila, I'd rather die than hurt her again. I'm back for good and my business *will* be a success and nothing's going to stop me from proving to my mom that I'm not the screw-up I was when I left." His eyes hardened. "I refuse to let anything get in my way again."

Photo by Jamilla Yip Photography

Mia P. Manansala is a writer and book coach from Chicago who loves books, baking, and badass women. She uses humor (and murder) to explore aspects of the Filipino diaspora, queerness, and her millennial love for pop culture. A lover of all things geeky, Mia spends her days procrastibaking, playing JRPGs and dating sims, reading cozy mysteries and diverse romance, and cuddling her dogs Gumiho and Max Power.

CONNECT ONLINE

MiaPManansala.com

MPMtheWriter